Sniper Fire

by

Kathy Lane

Love in the Crosshairs Series

Sniper Fire

Cover Art by *Debbie Taylor*

The Wild Rose Press, Inc.
PO Box 708
Adams Basin, NY 14410-0708
Visit us at www.thewildrosepress.com

Publishing History
First Crimson Rose Edition, 2014
Print ISBN 978-1-62830-472-5
Digital ISBN 978-1-62830-473-2

Love in the Crosshairs Series
Published in the United States of America

"Why in the world, when the stakes are so high, would you decide to give up now?"

Kyle ran a hand over his face, feeling the frustration leak out of every pore along with his sweat. "Farrah…I'm not giving up. I just…I'm trying to be realistic here."

He sucked in a deep breath and looked away. The silence stretched between them, broken only by Farrah's quiet sniffles. It took all his strength to meet her wounded gaze again.

"Look, I understand you want to make things better. I appreciate it. I really do. But you have to accept there are some things you can't fix. Trying to force the issue won't accomplish a damn thing. You don't know what I've been through, what I'm still—"

"I was there, remember? I'm a doctor, I know—"

Her words cut off as he moved into her personal space, forcing her to step back until she bumped against the fender of her car. He didn't stop until their bodies almost touched. Deliberately, he reached down and pressed a hand against her thigh, applying just a hint of pressure. The material of her gray dress pants kept him from touching skin, but the heat of her still seared him. He held her watery gaze as he slowly leaned to the side, moving his hand down, sliding his palm over her knee, then trailing searching fingers back up, up and around, until he stopped just shy of cupping her deliciously firm ass. Her heavy breathing matched his, their breaths mingling in the hot, August air.

"I don't feel a brace on your leg, Dr. Hastings," he said softly. "I don't feel any twisted muscles or hard scars. So how can you stand here and say you know what I'm going through? You can't."

Praise for Kathy Lane

SNIPER SHOTS is a "sit-on-the-edge-of-your-seat plot with unexpected twists and turns. There's enough action and sex to keep you turning the pages straight to the end."

> *~Lorelei Confer, Romantic Suspense Author*
> *~*~*

BLOODSWORN: BOUND BY MAGIC
"I like nothing better than to get my teeth into a nice juicy romance and this had all of my favorite elements, fantasy, adventure, action, and real depth to the plot. I was truly transported. I can't wait for my next chance to return to the planet Avalyr."

> *~Cyd, Night Owl Reviews (Top Pick)*
> *~*~*

"One book I wouldn't mind reading again. This is a great story about what happens when magic meets science...solid romance with a lot of action."

> *~Romfan Reviews (5 Stars)*
> *~*~*

BLOODSWORN 2: LINKED BY BLOOD
"This book has everything. I can't wait to read more from Kathy Lane. I'm definitely calling both Bloodsworn books the kind you keep and reread."

> *~Kathy F., The Romance Studio (5 Hearts)*
> *~*~*

"Ms. Lane's solidly brilliant storytelling skills had me captivated and entertained."

> *~Cyd, Night Owl Reviews (Top Pick)*

Dedication

A mother can't ask for more in life than that her children love and respect her. So saying, this book is dedicated to my sons, Joe and Jon. Joe, the oldest, is the more practical of the two and I look to him for all kinds of advice. He's my rock, and sometimes, I have to admit, my brakes. (Don't ask.) Jon, on the other hand, is a dreamer, something we both have in common. He wants more out of life than a nine-to-five job and is always reaching for the stars. The neat thing is that he encourages me to reach right along with him.

Both of these guys together make a great support team, something a mother—and a writer—is lucky to have. I clearly hit the jackpot with my children. They're both strong and independent young men, with big hearts like their father. I'll always be there for them, just like I know they're always there for me.

Acknowledgement

Writing a novel isn't always easy. Sometimes the words flow like water and sometimes they drip out onto the page with agonizing slowness. Either way, getting a book from concept to the hands of readers is hard work, folks—don't let anyone tell you different. You need a rock-solid support group to lend you encouragement when needed. Which is why I want to thank my beta reader, Mike, for pestering me like clockwork for the next chapter of *Sniper Fire*. It always helps to know I'm writing for someone who really enjoys the story.

It also doesn't hurt to have a super-fantastic editor on your side. Many, many, many thanks to my wonderful editor, Frances. Thanks for listening to me, encouraging me, and knocking me in the head when I needed it. Thanks for your patience and understanding when things got rocky, and for hanging in there with me. Most of all, thanks for believing in me and my writing. I couldn't get through all the editing phases without you.

Chapter One

"Find a perch, Flight One!"

Kyle Fagan froze at the urgent command coming over the tiny com tucked into his ear. Sweat rolled down his back as he scanned the narrow Cairo alley ahead and behind him, looking for anything remotely resembling a threat. Nothing moved. At least, nothing hostile. The quick "OK" sign he got from his partner crouched at the other end of the alley didn't count.

"Raptor, Ghost, you got incoming."

Of course they did. Kyle breathed out a string of swear words as he took cover, knowing his partner, Rashid Fehr, otherwise known as Raptor, was doing the same. He ducked behind a short pile of broken stone and wood that looked to have been part of a nearby building at some point. As soon as he crouched down, he almost changed his mind and stood up again, incoming be damned. The stench of decaying flesh wafting from the pile surrounded him like a noxious perfume. Something—or someone—lay dead beneath the impromptu burial mound. He swallowed hard, trying not to gag, and put his nose against his rifle just to breathe in the clean smell of metal and gun oil.

Seconds ticked by with nerve-fraying slowness. He finally caught the faint scuff of hard-soled boots against stone, the quiet murmur of male voices speaking Arabic. The sounds grew louder. Kyle tensed as the two-man patrol moved into view. Around him, the stench of death didn't so much fade as take a backseat to more pressing matters. A fresh kill was imminent, and he had no intention of ending up the next rotting corpse. He caressed the trigger of his rifle once before moving his hand to the smooth hilt of a throwing knife. Gunfire, especially this close to their target, would not only blow their whole operation, but also get him in deep shit with his boss. The Harrier had little use for trigger-happy fools.

The pair of soldiers paused at the mouth of the alley. Kyle tightened his grip on the knife as one man lit a cigarette. The flare of the lighter reached greedily into the darkness. Then the light snuffed out. The man drew deep on his coffin nail while his partner told a rude joke involving an American, a donkey, and a bunch of bananas. Despite his tension, Kyle's lips twitched. The joke wasn't half-bad, all things considered. Insulting, if you took the part about the American personally, but still damn funny.

The men started walking again, passing within six feet of his hiding place before disappearing out of sight. Kyle let out the breath he'd been holding, but kept his hand on his knife. Another minute crawled by before Capella, the NightHawks' communications specialist, graced the airwaves with his voice.

"All clear, Flight One." A brief pause. "Harrier advises a schedule change. All birds double time to rendezvous one. Avoid flying side trips. Repeat, no side trips. Eagle and Laptop will take to the air with eyes open."

Kyle couldn't hold back a grin as he tapped the acknowledge sequence into the com device in his ear.

Capella liked to live dangerously. The com specialist knew Dell Hudson hated the nickname Laptop, but he used it every chance he got in place of Dell's more sophisticated Peregrine. There'd be a round of payback when this job was over and they were all safe at home.

Signaling to Rashid, Kyle moved out, fast and quiet, grateful to leave the noisome alley behind. One by one, his teammates, the other members of the Special Ops unit codenamed Nighthawks, signaled acceptance of the new order. Worry niggled at Kyle as he and Rashid worked their way through the maze of crowded buildings on the outskirts of Cairo's east side. Their fearless leader only changed an operation's timetable if unexpected trouble popped up. Usually he'd give the team a head's up as to what that trouble was, but tonight the airwaves stayed quiet. Interesting. Maybe Kyle wasn't the only one who wanted out of this damn city. Ever since they'd set foot in the conglomeration of ancient and modern buildings that was Egypt's capital city, something had the fine hairs on the back of his neck standing at attention. And it damn sure wasn't the weather. No surprise the Harrier felt it, too.

Another voice broke the com's silence, the throaty bass rumbling as deep and dark as the speaker's skin. "Damn, no side trips? And here I was hoping to sneak in a couple of midnight mosque tours on the way."

Kyle grinned again at the half-serious complaint. No one was sure which had come first, Brick's love of architecture, or the joy he got from blowing it up. Either way, the explosives expert had a fascination with beautiful buildings of all types. And bridges. Hell, show the big man a bridge and he positively drooled.

"Look at it this way," said a third voice Kyle easily recognized as Gage, the unit's lead medic. "We get done early, and we'll have a longer layover at Winter Tree going home. Lots of bridges in that neck of the woods. Didn't you say you'd only profiled about half of them so far?"

"Mmm," Brick hummed. "There is that. There is that."

"Lots of sweet little birdies in those woods, too," Kyle murmured, thinking of a pair of eager ladies he hadn't had time to get to know last time the NightHawks had been through Brussels, or Winter Tree as the Hawks called it. He still had both their numbers tucked away in his wallet somewhere.

"Oh, yeah," Gage agreed. "Bet they'd appreciate a couple cock-o-the-walks visiting their nests."

A chorus of snickers and groans was closely followed by a no-nonsense, "Close beaks you bunch of limp-feathered ladybirds. Unless you're dying, I want radio silence from here on out."

"Roger that," Kyle snapped quickly. When Joshua Colby, a.k.a. the Harrier, used that tone of voice, playtime was over.

A quiet fifteen minutes passed while he and Rashid made their way to the rendezvous point, dodging pedestrians and what little traffic the narrow roads offered this late at night. He caught glimpses of his teammates the closer they got, but only because he knew where to look.

"I have the mouse's house in sight," announced Ty, their "Eagle" sniper. "Two on the roof, three on the ground. Southeast, Northwest, West, West, South. Have target in line of sight, second floor, southwest corner.

He's awake."

Kyle eased up to the final corner and squatted, back to the wall, before looking for his partner. Rash waved from his hiding place half a block away, signing that he was breaking off to carry out his part of the plan. Kyle waved back. He checked his watch. Twelve minutes after local midnight. That put them eighteen minutes ahead of schedule. Even with the slight adjustment, their target should have been fast asleep. Maybe it was better this way. At least now they had a positive ID before all the shooting started.

"Looks like the intel was good after all," Joshua murmured over the com.

Kyle wiped the sweat from his forehead with his sleeve. He and Josh had discussed the sketchy nature of the information they'd been given right up to go time. Wouldn't be the first time an operation was scrubbed due to poor intel. But neither he nor Joshua were prepared to leave a twenty-year-old kid in the hands of terrorists any longer than necessary. It helped that Joshua didn't sound the least worried, but then, he rarely did. Took a lot to rattle the Harrier, always had.

That's why he's in the driver's seat and I'm just one of the wheels, Kyle thought, perfectly happy with the way things were. From the time they were boys back home in North Carolina, Joshua had always led their adventures. Kyle's tendency to worry about details he couldn't control would have made him a basket case if the roles were reversed.

He checked his watch again and took a quick peek at the street beyond. Despite his nerves screaming at him that something was definitely off, he saw no surprises. The large building took up most of one block in the old sector. Many of the windows he could see on the south-facing ground floor were boarded up, as were all but one door. A single man patrolled this side, just like Ty said. The guard stood about thirty yards away, a dark shadow outlined against the building harboring their target.

Kyle touched the com, tapping in the signal that he was in position. Ten seconds later, a noise at the other end of the street drew the guard from his position by the building. Kyle ran, body low, sticking to shadows until he was almost in the exact spot where the guard had stood a moment earlier. He carefully shouldered his rifle and drew the seven-inch SOG SEAL knife from its sheath on his belt. Standing in the middle of the street, the guard called out a string of Arabic, asking one of his cronies on the roof if he saw anything. The roof guard answered, explaining that the noise was nothing more than a cat chasing a rat.

Kyle stilled, recognizing the voice despite the unusual cadence and rough edge. He swallowed a curse. Had everyone decided to break the damn rules this trip? Rashid should have taken out his target at the same time Kyle took out his, to avoid the risk of detection. He was three minutes ahead of schedule. Details, see, uncontrollable details. Just one more thing that hadn't gone according to plan. Still, all wasn't lost. While Kyle could speak and understand Arabic like a native, Rashid *was* a native, having lived just a few miles outside Cairo for twelve years before moving to the U.S. His Arabic was flawless, without a trace of accent. Question was, did the guard in the street know his buddies well enough to recognize voices?

The man seemed to hesitate, cocking his head to

the side. Kyle tensed. If he started acting like he knew something was fishy—shooting or running to warn his friends—he'd have to be silenced in short order.

The screech of a pissed off cat preceded the animal sprinting out into the street. Damn if Rashid hadn't been telling the truth. The guard relaxed, muttering and picking up a rock and throwing it at the cat before turning back to his post. Kyle clung to the shadows. He'd have only a small window of surprise before the guard noticed him. It didn't help that his target took his time returning, scanning the street, the narrow alley, and the surrounding buildings intently. Fortunately, he looked everywhere but the last place he'd been standing his watch.

Waiting until the guy was almost on top of him, Kyle launched himself in one fluid move. One hand went around the startled man's head, covering his mouth. With the other, Kyle shoved the knife deep into the man's chest just under the ribcage, aiming for the heart. A brief struggle, a muffled groan, and the long knife did its job. The man collapsed. Kyle pulled his knife free, wiped the blood on the guard's clothes, and put it away. Then he grabbed the body by an arm and leg and hefted it over his shoulders. It took less than a minute to dump the lifeless corpse in the blackness of a nearby alley and return to the guard's post. Shifting his rifle back to his hands, he took up position in the shadows.

Five long minutes passed. Time always seemed to crawl when things were quiet. Finally, a series of soft beeps came over his com, indicating that the next phase of their mission was about to begin. When he heard Joshua give the verbal order to go in, he had to lock his muscles to stay in place. Damn, how he hated this part. Waiting was a bitch. He'd much rather be inside with his best friend, facing death around every corner. Growing up together, they knew each other's moves, how the other thought in any given situation. But as second-in-command, Kyle had to stay on point. Josh and the others would exit this way in less than ten minutes. Someone had to keep the exit route free of any impediments, be they terrorists or civilians, and it was Kyle's turn to play watchdog. Still, he didn't have to like it.

Pulling his thoughts back to his job, he scanned the area. He got a glimpse of Rashid on the roof and stepped out of the shadows long enough to give him the all clear sign. Rash waved an all-clear back. Ty was up there somewhere, too, watching, waiting to provide cover fire if needed.

"What the… Shit! We got a hive!"

Joshua's vehement swearing came a split second before an explosion shook the building. Kyle staggered, caught himself, and sprinted for the door as the rapid staccato of automatic gunfire filled the night. Way the hell too much gunfire. Their intel had specified a cell of ten, tops. Five men were posted outside, which should have left the other five for Joshua and company to deal with. But from the sound of gunfire and shouts, there were a hell of a lot more than five terrorists inside.

Dread flooded him as he reached the door and wrenched it open. Dust and smoke poured out in a pale envelope, swallowing him, filling his lungs and making his eyes sting. He coughed, found a pocket of clean air that he sucked down like a drowning man, and started for the door again.

"Hold positions! Hold positions! Bastards have a whole platoon in here instead of just a handful. Damn it, Falcon, you and Stitch get the target to Ghost! Peregrine, you're with me! Brick, do us all a favor and blow these bastards to hell!"

Relief made Kyle sag against the doorframe before anger shot through him. How the hell did surveillance miss fifteen or twenty men?

Joshua growled. "Someone's got a hell of a lot of explaining to do. Don't wait for us, Ghost, go to plan B. Repeat, everyone go to plan Baker. Eagle, keep 'em company."

A quiet "Roger that." from Ty just before another explosion rocked the neighborhood. Kyle ducked away from the door, but couldn't escape the concussion that thumped his chest like a freakin' bass drum. Another cloud of dust and smoke whooshed out. Several smaller explosions followed, one right after the other. From somewhere in the building came Brick's deep, rumbling roar of pure joy. The operation might be going to hell, but at least one member of the team was having a good time.

Kyle shook his head to clear it and moved swiftly back along the wall until he could see down the side street. He took a knee, rifle up and ready, willing Gage and Sam to hurry. Shouts were coming from the surrounding buildings, though there wasn't a flood of civilians emerging onto the streets to see what was going on like there would be back in the states. That didn't mean the terrorists didn't have more backup stashed nearby.

Movement behind him. He swung the rifle around as two bodies burst out of the building at a dead run.

Kyle aimed, then lowered the barrel as he recognized Gage's blond ponytail flying in the wind. "Falcon! Here!" he shouted, stepping out of the shadows.

Gage spun, fired several rounds back through the doorway, then grabbed the arm of the figure stumbling beside him and headed for Kyle.

"Where's Stitch?" Kyle called.

"Pinned down at the bottom of the stairs. I think he's hit." Gage shoved the young man with him against the wall. "Stay there. Don't move."

Kyle swore. He wanted to be the one to head inside and bring his teammate out, but he had his orders. The safety of the target was his number one priority. Besides, if Sam was hit, Gage could get him up and running quicker than Kyle could. "Can you get to him?"

"Can falcons fly?"

He shot Gage a grin and nodded sharply. "Plan B means the rest are exiting on the north side. They won't be able to get to him. Go! Pry our boy out of there. I got this one." Gage was gone before Kyle finished speaking, sprinting for the door that was still spouting smoke. As soon as he was out of sight, Kyle caught their target's arm and jerked him to his feet. "Jeffery Waterhouse, I presume?" He didn't really have to ask, having recognized the younger brother of Alabama Senator Wade Waterhouse from the photos they'd been given. He didn't really expect an answer either, but the guy surprised him.

"Y-y-yes, that's me. Who are you people?"

"We're the good guys." He led his charge to the dubious cover of a burned out car sitting at the mouth of the first alley east of the building. From there he scanned the street that was his exit, noticing that a crowd was finally forming. Plan B hadn't counted on Brick's little explosive party drawing unwanted attention. He'd have to improvise.

A shout came from behind him. A quick glance showed at least a dozen men running in his direction. From what little he could see, those weren't umbrellas they were carrying. He waited half a second more to make sure the front-runners weren't part of his team. One of them gestured, shouting a string of Arabic. Kyle let the adrenaline settle into his bones as he aimed and fired. One by one, bodies jerked and fell, tumbling bonelessly like puppets with their strings cut. He smiled grimly when a couple of the terrorists diving for cover—ones he'd yet to aim at—suddenly hit the ground and stopped moving. Nice to know Ty was upstairs somewhere, keeping watch with those eagle-eyes of his.

Despite the double-team, some of the bad guys evidently made it to cover. Kyle ducked behind the dead car. "Stay flat!" he ordered Waterhouse. Bullets thudded around their hiding place, some of them pinging sharply against metal.

Another explosion. Kyle chanced a quick peek just in time to see dust and debris rain down on the terrorists from a large hole in the second story of their hideout. Perfect cover. He grabbed Waterhouse's arm and pulled him up before the last piece of wreckage hit the ground. "Come on!" He glanced back once at the rubble clogging the street. Damn if Brick wasn't milking the situation for all it was worth. Still, the building hadn't collapsed yet, so at least the big man was showing a little restraint.

They'd run the length of several alleys and taken a

handful of twisty streets when the com beeped. "Approaching from your nine, Ghost. Don't shoot us."

About damn time. Hearing Joshua's voice loosened some of the tension in Kyle's chest. He drew his winded charge to a halt in the shadow of a second story overhang. Exactly ten seconds later, his team poured out of the alley to his left. Joshua, Gage, Brick, and Dell looked like they had a few bumps and scrapes, but otherwise, were fine. Sam, codenamed Stitch, on the other hand, looked a mess. His right arm was cradled in a makeshift sling and he leaned against a wall forcing air in and out past clenched teeth. The hit he took must have been pretty bad judging from the wide trail of blood darkening his clothes. Gage hovered, ready to steady his partner if necessary.

"Remind me to kill someone when we get back to base," Joshua snarled, flattening himself against the wall next to Kyle.

"Anyone in particular?" The echo of distant shouting had Kyle peering back around the corner.

"Yeah, whoever was in charge of gathering the data for this poor excuse of a mission. A five-year-old could have done better. Damn it, I'd swear they knew when and how we were coming in. There was no other reason for all of those terrorists to be in that one building. That's not how they operate."

"Agreed," Kyle said. "We've been dodging way too many bullets for them not to know exactly what streets we were going to take."

Everyone fell silent. The implication wasn't pretty. No one liked the idea of a traitor in their midst. More shouts in the distance, closer now. Time was running out. They'd have to break cover soon.

Kyle meet Joshua's gaze. "Time to go off the rails?"

"Definitely," Joshua said. He tapped the com, including Ty, Rash, and the others not huddled with them in the shadows. "Attention Hawks, this is the Harrier. Scrap all tickets for this ride. Repeat, this ride is a bust. P2 is still the goal, but we're going to enjoy a night at the improv. Have fun."

As if on cue, gunfire burst over their heads.

"Down! Down! Everybody down!"

Kyle dived for the hard cobbles, using a handful of shirt to jerk the senator's brother down with him. Thankfully, the young man didn't fight him, not even when Kyle rolled on top of him to act as a living shield against the bullets whizzing by overhead. Most people usually reacted one of two ways when getting shot at. They either went to pieces and started running and babbling like a lunatic, or they went wordless, their brains and body shutting down to robotic level. Nice that the senator's brother fell into the latter category. Easier to handle that way. Would have been nicer if they'd never had to find out which category he fell into.

So much for a smooth, quick operation with minimum exposure. This job was just full of nasty surprises. He glanced across to where Joshua crouched in a shallow doorway, returning fire. His expression didn't bode well for whoever had gotten the intel wrong on this particular terrorist cell. The new pickup point was still several miles away. Anything could happen.

More shots. Cover fire from above this time by the sound of it. Kyle traded a quick grin with Josh. You had to love the efficiency of snipers, especially when they were on your side. He'd definitely be buying Ty and

Rash a beer first chance he got.

Joshua's voice rose over the noise of automatic weapons. "Get him out of here, Ghost!" A tap of the com. "Raptor, Ghost is leaving the party. Go with!"

Kyle nodded and pulled Waterhouse to his feet. Fifteen minutes later, the two of them sat huddled out of sight in the back of a stolen vehicle while Rash, in "borrowed" civvies, drove the narrow streets of Cairo like a mad man. It was well after midnight, but they still had to deal with some traffic. Rash swore in Arabic, gesturing with the best of them. Kyle waited another twenty minutes of roundabout driving to make sure they weren't being followed before checking his GPS. Almost there.

He tapped Rash on the shoulder to get his attention. "Take the next left. Time to find a nice quiet alley where we can ditch the car," he said.

"You got it, bro," Rash replied, the inflection pure Boston southie. "One deserted alley, coming up." The car accelerated, swerved left, right, then left again, all to the tune of a steady stream of Arabic.

Kyle tucked the GPS away, grinning at the occasional swear word he picked out of his friend's running monologue. He and Rash had a habit of trading cuss words ever since the Arab-American joined the NightHawks a year ago. Nothing like a little cultural exchange.

The young man beside him shifted in his crouch. Kyle gave him the once over. Pale face, dazed, wide eyes, bloodless lips. Yeah, still in shock mode, poor kid. Feeling like he needed to do something about that, he reached over and patted the kid's shoulder. "Almost at the pickup point, sir. You'll be safe and on your way home very soon."

The car screeched to a halt, throwing them forward into the back of the front seat.

"Last stop. All out for the whirly-bird express. Women, children, and brothers of U.S. Senators first," Rash quipped as he opened his door.

"That would be you," Kyle said, grabbing a handful of shirt and tugging when Waterhouse showed no sign of moving on his own.

Once in the narrow alley, Kyle parked the senator's brother in a convenient doorway and motioned Rash to take the high ground. They needed to reach the rooftop where the chopper was due to land in the next ten minutes.

The tiny com in his ear clicked once. "Rats closing at nine o'clock, oh ghostly phantom. Time to do your disappearing act."

Kyle swore softly at Rash's warning. He would have bet money they hadn't been followed. How the hell had the terrorists found them so quickly?

Face it, Fagan. The rats aren't limited to Cairo's back alleys.

Someone had to have tipped off the terrorists that the Hawks were coming. Someone who knew times, dates, and apparently pickup points. There was no other explanation for the extra manpower back where the senator's brother was being held, or for the ones closing in now. The NightHawks had been betrayed.

He slipped quietly into the dark doorway with his charge.

"I just want to go home. Please, you said I could go home."

Wonderful, his robot was turning into a real boy.

Now was definitely not the time for him to come to life.

Eyes still on the alley, Kyle put his lips to the kid's ear. "We'll get you home. You just need to stay quiet a little longer and do exactly what I tell you when I tell you. Nod if you understand me."

A couple of heartbeats passed before the nod came.

"Good." He straightened and tapped his earpiece. "Rash—"

The sniper fire came out of nowhere. The first bullet slammed into his knee with the impact of a sledge hammer. Kyle bit off the roar of pain that burst out of his throat as he returned fire. More bullets tore into him. Pain exploded, white hot starbursts that expanded and merged, trying to block out everything else. He fought his way past it. Joshua was depending on him. He had to get their target to the roof. He had to get the kid on that chopper.

Rashid's voice on the com. "I think I got him. You two okay? Ghost, anyone hit? Ghost!"

Kyle fell back, eyes squeezed tight against the pain. He wanted to answer Rashid's frantic call, but couldn't. He could only suck air in through gritted teeth, pushing back the unconsciousness that threatened. He didn't dare pass out now, but oh, how he wanted to. Anything to escape the pain that only promised to get worse, *did get worse*, as something pressed hard on his leg. He swore, swinging his fist and opening his eyes at the same time. Luckily, the kid knew how to duck.

"Sorry," Kyle gasped, letting himself sag against the doorway. His estimation of the senator's little brother went up a notch when he realized that throughout the swing and duck, the guy's hands had stayed put, applying pressure to the worst of Kyle's wounds.

"Y-you're bleeding," the kid stammered. "I-I know first aid. Took a course in college last spring." His gaze dropped to his red-stained hands. "This is bad," he whispered. "Really bad."

Kyle didn't doubt the kid's diagnosis for a second. He could already feel the blood, hot and sticky, soaking his pants. Lots of blood. Another bullet zinged down the alley. Cradling his rifle in one arm, he tried to scoot deeper into the doorway. Cover was at a premium, and he wanted his impromptu field medic to have as much as possible.

He knew he'd made a mistake trying to move at the first sensation of bones grating beneath skin. He grabbed reflexively for the worst area of pain. A firestorm of agony from his busted knee plunged him into a mini hell. The searing pain swamped him, taking breath, sight, and finally, against every bit of willpower he had, consciousness.

Voices roused Kyle. Gruff, hard, urgent. Impossible to ignore. So was the constant agony pounding through him with every beat of his heart. For a moment he could barely breathe, much less think. When his mind finally did decide to work, it locked on one vague thought: something to do with the helicopter. Something he desperately needed to remember.

Have to get the senator's brother on the chopper!

The thought jolted him. Kyle tried to roll, to sit up, but didn't get far. Just that first, brief tensing of muscles sent a fresh wave of pain through his body sharp enough to slice steel. He wanted to scream, to howl, to swear the world a solid blue streak. Somehow, he kept everything behind locked lips and gritted teeth. *Stay quiet. Don't let the enemy know where you are. No matter what, stay hidden.*

Hands pressed his shoulders flat. Another one grabbed his hand in a tight grip as a voice said, "Easy Kyle, take it easy. You're safe, buddy. Go ahead and cuss if you need to, just keep it low."

Kyle gripped the hand in his like a life line and squeezed, feeling a ridiculous urge to smile despite the sea of pain he was drowning in. Only one person knew him so well. He forced his eyes open. His brother in all but name stared down at him with a flat expression that might have fooled anyone else.

"That bad?" he tried to ask, feeling the words lodge in his throat. Joshua must have read his lips.

"Bad enough," Joshua said. "You just hang in there, you hear me? Gage is getting ready to work you over. We'll get you to a hospital as soon as we can."

"The kid?"

Joshua's gaze slipped to the side then back again. "He'll make it. We'll make sure. We owe him for keeping you from bleeding out."

Some of the urgency left Kyle. Waterhouse was safe. That was good. Joshua would make sure the kid got home in one piece. Whether Kyle himself made it really didn't matter. He accepted long ago that he'd probably get his ticket punched in the middle of an operation. Bleeding out from a nicked artery was just following the script.

Pain flared as he felt hands moving fast over his leg, cutting fabric, wiping away excess blood. Every touch, however minor, was agony. He screwed his eyes closed and ground his teeth until he thought they'd crack.

"Damn it, give him something for the pain, Gage. Do it now!"

Kyle wanted to tell Joshua not to worry, that he wouldn't be awake much longer anyway. He could already feel his heart struggling, the heavy thump slowing down like a chopper's rotors coasting to a stop.

Someone shoved a needle into his arm. Kyle opened his eyes again, looking for Joshua. All he saw was a sea of swirling black dots growing larger. He heaved a sigh as the morphine began to put a cap on the pain. At least he wouldn't take his last breath in mortal agony.

Kyle closed his eyes, feeling himself starting to drift. Everything began to fade in and out, leaving bits and pieces of sentences behind.

"…bloody mess…"

"…not sure if I…"

"…artery's hit too bad…"

"…lose the leg…"

A surge of panic washed over him at those three words, followed by a fatalistic calm. Well, what had he expected? He knew the damage something like a sniper's bullet could do to a body. Shredded veins and arteries, shattered bone, massive tissue and nerve damage. The image that the grim list brought up wasn't pretty. Cripple wasn't a word any soldier wanted in his vocabulary. Neither were endless surgeries and hospital stays. Damn, he hated hospitals…and if the surgeries didn't work?

Retirement at best. A VA facility at worst.

Could he live confined to a wheelchair?

The thought sent a wave of denial through him so

violent he jerked.

"Easy, Kyle, you're going to be okay."

No. No, he wasn't. He was going to be a cripple, a burden, and that was totally not okay. If he couldn't make it under his own power, he may as well be dead. Better to go down fighting, doing what he'd been born to do. With a little luck and a nicked artery, that could happen. Couldn't it?

The com still in his ear crackled to life. "Bad news, big H," Capella said. "T-Bird was made in the air and got sidelined. Onlookers advise a trip to P3. Time out twenty-two sixties."

If the morphine didn't have such a tight hold, Kyle would have cursed. The chopper wasn't coming. Next pick up was twenty-two hours away. He couldn't remember where P3 was, but knew it wasn't anywhere close. Not only was he not going to make it, his team, men he thought of as brothers, were going to be in danger because of him. Hard to run and hide if you're carrying a body.

"Josh…"

"Kyle, shut the hell up. I know what you're thinking and so help me, if you say one word about leaving you here I'm going to kick your sorry ass into next month. Just be still, will you, and concentrate on staying alive. I need to think."

****

Joshua gave Kyle's hand a hard squeeze before letting go. He didn't have to be a mind reader to know what his buddy had been thinking. Damn idiot knew better. None of them would even think about leaving a fellow Hawk behind. "Get him ready to move," he ordered Gage.

"Cap, P3 is miles away. And he doesn't have an hour, much less twenty-two."

"Damn it, don't you think I know that? Just get him ready."

"All right. I'll need to immobilize the leg. The tourniquet Waterhouse put on the nicked artery should hold for now, but the knee's in pieces. Can't risk the bone shifting and cutting things up worse than they already are."

"You've got three minutes." He tapped the com. "Eagle, how's the terrain look from up there?" They'd neutralized the enemy lying in wait at the second pickup zone, but that didn't mean they were safe. Between now and dawn, they had to find a bolt hole to lie low in. Someplace where Sam, and especially Kyle, could get the help they needed. And he knew of only one place like that within walking distance. Problem was, he wasn't sure of their welcome once they got there.

Ty's voice came back, as unflappable as ever. The man had nerves of raw steel. "Party forming at your six about two blocks out. Advise a move ASAP."

"Roger that. We're mobile in two." He pulled a folded map out of a pocket and motioned Dell and Rashid closer. Unfolding the creased paper, he pointed. "I need recon along this route. Let me know if you see anyone remotely resembling our terrorist friends, Cairo cops, or Egyptian military. This is your objective."

Dell whistled low. "Sure you want to go there?"

"Go where?" Brick asked, glancing over at them from where he guarded the entrance to the small deserted house they'd pulled Kyle into.

Joshua stayed silent and refolded the map, letting

Rashid answer Brick. "What's the one place he told us to stay clear of before we started this gig?"

Brick groaned. "Ah hell, boss."

"You'd rather we let Kyle bleed out," Joshua snapped.

"Hell no! Just..." The big man fixed his worried gaze on Joshua. "Won't this put her in danger, too?"

Joshua thought of the woman he and Kyle had grown up with, the woman they'd come to love like a sister. Putting Farrah Hastings in danger went against everything inside him. But what choice did he have? It was either that or let Kyle die.

"Go," he said to Dell and Rash. "We'll be right behind you."

Chapter Two

Something pressed against her face.

"Don't scream."

Farrah jerked wide awake at the quiet order, her heart slamming into her throat. Her first instinct was to do exactly what the voice told her not to. She grabbed the hand over her mouth and tried to pull it away. Her assailant leaned more weight onto her, pinning her down while his big hand smothered her. Panic surged.

"Farrah, it's me, Joshua."

Farrah stilled, not quite ready to believe her ears. Joshua Colby? Here? Why would Joshua be in Cairo? More importantly, why would he be sneaking into her room in the middle of the night? She reached for the bedside lamp, needing to see his face.

"No," he whispered. "No lights. No one can know we're here." His hand moved off her mouth hesitantly, as if ready to silence her again if need be. She wasn't a fool. Whatever had brought Joshua to her room situated above the World Health Organization clinic on the edge of Cairo's rundown east side had to be serious. He'd never have approached her otherwise.

"What are you doing here?" she demanded. He eased off her to stand beside her bed. It was night, but the darkness in her room wasn't absolute. She could see his outline against the window. Tall, broad shoulders, his flat stomach and narrow waist bulked out by a belt heavy with pouches and weapons. Instead of answering her question, he flipped her covers back and pulled her up, into his arms. Hot breath against her cheek made her shiver.

"One of my men needs a doctor."

That didn't explain why he'd come to her. She'd completed her residency only months ago. While she'd graduated at the top of her class, her practical experience was limited. Hence, her decision to sign up for a year with the WHO before she opened her own practice. To top things off, Joshua knew first-hand about her aversion to all things military. He knew better than to bring that kind of trouble to her door.

He gave her a little shake. "Come on, Farrah, wake up. You know I wouldn't be here if it wasn't life or death."

"All right. All right! Stop shaking me. I'm awake," she grumbled. She didn't usually snap at people, but it was his own fault. He'd scared her. Some of the adrenaline flooding her body had already drained away, leaving her limbs shaking. She didn't like the feeling one bit. She badly needed a minute to catch her breath, especially if Joshua truly had a patient for her to treat. "Just…let me get dressed and I'll come with you. How far away is he?" She looked around the dark room, trying to remember where she'd put her clothes when she'd gone to bed.

"He's here."

"What?" Farrah shoved her hair back from her face, not sure she heard right. Joshua didn't just tell her he brought a member of the U.S. military to the WHO clinic. If the Egyptian government found out, she'd be lucky just to be tossed out of the country.

"We've got him downstairs in the exam room next to the exit." Hands squeezed her shoulders. "Hurry, Farrah, it's Kyle, and I don't think he has much time."

Kyle? Farrah couldn't move when Joshua released her. She couldn't even draw a breath until the door to her room eased closed behind him. Only then did she jerk into motion. Not bothering to change out of her sleep shorts and t-shirt, she snatched her medical coat from the hook on the door and shoved her bare feet into shoes. She almost flung the door open, but caught herself, easing it open and closed again with the same care Joshua had taken. All she could think of as she made her way quietly down the stairs was Joshua's last words. *It's Kyle, and I don't think he has much time.*

She hit the last stair step almost running, not slowing down until she reached the exam wing. The clinic was actually made up of several small buildings built side-by-side. Parts of the common walls had been removed to create enough space to handle the huge influx of daily patients. Joshua waited for her at the end of the long hallway. She slipped inside the dimly lit room as soon as he opened the door.

Farrah blinked, her eyes adjusting to the light coming from a couple of small flashlights. Her first thought was that the room was crowded, even though she counted only three men besides Joshua and the one on the exam table. Two of the men were obviously soldiers, one with an arm in a sling. The third, dressed in jeans and a blood-smeared t-shirt, stood in a corner with his face in shadows, arms wrapped tight around himself. Joshua hadn't mentioned more than one patient, but two of these men obviously needed attention.

Kyle came first, however, and she shifted her gaze to where he lay prone in front of her. His face was pale, his eyes closed. There was blood smeared on his face and hands. An IV bag of clear saline hung from the pole at the head of the table. A small tube twisted its way from the bag to the needle taped to Kyle's arm. A blood-pressure cuff curled around his other arm.

After watching his chest rise and fall a few times, Farrah went to work. The first thing she did was remove the slats of wood secured to both sides of his right leg. She didn't have to ask why they were there. Kyle's knee was almost the size of a basketball. What looked like a whole box of gauze pads was taped around the swelling flesh. She understood why when she peeked beneath the bloody bandages. Farrah swallowed hard. So much damage. She'd dealt with a few bullet wounds before, but nothing quite so…massive. And Kyle had more than one wound.

Farrah examined them all, cataloging the injuries in her head. The one wound she didn't examine lay beneath a blood-soaked piece of cloth held in place by a makeshift tourniquet cinched tight around Kyle's thigh. The material might have been white at one time, but was now a solid red. *Has to be a damaged femoral artery under there. Too much blood for anything else.*

"I can't believe you brought him here!" she muttered fiercely. Moving him in this condition was the last thing she would have recommended.

The silence in the room suddenly grew heavy. She didn't know why until Joshua stalked around to stand opposite her on the other side of the table. "He's dying, Farrah," he said harshly. "Sorry to interrupt your little save-the-world campaign, but you're the only one within a hundred klicks I can trust. You don't want us here, fine, we'll go. But not before you do your doctor thing and get him stable enough to move. Do *that*, and I promise we'll be gone before sunrise. No one need ever know you helped us."

Farrah fought the urge to slap Joshua the way his words hit her. Stupid, stupid man. Did he really think so little of her? She shot him a glare before returning to her assessment. "I thought you knew me better than that, Josh Colby. It's not me I'm worried about, you idiot." She motioned to Kyle's leg with her blood-stained hand. "Moving him in this condition could have killed him. I would rather have gone to him."

Another long silence, this one not so heavy. Finally, Joshua cleared his throat. "Wasn't safe."

"Well, it's not very safe here, either. The Egyptian government sends people to check on us almost every day. If they find any of you here, the least they'll do is shut us down."

"We'll stay out of sight."

"See that you do." She didn't waste any more time berating him. Just looking at Kyle told her Joshua had made the only call possible. Blood leaked from the ragged wounds every precious second, pooling on the exam table. Blood Kyle couldn't afford to lose. Pulling a penlight from her coat pocket, she leaned over and checked his pupils, then felt the pulse in his neck. Dear God, Joshua was right. They were losing him.

"I need to go in and stop the bleeding." She shuffled her mental list of the injuries, putting them in order of importance. The nicked artery came first. If she couldn't get that plugged, all the others wouldn't matter. He'd bleed out right in her hands.

"What's his blood type?" She pulled the little chain from under her coat and nightshirt. Several keys jingled until she found the one she wanted.

"O-positive," Joshua and one of the men said together.

Farrah nodded and unlocked the small cooler bolted to the floor. Donated blood was precious and closely monitored. She'd have to explain the shortage somehow, but that was the least of her worries. Stitching flesh back together was one thing. She was good at that. Stitching arteries? That was another matter entirely. She wasn't yet comfortable doing something that delicate without a more seasoned doctor looking over her shoulder.

"I want to wake one of the other doctors," she said, removing three bags of O-positive from the cooler. "That arterial wound could get tricky."

"Are you saying he'll die if you operate on him?"

She shook her head and tucked one of the bags of blood under her arm to start warming it. "No, that's not what I'm saying. I'd just rather he have someone more experienced." She locked the cooler and grabbed another IV line from a drawer.

"Too risky. It's best if no one else knows we were even here." Joshua touched her shoulder as she stopped at Kyle's side. "You'll do fine, Farrah. If I didn't believe that, I wouldn't have brought him to you."

Farrah let the matter drop. Arguing with him would only waste precious minutes Kyle didn't have to spare. She only wished she had as much confidence in herself as Joshua did. She hated that her first solo experience at arterial repair was going to be on someone she really cared for. It was going to make it so much harder to maintain that professional level where she viewed things dispassionately. That was the only way she could deal with the severe trauma cases. She had to tuck her emotions deep inside behind a thick wall of concentration.

As soon as she had the second IV hooked up and running, Farrah checked Kyle's pulse again. Slow and thready. The need to hurry pressed down on her. She glanced at Joshua as she pulled a rolling instrument tray from a corner and started piling on sterilized packs of scalpels, forceps, and sutures. "You have a medic with you? Someone who knows a retractor from a scalpel?"

"Gage."

One of the scary-looking soldiers stepped forward. She paused and looked him up and down. Tall, broad shoulders, slim build. His blond hair, blue eyes, and tanned skin reminded her of the proverbial surfer type. Her gaze moved on, snagging on the stethoscope hanging around his neck. She hadn't noticed it before. The dangling ends tapped the barrel of the rifle he cradled across his chest. The other soldier, the one with the sling, moved up beside him. He was the dark to Gage's light, with black hair, black eyes, and bronzed skin. The sculpted goatee he wore gave him a rakish air. Farrah met his determined stare and arched a brow in question.

"Name's Sam. I can't sew him up," he said, lifting his wounded arm slightly, a wince of pain flashing across his face. "But I can monitor vitals."

"Good." She tilted her head at the sink in the corner. "Both of you wash up. And for goodness sake, put away that gun. That goes for all of you. There'll be no shooting in here. I've got a couple of sick patients sleeping down the hall." Patients who would be awake in a few hours. People would crowd the clinic's halls shortly after that. More patients, nurses, doctors.

Officials.

Thoughts of getting caught, of the damage to not only her reputation, but the WHO's, flitted through Farrah's mind. She firmly pushed such worries aside as she set about cutting the rest of the blood-soaked clothing off her patient.

Her patient. She had to think of him as just another patient, one of the many she treated every day, nothing more. Not the close friend she'd gone to school with. Not the laughing, joking young man she'd watched go off to boot camp as eager as a kid on his first day of school. No, this wasn't Kyle Fagan, one of two men she held close to her heart. This was a stranger, just a face-less stranger. If she let herself think the shredded flesh under her hands belonged to Kyle, she'd throw up.

"Is there anything I can do to help?"

The softly spoken voice was so out of place, she started. Looking up, she found the man in jeans and t-shirt standing on the other side of the table. He was younger than she'd first thought, late teens, early twenties. Too young to be part of Joshua's crew. Joshua laid a hand on the young man's shoulder. "No, you stay—"

"Yes. Yes, you can help." Farrah didn't care that she overrode Joshua. He might be in charge of this band of misfits, but this was her clinic. At least it was as long as no one found out she was treating a member of the U.S. military. Noting the blood stains again, she asked, "Are you hurt?"

He quickly shook his head and pointed at Kyle.

"It's his blood."

"Okay. You can wash up, too. Gage and I will need someone to hand us instruments. There's a scrub top in the cabinet next to the sink. Change your shirt." She ignored Joshua's questioning gaze and went back to prepping Kyle's leg, swabbing every inch of unbroken skin with antiseptic. The dark orange stain of the liquid looked bloody in the dim light.

"I'm going to need more than flashlights. Can we turn on the overhead?" She looked up in time to catch Joshua exchange glances with his men. Finally, he moved to the light switch.

"We'll risk it."

Farrah closed her eyes briefly as the bright lights flickered on. When she could see, she pointed to a small placard hanging from a nail beside the door that read, QUARANTINED. "Put that on the door. No one will come in without knocking." She heard the door open and close as she moved to the sink. Both Gage and Sam had finished washing up and were helping each other into gloves. The young man with the quiet voice moved to the side to make room for her.

"My name's Jeff, by the way," he said.

"Nice to meet you, Jeff. Don't forget to scrub under your nails."

He dutifully obeyed as she soaped up her arms. "Do you really think you can save him, Ms. Hastings?"

"That's Dr. Hastings," she corrected gently, "and I'm going to try my best."

When she was done washing, her hands gloved, she moved back to the table. Gage, she saw, did indeed know a little about medicine. He'd set up the anesthesia, the mask ready to go over Kyle's face, and changed the saline bag. Sam, stethoscope now dangling from his ears, pulled up a rolling chair with his foot and made himself comfortable. He held the end of the scope to Kyle's inner arm, then began pumping the blood-pressure cuff with his good hand. Air hissed. A few seconds later, he said, "Seventy over forty."

Good enough. Farrah pointed to the belt cinched tightly around Kyle's upper thigh. "That artery is going to be the deciding factor. If it's too damaged to fix, there's no use working on the knee. I'll have to amputate." She said it quickly, dispassionately, but still couldn't keep from cringing inside. She'd only assisted in a handful of amputations in her short career, and those had been bad enough. This? Taking the leg of one of her best friends? This would stay with her forever. If it came down to it, she'd have to shove all her doubts aside and work fast. And hope she could control the bleeding.

"No."

She and Josh both stepped to the head of the table at the whispered word. Kyle's eyelids flickered and opened. His pain-filled gaze seemed to roll around the room unseeing until it landed on Joshua. He raised his hand, reaching, the weak tremble of his muscles making her want to cry. She'd never seen him so vulnerable before.

"Kyle, what—"

"No amputation, Josh…swear."

Joshua frowned. "A lost limb against your life, brother. Think about it."

"Have. Can't work…rather be dead."

Anger rose in Farrah at the ridiculous words. She'd have shaken him if her hands weren't already gloved.

Instead, she jostled his shoulder with her elbow and leaned over him so he could see her. "Hey. Kyle Fagan. You are not going to lay there on my table and spout that melodramatic garbage. I won't allow it."

His head rolled until he faced her. He blinked those dark eyes of his slowly. His brows drew down, eyes narrowing. Then they widened in alarm. With a strength that surprised her, he jerked his hand free of Joshua, pulled back, and punched his friend in the stomach. The angle was awkward and the force almost non-existent, but Joshua still took a step back. "What the hell was that for?"

"Lost your…fuckin' mind?" Kyle gasped and closed his eyes, as if the punch had taken the last of his strength. "Can't believe…you brought me to her. Such an idiot."

Torn between laughing at the offended look on Joshua's face and being offended herself, Farrah said, "Well, you're here now, so we're just going to make the best of it. Now, no more talk about dying. Let's get started, shall we?" She nodded for Sam to turn on the anesthesia. Gage lifted the mask.

"No." Kyle turned his head, dodging the mask with an urgency she didn't understand. Not until he spoke again. "No. Not her. Someone else. Anyone but her."

Farrah bit her lip, willing away the hot sting of tears behind her eyes. Amazing the pain three little words could cause. *Anyone but her.* As if he didn't trust her. As if he didn't think her competent enough to take care of him.

She glanced up, easily reading the apology in Joshua's gaze. She'd like nothing better than to be able to give Kyle what he wanted. To march right out and

33

send in someone older, someone with a lot more experience. Only they didn't have anyone else, did they? Like Joshua said, she didn't dare involve one of the other doctors. There was just her.

She squared her shoulders. Okay, she'd treated reluctant patients before. Poor people who'd never once been to a doctor, who feared the shiny metal instruments, strange beeping machines, and the young woman who couldn't speak one word of their language. She'd overcome many an unwilling patient with a show of confidence. And sometimes, only when the case called for it, a little gentle force. She nodded firmly to Joshua. "We don't have time for this. Hold him."

Kyle got out one snarled, "Bastards!" before Gage pressed the mask over his face. Weak as he was, it still took all of them to keep him in place on the table until he'd breathed in enough gas. Farrah sighed along with the rest of them when his eyelids finally fluttered closed and his breathing evened out.

"Gracious, such dramatics." She tried to sound like the cause of those dramatics meant nothing. Like the fact Kyle didn't trust her to treat him didn't hurt at all. You'd think he'd at least trust Joshua's decision to bring him to her. But then, she was a last resort, wasn't she? They'd never have come if they had a choice.

She waited until Gage fit the elastic band of the mask around Kyle's head to keep it in place. "BP every two minutes while we're on the artery," she instructed Sam. "Gage, you stand over here please, I may need an extra hand. Jeff, if you don't know what something is when I ask for it, say so, don't guess. And you." She pointed at Joshua. "Guard the door and stay out of the way."

He gave her a little salute with a slight quirk of his lips that looked odd against the background of his worry. Farrah reached for the belt. "All right, everyone, let's see what we've got."

Chapter Three

Kyle wasn't sure what the noise was that roused him. All he knew was that it pulled him out of a blissfully numb state back into the pain-filled real world. He didn't like it one damn bit. He wanted to shoot the person responsible, was already feeling around for his gun, when he realized the noise was the sound of someone crying. Not boo-hoo wailing out loud crying, but the soft little sobs his Granny Fagan used to refer to as weeping.

He listened to the sound, half-afraid the crying came from him. No, too feminine. Had to be a woman. And damn if the quiet little sobs didn't threaten to break his heart. He didn't have a choice now, he had to wake up. Had to see what he could do to stop those tears.

After several seconds of struggling to push his eyelids open, Kyle finally got them lifted enough to look around. He didn't have to look far. The distressed woman stood not three feet away, almost within touching distance, a slim figure covered in a white coat with miles of red-gold hair tumbling down her back. A man held her in the circle of his arms. A man Kyle easily recognized. Some of the urgency pushing at him eased. Good. Whoever she was, Joshua would take care of her. He'd—

The woman lifted her face, smiling weakly at something Joshua said. Kyle's heart skipped a beat.

God help him, he hadn't been dreaming earlier. It really was Farrah!

He watched, helpless, as Joshua leaned down and gently kissed her tears away. Pain tore through Kyle. Not the physical kind, the one a good dose of morphine could take care of. Oh no. This kind went too deep, had been a part of him for too long. This kind went all the way back to his high school days. To the very day he planned to ask cute little Farrah Hastings to go out with him…only to have someone else ask her first. It only made it worse when that someone turned out to be his best friend. It was the first and only time Kyle had ever been tempted to cut Joshua out of his life, because Josh never had to ask a girl twice. Farrah had been his from that day on. Off limits. Out of reach. Even when she broke up with Josh, Kyle knew he didn't have a chance. The military was as much a part of his life as Joshua's. No safe, civilian job, no Farrah.

If asked, Kyle would have said that was one fast rule Farrah Marie Hastings would never break. But from the look of things, Joshua just about had her convinced otherwise.

He let his eyes close, the lids suddenly way too heavy.

Too late again, Fagan. Always too damn late.

He was drifting back toward sleep when more noise dragged him into consciousness once again. He tried ignoring the arguing voices, letting the sounds roll over him without actually focusing on the words. He thought it was working until cool, trembling fingers pressed against his wrist. Then he heard every word loud and clear.

"—don't tell me he can't be moved."

Kyle grinned. Joshua was in full Harrier mode. He pitied the person on the other end of that tone.

"I just did."

Damn, that was Farrah. If Josh was using that tone with her, maybe he'd imagined that tender scene earlier. Either that, or the situation had sure gone to hell in a hurry.

Kyle forced his eyes open, searching the dim room until he found Farrah's sweet face. Only she wasn't looking very sweet at the moment. The glare she had pinned on Joshua was as sharp as one of her scalpels.

"You brought him to me so I could save his life. I refuse to let you put that life in jeopardy again."

If not for the drugs dulling his senses, Kyle would have laughed at the look of frustration screwing with Joshua's usual stoic expression. The Harrier wasn't used to anyone questioning his orders. Not since he'd taken over the Hawks two years ago. The look he turned on Farrah was just as sharp as hers, just as cutting, revealing a ruthlessness Kyle was surprised Joshua let Farrah see. Hell, the man was just holding this woman in a tender embrace a moment ago. Now he was trying to intimidate her?

"He's a soldier, Farrah. This is his job. He'd be the first to tell you he can't stay here. I need you to move aside, now. Dawn is almost on top of us. We have to go."

Her chin lifted. Kyle would have liked to lay there and listen to the impending fight, but knew there wasn't time. Joshua was right. If he stayed, he'd just be putting her in more danger. He twisted his wrist under her hand, capturing her fingers. Her gaze dropped immediately, first to their joined hands, then his face.

Her smile warmed him like the sun on a spring day. He felt his heart respond, wretched organ that it was.

"Kyle! You're awake."

He tried to force his lips to curve up to take the sting from his words. No time for pleasantries. "Josh is right, sweetheart. I have to go with them."

Her smile disappeared, damn it, just like he knew it would.

"No."

Kyle felt a familiar hand land on his shoulder. The slight squeeze was encouraging. "My eyes outside," Joshua said, his tone clipped, "have already spotted several men with guns a few blocks over. They're searching building by building, Farrah. We couldn't erase all the blood where Kyle was shot, so they'll be looking for anyone injured. You won't be able to cover for him. He stays, he's as good as dead."

Kyle watched Farrah's forehead wrinkle, her lips tighten. She opened her mouth, then closed it again without speaking. Straight, white teeth tugged on her bottom lip. Her gaze circled the room before settling on him once more. He could see the moment the fight went out of her. Her next words weren't what he expected.

"There's another alternative."

Joshua muttered a swear word. "We don't have time for this. Gage, get the stretcher." He tried to muscle his way between Farrah and Kyle. Farrah's grip on his hand tightened, and Kyle squeezed back, unwilling to let her go.

"There's a safe room," Farrah said quickly. Joshua stopped trying to push her aside and took a step back. His gaze locked with hers.

"Safe room?"

She nodded. "Yes. Only WHO personnel know about it. It's not very big, about the size of this room, but we can hide Kyle there. All of you can hide there. You can stay till night fall. The searchers will be long gone by then."

"Where's this room?" Joshua asked.

Focused as he was on the woman holding his hand, Kyle saw the hesitation in her gaze, the shadow of something close to fear. She licked her lips. "Underground. There's a tunnel access."

Kyle closed his eyes. No wonder she was so hesitant. Farrah had a bad case of claustrophobia. Joshua had once told him she'd even freaked out in an elevator once. The words underground and tunnel were definitely not her friend.

He opened his eyes. "You stay up here," he said as clearly as the drugs let him. "You don't have to go down with us." The squaring of her shoulders and hardening of her expression reminded him that he'd forgotten who he was talking to. He wanted to swear again when she twisted her hand free of his and shoved her hands into her coat pockets.

"I'm a doctor. I need to stay with my patient."

"Damn it, Farrah!"

"Don't swear, Kyle," she said, a sudden brisk confidence in her voice that he didn't believe for an instant. "Joshua, you need to call in your other men right away," she continued, suddenly moving around the room with quiet efficiency. She grabbed a canvas bag from a cabinet and started stuffing things into it. Kyle closed his eyes again and listened to her voice, knowing there was no stopping her now. The Harrier could order her to stand down all damn day and it wouldn't do any good. When Farrah Hastings decided she needed to do something, she did it, consequences and fears be damned.

"Have them come in through the side door at the end of the hall. Less chance of anyone seeing them. Gage, please bring the stretcher. We'll have to be very careful getting Kyle down the stairs."

Beside him, he heard a deep, frustrated sigh. "If I had more time," Joshua said quietly, "I'd turn her over my knee." A light pat on his shoulder, then his friend was gone. From around him came the sound of bodies in motion. Kyle tried not to focus for the next few minutes as he was transferred to a stretcher. Jagged shards of pain shot through the barrier of painkillers in random strikes, leaving him gasping. A cool hand smoothed once over his forehead. Instantly he felt comforted, tension from the pain leaking out of his muscles like water through a sieve. Farrah's hand left him and he listened, straining his hearing for her light step, tracking her as best he could. There, to his left, down around his feet, up and to the right, back down and around his feet, again to the right…

Kyle smiled to himself, recalling the level of frustration in Joshua's voice when he'd threatened to spank Farrah. Maybe he was wrong. Maybe the two of them weren't getting back together. He'd always thought they were more like oil and water than a cohesive pair anyway. Maybe, just maybe, if he got his act together, he might be the one to convince Farrah to take a chance on loving a soldier.

Then the stretcher he was on was lifted. Just that slight movement caused more pain than the drugs could mask and knocked some sense into him. His leg was a mess. Despite Farrah's tender ministrations, there was still a chance he'd lose it, if not his life. He had no business dreaming of a future, much less one with Farrah. One day, hell, one hour at a time, was all he should be thinking about right now.

He cracked his eyes open as they exited the room. The hallway was dim. Still dark outside, then, but something told him dawn wasn't far off. There was more noise coming from behind the closed doors of the occupied patient rooms they passed than from the men walking quickly and quietly down the hall. He tilted his head up a little when they stopped. Farrah opened a door to a closet-sized space. She bent and lifted out a rolling mop bucket, setting it aside as quietly as possible. Then she squatted, her fingers running along a strip of wood marking the closet's threshold. Next thing he knew, she was lifting a section of the closet's floor on nearly silent hinges. Farrah stared down into the dark hole in the floor, but didn't move. Kyle let his head fall back. He'd give anything to be able to stand up right now. He'd walk over to her, take her in his arms, and tell her she damn well wouldn't ever have to hide in a hole in the ground. Yet, here she was, willing to do just that—because of him. Damn if the guilt didn't hurt almost as bad as his leg.

****

Farrah tried to stop her insides from shaking apart. Just the thought of walking down those steps, of being boxed in by those narrow walls made her sick to her stomach. "There's a light switch at the bottom," she whispered.

She caught Joshua's nod, saw him motion to one of his men—a slight, brown-skinned man she would have taken as a native—to go down first. The soldier navigated the stairs with ease, disappearing quietly into the darkness. Several seconds later, the light came on. Another few seconds and the man appeared at the bottom of the stairway. He made a motion with his hand and she saw Joshua make one with his.

"Go," he said, squeezing back so Gage and another man could carry Kyle down. She was afraid the steep stairs would be a problem, but the men handled the stretcher and its burden with ridiculous ease. The others quickly followed until it was just her and Joshua. He gestured to the stairs. "Is this the only entrance?"

"No, there's another tunnel through a door in the far wall. It's locked, but I have a set of keys. The tunnel comes up a few houses down where we keep the vehicles. You won't be trapped down there." She let those words repeat over and over in her mind, hoping she could somehow make herself believe them by the time it was her turn to go down the stairs.

"Good," Joshua said.

The sound of voices came from down the hall. Joshua stiffened, his hand going to the gun on his hip.

"No." Farrah put a hand on his and squeezed. "It's only the shift change. I recognize the voices. Hurry."

"What about you?"

"I need to clear my schedule so I'm not missed before I can join you. And I have to get the keys. Give me an hour."

He nodded. "All right, but don't take any chances. Things get tense up here, you stay put and play dumb blond. I don't want you getting hurt. And no more tears, hear? I promise you we're getting through this."

Before she could even take him to task about the

dumb blond comment, he was down the stairs. Farrah eased the trapdoor closed. She shook her head at his order not to shed any more tears. Joshua never knew what to do when she cried except hold her until her tears ran out. Kyle, on the other hand, was too impatient. He knew just how to gently tease her out of a crying jag. She missed that teasing. Even when he took it a step too far and riled her temper. She could only hope she'd done enough so he'd one day be able to tease her again. She'd managed to temporarily stitch the damaged artery back together, enough, at least, to save his leg and his life, but she knew it wouldn't last. The tissue was too damaged. A graft was needed, something that was beyond her skill as well as their current circumstances. And his knee! She wasn't an orthopedic surgeon, but she wasn't sure anything could save the damaged joint short of a complete replacement.

She returned the mop bucket and closed the closet door just as one of the aides, a local man, came around the corner. At first he smiled at her, then his eyes widened as he took in her appearance. Glancing down at herself, Farrah barely managed not to wince. Fresh blood stains marred the white of her coat. She needed to hurry and change before one of the other doctors saw her and started asking questions.

"Good morning," she said, hurrying past man. Once around the corner, she dashed for the back stairs.

****

The clinic was busy when Farrah made it back down to the main floor. She was a little later than usual, but decided to keep to her normal routine. She smiled and nodded to those she encountered on her way to the dining room. The clinic's cook, an older woman who knew her way around a kitchen the way a surgeon did an operating room, waved to her as she entered.

"Morning almost gone, Doctor Hastings. Good you come now. You eat today? I will wait and come back." She gestured to the nearly empty trays on the buffet with a big smile. She was always trying to get Farrah to eat more.

"Thank you, Mrs. Diab. I am a little hungry this morning. Is there any coffee left?"

"Of course, yes. I bring some fresh right away." Still smiling, she inclined her head and hurried through the door to the kitchen.

Farrah quickly moved to the buffet. She used two napkins to gather as much portable food as possible, including a small covered bowl of fuul, mashed fava beans that reminded her of Spanish refried beans. There were some emergency rations in the safe room Joshua and his men could eat, but she'd rather not use any more of the WHO supplies than necessary. Replacing them would be difficult. Glancing around to make sure she was still alone, she slipped the bulging packs inside the light jacket she wore under her doctor's coat. Unlike the coat she'd worn earlier, this one was a little large for her and hid the smuggled food well. Footsteps announced the cook's return. Farrah had just enough time to snatch a plate, pile on some food, and sit down before Mrs. Diab came in with the coffee. The cook paused beside Farrah's chair, took in her piled plate, and blinked.

"Thank you," Farrah said, gently removing the cup from the woman's hand. Mrs. Diab seemed to shake herself and recovered her grin.

"You enjoy eating, Doctor Hastings, yes? Tell me

if you need more."

"I will, Mrs. Diab, thank you." She smiled and took a big bite of fresh bread, hoping to forestall any more conversation. The cook inclined her head again and left. Farrah sighed in relief and took a sip of the hot coffee. This sneaking around business was hard. She couldn't imagine how Joshua and Kyle managed without getting caught. She stared at the food on her plate. This was definitely not her normal routine. She usually ate sparingly at breakfast, if at all. No wonder Mrs. Diab had seemed so surprised. Well, it couldn't be helped now.

She used a third napkin and stowed away as much of the food as possible. She'd have to make sure no one brushed up against her or they'd surely feel all the lumps surrounding her waist. She took a final sip of coffee and hurried out into the main hall, conscious of the passing minutes. Joshua would be looking for her soon. She needed to make her excuse to the head of the clinic, Dr. Couruy, and somehow sneak back into the hall closet without anyone seeing her.

Fingering the set of keys in her pocket, she turned a corner and stopped short. People crowded the hall, their backs to her. Beyond them, Dr. Couruy confronted several armed men. His round face was suffused with color. He shook his finger in the face of the man who seemed to be in charge of the soldiers.

"You have no right to burst in here scaring my employees and patients. We have the Ministry's full approval to operate this clinic. I'll see that you are severely punished."

Farrah sucked in a breath. Even she knew better than to threaten a man with a weapon. She gasped again when the man Dr. Couruy was facing suddenly grabbed the doctor by the throat and shoved him against the wall. The people around her cried out and one woman crumpled in a faint.

"We search for American terrorists," the man said in clipped English. "One or more wounded. I ask again, did you or any of your people treat an injured man last night or this morning? Do you have Americans here?" He punctuated the last question by pulling the doctor up and slamming him against the wall again.

Farrah trembled. There was no mistaking the man's determination. He wanted Joshua and his men very badly. Had she made a mistake insisting they stay in the safe room? Dear Lord, she hoped not. She wanted to run herself, but locked her muscles, refusing to give in to the urgent desire to flee. With everyone looking around at each other fearfully, any move she made would draw quick attention. She caught a glimpse of the man she'd passed earlier on the other side of the crowd of clinic workers. Cold washed over her, leaving her light-headed. He'd seen the fresh blood on her coat quite clearly. One word from him, and she was as good as dead. These men didn't look like Egyptian military or even special police. They were terrorists, just like Joshua had said. There would be no diplomatic rescue for her if they took her.

The sound of flesh smacking flesh jerked her attention back to the confrontation. Dr. Couruy lay on the floor, conscious, but dazed. The leader of the terrorists stood over him, gesturing and issuing orders in Arabic too quickly for her to translate. Suddenly the hallway was flooded by men with guns, shouting and shoving the clinic personnel. One by one, each person was pushed against the wall face first and roughly searched before being forced to sit. Farrah took a step back. If they searched her, they'd find the food she'd stashed. She might be able to convince them she was smuggling food out to a hungry family—goodness knows there were plenty of those for it to be plausible—but she preferred not to have to lie. She'd never been good at it.

She took another step back. Something hard poked her in the back and shoved her forward. Farrah gasped. She'd been so occupied with what was going on in front of her, she hadn't noticed the two men who'd come up from behind. She glanced at them both, then quickly looked down. This wasn't the time to flout custom. If they thought her nothing more than a subservient woman, they might let their guard down long enough for her to get past them.

One of the men shoved her roughly against the wall. Just as he grabbed her shoulder, more shouts joined the cacophony. The Arabic came fast and thick, the noise reaching a crescendo as a group of people carrying a bloody body rushed into the clinic. The two men who were about to search her turned their attention to the new arrivals. Farrah caught enough of the Arabic flung around to know the man was a car accident victim. Bad for him, but the timing couldn't be better as far as she was concerned. She held her breath and inched back along the wall. There was no way for her to reach the dubious safety of the hidden room via the closet. She'd have to take the long route and hope there weren't any soldiers waiting outside to stop her. Taking a deep breath, she ducked out of the hall and ran.

The kitchen was empty. Farrah didn't pause until

she reached the back door. She opened it cautiously. The narrow alley running the length of the clinic was empty for the moment. She stepped out quickly and closed the door. Something told her going to either end of the alley would be a mistake. Instead, she darted straight across to a deep archway in the building next door. She knocked on the half-hidden door. When no one answered, she turned the knob and ducked inside. The room was dim. No lights were on and the windows were shuttered. Still, she could make out Mrs. Diab and her family huddled in a corner. The woman had her arms around the heads of two children, tucking them in tightly to her body as if trying to hide them. She met Farrah's eyes for a moment, then motioned sharply to the other doorway out of the room with her chin.

Farrah couldn't blame the woman for wanting her gone. Without saying a word, she nodded once and hurried out of the room, conscious of the frightened gazes of the children following her. She needed to hurry. Mrs. Diab wouldn't lie to protect her, not if her family were threatened.

She grabbed a scarf hanging from a hook on the wall and wrapped it around her head before leaving. Hopefully it would make her less conspicuous, though a woman in a white medical coat and pants was sure to stick in the memory of anyone who saw her. Trying to blend in with the early morning foot traffic, she forced herself not to run. Distant gunfire broke the morning's peace. Around her, people started, paused, and then hurried on their way, some changing direction away from the ominous noise. Farrah broke into a trot along with the rest of them and was soon at her destination.

The old barn had been remodeled some years ago

into a garage of sorts. She used one of the keys on her ring to gain entry, closing and locking the door behind her. Several windows set high in the walls flooded the medium-sized building with dusty light. Farrah slipped between the converted van, which served as the Clinic's ambulance, and Dr. Couruy's compact little sedan. The other entrance to the safe room was hidden in a corner behind a wheeled tool chest. She tugged and pushed the heavy chest away from the wall just enough to get the door opened. She stood for several seconds, staring at the steep stairs that disappeared into darkness. Her panting was all she could hear, the rush of air in and out seeming to drown out everything else.

Farrah pressed a hand to her chest. She had to do this. Kyle was down there, hurting, possibly bleeding. She needed to be with him. Too bad there wasn't another brave soldier to go down first and turn on the lights for her.

"You're not a baby," she scolded herself in a harsh whisper. "You're a full grown woman, a doctor for Pete's sake. Grow a spine, Hastings."

Swallowing hard, she forced herself to put one foot in front of the other. Getting the door closed again was awkward. She could only pull the chest back so far without trapping her hand. She sat on the steps when the door was firmly closed, blocking out all light. The darkness seemed to hang like a thick shroud around her, making it hard to breathe. Sweat trickled down her back and dust tickled her nose. Only the knowledge that Kyle was waiting for her kept her from shoving the door open again.

She finally made herself stand, one hand pressed against the wall, the other out in front of her. One step.

Two steps. Her legs shook hard, threatening to give out. Farrah sat abruptly. She buried her face in her hands and caught back a sob. Why in the world hadn't she brought a flashlight? It wouldn't be so bad if she could see something.

Deciding to stay low instead of risking a tumble, she inched her way down several more steps. When she reached the bottom, she stood up cautiously, staying close to the wall. There was a light switch here somewhere. She blinked back tears as she ran her hands over the rough surface. It had to be here. She had to have light. The darkness was so absolute, adding to her feeling of suffocation. She could feel the press of the earth above her, the buildings, two and three stories high, sitting heavy on their foundations. Crowds of people stomping back and forth. Vehicles rolling along, their metal bodies pounding over the uneven roads. The thought of all that weight pressing down on top of her made her cringe. Dear Lord, the ceiling could give way at any moment!

Caught on the edge of panic, Farrah closed her eyes and hugged the cool wall. She knew she'd have to go down the sloping tunnel to the safe room eventually, with or without light. She couldn't stay here. But right now, she simply couldn't move another inch.

"Farrah?"

She jumped at the voice, even as she recognized it as Joshua's. Opening her eyes, she saw him standing in front of her, a glowing light stick in his hand. With a gasp, she threw herself into his arms.

"Easy, easy there. Are you all right? Damn, Farrah, you're shaking all over. Calm down, sweetheart. You know you don't have to do this. You can stay up top.

We'll take care of Kyle."

She shook her head against his shoulder, not yet ready to let him go. "The terrorists are looking for you very hard. They're questioning everyone. Someone saw me this morning before I could change out of the coat stained with Kyle's blood. I couldn't take the chance on him keeping quiet. If they searched me, they'd find the food I was bringing to you and your men and I don't think I could really make them believe it was for some poor hungry family, especially if the man who saw me said anything, and I just couldn't, I couldn't…"

"Hush, sweetheart, hush." He held her tighter, stroking one hand over her hair. "It's all right. You did the right thing." His tone hardened. "I'm just so sorry I had to drag you into this."

"No." Farrah pushed back, easing out of his hold. With Joshua's presence and the light from his glow stick, she felt her courage returning. Or at least the panic faded to manageable proportions. She wiped at her wet cheeks with the back of her hand, feeling thoroughly embarrassed. "No, don't be sorry. I'm glad you thought to bring Kyle to me. Even if you hadn't, those men would still be at the clinic searching for you. There's no telling what they'll do to Dr. Couruy and the others. I should be there."

Joshua gripped her shoulders and shook her slightly. "No, Farrah, don't ever feel guilty for looking out for yourself. Kyle and I need to know you're safe, that you don't take any hurt from this. From what you've said, you're better off down here with us." He cupped her cheek. "Now come on. Your patient was getting restless when I left. You know Kyle. I wouldn't put it past him to try and come after you himself."

Chapter Four

One of Joshua's men stood at the entrance to the safe room. Farrah pointed to the heavy metal door standing ajar behind him. "That was supposed to be locked." The man smiled, dipped his head and raised a shoulder in a slight shrug. "I don't like locked doors, ma'am."

Joshua chuckled softly. "Don't let him fool you, Farrah. Laptop here loves locked doors. The harder to unlock, the better." He focused on the soldier. "Any change?"

The man snorted. "Just a bunch of swearing. Same old Kyle. And it's Peregrine, ma'am, not Laptop." He threw Joshua a scowl. "I am not a fu—" He cut himself off and shot her an apologetic glance. "I'm not a blasted computer. That's Capella's gig."

Farrah bit her lip to keep from smiling at his sudden switch of words. Joshua must have warned his men that she didn't like foul language. "Peregrine, as in the falcon?"

"Partially. Since we're the NightHawks, it made sense. But it's more because we travel around a lot. Peregrine means wandering pilgrim."

Joshua put a hand on her back and urged her past the soldier. "Which is too much of a mouthful when we're running a mission. We tried shortening it to Grin, but he wouldn't answer to that either."

The young soldier winced. "Come on, Cap, Grin? Like I'm a stupid clown or something?"

Joshua chuckled again and slapped him on the shoulder as they entered the safe room. Farrah immediately looked for Kyle. The men had placed his stretcher on top of a couple of storage boxes pushed together. He was looking in her direction when she entered the room, eyes fever bright. He lifted an arm, reaching for her. She focused on his hand, blocking out everything else; the walls, the dim light, the crowd of men who seemed to take up every inch of space. Taking his hand, she whispered, "I'm here. It's okay."

Which was half a lie. It was very much not okay. She could still feel the weight of the sand and dirt pressing all around them, enclosing them, suffocating them. She tried to take a deep, calming breath, anything to loosen the sudden tightness in her chest. Even as her lungs told her there was no air, she knew it was ridiculous. From what she'd been told, the little room was well ventilated. There should have been—*there was*—plenty of air to breath. Only her body didn't agree with her brain.

Kyle squeezed her hand. "Look at me!" he growled. "Breathe, Farrah. That's an order!"

An order? Farrah drew in a harsh breath on a laugh damp with tears. Trust Kyle Fagan to think ordering her to do something was going to work. His struggle to sit up did what his words couldn't, focusing her attention on him instead of the false sense of suffocation. "Stop that." Other concerned hands joined hers in pushing him back down. Bodies crowded close. Too close. "Would you all please step back," she said, trying to keep her voice from shaking. "My patient needs air."

"At ease, everyone. She's got this." Joshua's rough command came on top of her request.

The other men quickly stepped away. Farrah sucked in a steadying breath and met Kyle's pain-filled gaze. "Now you stay there," she ordered, brushing sweat dampened hair off his forehead. "If you tear any of those stitches, I'll have your hide. And I've got just the scalpel to do the job."

"Yes, ma'am."

The weakness of his reply—when he'd sounded so strong a few seconds earlier—had her worried. "No more talking," she said, lifting the edge of the light blanket covering him to check his bandages for any sign of fresh bleeding. "You need to rest."

His fingers brushed her arm, sending a rush of unexpected chill bumps across her skin. She stifled a shiver as he said, "So do you. You've been up half the night."

"I'll grab a cat-nap in a bit." She took his hand and tucked his arm back under the covers. Though the sun was well into heating the city above, the air in the little underground room was cool. Kyle nodded his head and closed his eyes. She saw him swallow hard.

"Would you like a sip of water?"

"Yeah," he said. "Just to wash the sand out of my mouth. Stomach isn't too happy with me right now."

"Probably a reaction to the anesthesia. Hang on." She walked over to a small table tucked in a corner. "Excuse me," she said to the man she'd taken for an Egyptian native earlier. He grinned at her and slid to the side, giving her access to the table. She opened her lab coat and started pulling out the bundled food. As soon as she set out the small covered bowl, the man beside her leaned over and sniffed. "Is that fuul?"

She smiled at him. "Yes. And bread and fruit and a few honey rolls I snatched at breakfast. I thought you guys would like something fresh." The man moaned dramatically and dropped to his knees.

"Ah, sweet lady, for fuul and fresh bread, I am your slave for life."

Another man slipped up beside her, his big body crowding her a bit. She started to ask him to back off, but the little-boy smile he turned on her melted her heart.

"Did I hear you say you had some honey rolls, ma'am? I do like honey rolls."

"Of course," she said laying the last of the food on the table. "Just let me get some water for Kyle and you guys can have at it." She reached down to the box tucked under the table and retrieved a couple of bottles. Then she left the corner, biting back a smile at the quiet, but intense feeding frenzy going on behind her. She handed Joshua a bottle and cracked the other one for Kyle. "You're going to miss out if you don't hurry," she told Joshua.

"I'm fine." His gaze swept over her. "I thought you felt a little lumpy earlier. Thank you for the food."

She twisted her lips. "Yes, well, if I'd had more time to think about it," she said, slipping an arm under Kyle's head so he could drink, "you and your men might have had to settle for the granola bars and jerky stored down here. The terrorists were searching everyone pretty thoroughly right before I got away."

"You shouldn't have taken the chance," Kyle said between sips.

"Hush and drink." She tipped the bottle against his

lips, practically forcing him to open his mouth. He managed about three more small sips, pausing between each one to swish the water around before swallowing. When he nodded that he was through, she eased him back down. She smoothed back his hair again, noting the heat coming off his skin. "How's the pain?"

He closed his eyes. "Manageable."

"Tough guy, huh?" She moved to another storage box and rooted inside, pulling out a small vial of morphine and a syringe.

"No," Kyle said, seeing the needle. "No drugs. When we move, I need to be conscious."

Farrah huffed quietly, not pausing in prepping the shot. "When you're moved you should be sedated up to your gills, but I have no doubt that won't happen. As it is, you can't lay there in pain for hours. It'll cause too much stress on your body." She pressed a couple of fingers to his lips when he started to speak again, and looked to Joshua. "When do you have to leave here?"

"Not for at least fourteen hours. That'll give us plenty of time to make the pickup zone by midnight."

"Where's the pickup zone?"

When Joshua hesitated, Farrah lowered her gaze and concentrated on filling the syringe. A small knot of hurt curdled the coffee in her stomach that she'd had at breakfast. He didn't trust her. She could understand—he had more lives to consider than just his and Kyle's—but it didn't make it any easier to swallow. She held up the filled syringe. "Don't worry," she told Kyle. "This will help you rest now and should wear off in about four to six hours. Okay?"

At his nod she swabbed the intake on his IV line with alcohol before slowly injecting the morphine. She stood quietly as the drug took hold. Her own tension eased as the tight muscles in Kyle's face relaxed. Fingers brushed her arm again. Joshua's touch, warm and comforting, the touch of a dear friend. No goose bumps danced over her skin this time. Seemed those were reserved just for Kyle, she noted wryly, a man who had never shown the slightest interest in her.

"Sorry," Joshua said when she met his gaze. "Secrecy is a habit, Farrah. It's what keeps us alive most days. The chopper is picking us up about six miles outside the city. Normally it wouldn't take us four hours to cover that distance, but with packing out Kyle—"

"What do you mean by packing him out?" She couldn't have heard him right.

"Just what I said. We'll have to carry him. Don't worry, we'll keep him on the stretcher as long as possible. Even I know that's better for him than a fireman's carry, considering his condition."

"A fireman's—Joshua, have you lost your mind?" she hissed, trying to keep her voice down when she wanted to yell at him. "You can't carry Kyle anywhere. Not in his condition, as you so succinctly put it."

"Farrah—"

"No, Joshua, you aren't listening. You can't move him six miles on foot, in the dark, dodging patrols or police or whoever. It's just too dangerous."

"And leaving him here isn't? Look, Farrah, I know you're worried about him. So am I. But he needs more medical attention than we've safely got here. Even if you were able to transfer him to a civilian hospital to get that attention, the terrorists probably have all medical facilities monitored by now. They'll find him.

We're not leaving him behind."

She pointed to Kyle's leg. "You don't think I know he needs more help than I can give him? That limb has to be kept as stable as possible so better qualified surgeons can fix it. Bouncing him all over the place on a flimsy stretcher is not what I call keeping it stable."

"It will have to be enough."

"No, it won't. I can take you all in a vehicle."

His expression hardened into one she rarely saw. This was the soldier he'd become. Not just her friend, but a man trained in the art of war. "No, absolutely not. You've done enough. If Kyle's life wasn't on the line, we wouldn't even be here. Fourteen hours and we're gone. The sooner we leave you alone, the less danger you'll be in."

The coldness in his voice made her want to back down, but she couldn't do that. Like he said, Kyle's life was on the line. "Stop being so stubborn, Joshua. I won't be in any danger. We can go out through the tunnel to the garage without anyone seeing us. I can transport you all in the clinic's ambulance. It'll be tight, but the ambulance is a converted van, so everyone should fit." He opened his mouth and she rushed on to cut him off. "If we turn the emergency lights on, everyone will think twice about stopping us. You won't have to hide from the military or the police, and Kyle will get a smooth ride." She saw his jaw tighten, could almost hear his teeth grinding together. Joshua had always hated giving in to anyone.

Finally, he blew out a long breath, one hand coming up to rub across his face. "There'd be more room if you stayed here."

Farrah crossed her arms, letting him see her

determination. "I can't. Physician's oath, remember? Kyle's my patient. He's my responsibility until another doctor takes over his care. Will there be a doctor on the helicopter that picks you up?"

Joshua nodded. "They know he's critical, so yes, they'll send a doc. Gage can watch him between here and there."

"From what I've seen, Gage is a great medic, but he's not a surgeon." She glanced at the blond-haired soldier standing by the door, munching on a sweet roll. "No offence intended."

"None taken ma'am. I know my limitations." His sharp blue eyes looked over her head at Joshua. "That artery blows, I won't be able to fix it, boss. Stitch could, but he's out of commission."

A long moment of silence passed. "Fine." Joshua glared down at her. "Just so you know, if there's so much as a hint of hostiles within a mile of P3, me and the guys are gone. We'll finish on foot and you'll get yourself back here in one piece."

"But—"

"No buts, Farrah." He pointed a finger at Kyle's sleeping figure. "I'm going to catch hell from him for involving you as it is. You get hurt in this, and I won't have to worry about having a retirement plan. That man will gut me in my sleep, and I wouldn't blame him a damn bit."

"That's a bit dramatic, don't you think?"

"But true. So you'll do what I tell you when I tell you, for both our sakes. Agreed?"

Farrah held his dark gaze for several seconds, but knew she'd already lost on this point. "Agreed," she said finally. Even though she didn't agree at all. The idea of these men carrying Kyle over rough ground—while possibly dodging bullets—scared her to death. Too much could go wrong. A stitch could slip or a weak part of the damaged artery give way. A bone splinter could shift a millimeter too far, causing more damage. Worse, a blood clot could develop, shooting straight to Kyle's heart or lung, snuffing out his life before she, or anyone else, could do a darn thing.

No, if she had her way, Kyle Fagan wouldn't be going anywhere any time soon.

****

Farrah dozed, her head resting on the edge of Kyle's stretcher, when the creaking of the stairs drew her eyes open. The first thing she saw was Joshua and one of his men, deep in a whispered conversation. From the look on their faces, something was wrong.

Joshua glanced up, met her gaze, then said sharply, "Gear up, Hawks. We're moving out now."

Farrah glanced at her watch as the men who'd been dozing where they sat immediately roused. Barely four hours had passed since she'd incarcerated herself with the soldiers. It was broad daylight outside.

"What's wrong?" she asked. Around her, the men silently gathered packs and checked weapons. The medic, Gage, began wrapping some kind of long strap around Kyle, securing him to the stretcher. "Joshua?"

He motioned to the man who had come down the steps. "Rashid had his ear to the door, listening for trouble. He heard someone arguing and caught the words *secret room*."

"That's not possible. Dr. Couruy and the others would never reveal this room's location."

"Why not? If the terrorists have invaded the clinic

like you said, the others might say anything to save their lives. Especially if they thought this room was empty."

"Or they might be headed down here themselves to escape the bad guys," said the big, dark-skinned man the others called Brick.

Farrah nodded. That she could believe. She'd been a fool to think no one else would look to the room for safety. But then, she hadn't counted on the terrorists being so persistent. Dear God, she'd led these men right into a trap.

"I jammed the hinges on the trap door," Rashid said. "But there's no telling how long it will hold. We need to leave pronto, Cap."

"Right," Joshua said, "Dell, you and Ty take point. Brick, Gage, you two are on stretcher duty. Farrah, stay close to them. Sam, you're in charge of Waterhouse. Rash and I will bring up the rear." His gaze stopped on her. "Farrah, you said the tunnel comes out in a garage. Is it enclosed? Is the clinic's ambulance inside?"

"Yes, to both. Assuming the garage is still empty, we should be able to load up without anyone seeing us. I can open the garage door after everyone is in the van."

"Good. We'll have to move fast. They may already have men on the way to block the exit. Let's go."

Farrah grabbed the bag of supplies she'd filled earlier, slipping the wide strap over her head and shoulder to free her arms. She followed the others into the long, dark tunnel, only vaguely conscious of the claustrophobia that normally paralyzed her. Too much adrenaline, she thought, trying to distract herself. Why worry about a little claustrophobia when she could have someone shooting at her at any second.

They reached the end of the tunnel all too soon. After a brief wait, Dell came back and motioned them out without a word. Farrah fumbled for the keys in her pocket as they converged on the large white vehicle with the red cross and blue and white WHO insignia painted on the side. She headed for the driver's door, but Rashid stepped in front of her and bowed, palm out for the keys. Not wanting to argue, she dropped them into his hand with a sigh. It took a minute for all the men to move into the back and get situated. Joshua waited at the back. The soldier named Ty seemed to appear from nowhere. He eyed the stuffed van before turning to Joshua.

"All clear outside from what I can see from in here," he reported. "I'd feel better if I could get a good view from the roof. In fact, I volunteer to make the hike to P3 on foot."

Joshua pointed a thumb inside the ambulance. "Get your butt inside Eagle. Now isn't the time to separate. We'll have Capella direct us to a safe spot to hold up while we wait for the rendezvous time. You won't have to make like a sardine for long." He nodded to Farrah as Ty huffed and pushed his way into the already crowded van.

"Try to act natural," he told her. "If anyone pops up to question you, you're transferring a patient. They get violent, you hit the deck, face down, and cover your head. We'll take care of them. Got it?"

Take care of them. Those words slid through Farrah, leaving her cold and shaking inside. She knew what Joshua meant. This right here was one of the reasons she'd broken things off with him when he joined the Army. Death always seemed to be the answer to a soldier's problems.

"Farrah?"

He wanted her to answer, but she wasn't sure what to say. Then she caught sight of Jeffery Waterhouse's strained face. They'd talked for a bit after Kyle's surgery while she was sewing up Sam. He'd told her about his terrifying capture and about his more terrifying rescue. How Joshua and his men had literally shot their way out of a trap meant to kill them all. They'd saved his life, these men who seemed ready to kill at the slightest provocation. She glanced around at each man she could see. All of them seemed to be holding their breaths, watching her, waiting for her answer. Their eyes told her they expected her revulsion, maybe even her condemnation.

"Yes, I understand," she said, feeling like she did understand for the first time in her life. A solider didn't have to be just a killing machine. Not these soldiers. These men valued life just as much as she did. They killed in order to keep innocents safe. They killed, so people like her and Jeffery Waterhouse didn't have to. "I've got it," she said more firmly, finally meeting Joshua's gaze. "You do what you have to, Joshua, and so will I. We'll get Kyle out together."

The corner of Joshua's lips kicked up. His gaze never left hers as he said, "See guys, that's how they grow ladies in North Carolina. Tough and loyal to the bone."

Farrah choked on a laugh and shook her head as she turned away. "Stop making me sound like a hound dog, Colby."

A few chuckles followed her to the large garage door. She took a deep breath to steady her hands before unlocking and pulling on the handle. The one-piece door rose on its track. Farrah tried not to wince at the sharp squeal of metal on metal. She half-expected a row of terrorists to pop up in front of her, guns raised. Fortunately, the small street outside appeared empty of threats. She motioned for Rashid to pull the van out. Part of her was aware that this was the perfect opportunity for Joshua to leave her behind. She didn't think he would, but she wasted no time pulling the door back into place and hurrying to the ambulance. No sense tempting the man.

She'd expected to drive, but Rashid waved her to the passenger side. He had the vehicle moving before her door was closed. She glanced over at him and did a double take when she saw he'd donned one of the WHO coats. She didn't ask him where he'd found it. The buttons were done up over his sandy gray fatigues. Instead of an American soldier, he looked like any other Egyptian man the clinic might hire as a driver. With a quick little bow in her direction, he reached to the dashboard and flicked on the lights and siren.

****

Kyle knew without a doubt that he was dreaming. For one thing, he was lying naked on a blanket in a secluded glen he knew was on the other side of the world from his last location. The sun was high overhead, warming his skin just this side of uncomfortable. He was thinking of moving into the shade when a figure leaned over him, blocking the light.

Yep, definitely a dream. Not that he minded one damn bit. The scraps of emerald green lace that Farrah wore might be called a bra and panty set in some circles. To him they were pure seduction. He let a welcoming smile tug his lips up. Only in his imagination had he ever seen her like this; red-gold curls tumbling around her face and shoulders, caressing bare, sun-kissed skin. Smoky hazel eyes heavy with passion, lips plump and slightly damp, as if they'd already been thoroughly kissed. He sucked in a breath and felt himself harden.

His dream Farrah raised a leg and straddled him, her fingers flexing on his chest like a purring kitten. Oh yeah, this was what he needed. She settled down over his hips; her slight weight so near his crotch it caused him to jerk in her direction. He ran his hands up her thighs to those hips, holding her in place. If they were doing this, he wanted to live in this moment, savor it, draw it out 'til the end of time. He never wanted it to end.

Farrah leaned down and pressed her lips to his. Even as he groaned and reached for more, a hated voice started up in his head accompanied by a warning siren.

She's not yours. She'll never be yours. She belongs to Joshua. You're betraying him. You're betraying them both!

Guilt, heavy and relentless, rose like an oily tide, wiping out his desire between one breath and the next. As usual, anger followed. Why did he have to stand silently by while Joshua romanced the one woman in the world who set him on fire? True, he and Joshua were as close as any brothers born, but did that mean he had to step aside without a fight? He wanted Farrah, *needed* her, like clover needed sunshine.

The warning siren grew louder. He might want Farrah, but there was no guarantee she wanted him in return, was there? No sure way to know if, back in high school, if Kyle had asked her out first instead of Joshua, her heart would lean more toward him than his best friend.

Besides, he thought bitterly as reality began blotting out his dream, she didn't like soldiers. Soldiers, killers, they were all the same to her.

Above him, the woman of his dreams gave him a sad smile before fading to mist.

A thump and bump, followed by a stab of physical pain jolted Kyle awake. He grimaced, partly because of the pain, and partly because the shrill siren of his dream became all too real. The noise drilled into his head, making it throb. A soft, cool hand slipped across his forehead, gentle fingers smoothing away the wrinkles gathered there. The hand slid its way to his cheek and he turned his face into its soothing presence. He breathed in. Alcohol, latex, some kind of strong soap, and…Farrah?

"Hey, you awake?"

Yeah…Farrah. He'd know that sweet voice anywhere. Even if he could barely hear her over the annoying siren. Kyle forced his eyes open. Darkness surrounded him. He was in a vehicle. Dim light from the dashboard came from somewhere over his head. The constant glow was augmented by a periodic flash that seemed to come from the rooftop. Why was he in an ambulance?

He let the puzzle go as Farrah leaned over him, just like in his dream. Lingering guilt made a last push at his conscience, but he shoved back hard, squelching it ruthlessly. His or not, she was a damn fine sight to wake up to.

"Hey," she said. "You back with us? Joshua says we're almost at the pickup point."

Pickup point?

The gates to his memory popped open, spilling out the last couple of shitty days in a mad flood. And like flood waters, some of the memories weren't very clear at all.

"Where…" His voice came out a croak and he stopped.

She quickly slipped her hand beneath his head and raised it so he could sip water from the bottle she held. Déjà vu. They'd done his before, and recently. Ah, yes, the safe room. But they weren't in the safe room under the WHO clinic now. They were in a vehicle, an ambulance by the sound of it. For some reason, the fact Farrah was beside him bothered him, but he wasn't sure why. Things were still a bit fuzzy.

He let the thought go for the moment, concentrating on the water bottle pressed to his lips. He rolled the tepid liquid around in his mouth, wetting every dry spot before letting it slide down his throat. When he'd had enough, Farrah lowered his head gently. She leaned back a little and Kyle finally looked past the beautiful woman busy taking his pulse. A sense of safety settled over him like a comfy warm blanket. Nothing like waking up surrounded by NightHawks.

He met Joshua's concerned gaze and gave his friend a weak smile. Habit had him counting the others he could see like a damn mother hen with her chicks. Finishing his count, he muttered a few quiet swear words. Even adding in one young, pale-faced Waterhouse, he came up two chicks short.

"Rash and Dell?"

Joshua shifted in the cramped space to face him. "Up front. Don't worry, all personnel are present and accounted for."

Good. That was good. He searched the group again until he found Sam braced in a corner next to Waterhouse. "You okay, Stitch?"

The taciturn man nodded once. "Been better, but I'm not complaining." His head tipped in Farrah's direction. "Doc here sewed me up tight. You, too. Trust me, nothing's getting past her stitches."

Kyle grunted. High praise, indeed. Sam wasn't codenamed Stitch after the little blue cartoon character. The man was a magician with a needle and thread.

Another bump and thump. Swearing joined the siren, as everyone bounced off the seats. A few heads connected painfully with the metal roof. Kyle added a few of his own choice words. He was strapped down, but the stretcher he lay on wasn't. Pain shot up his leg, making him wish, just for a split second, that Farrah had taken the damn thing off after all.

"Rash!" Joshua growled. "Stop driving like an Egyptian, damn it. You're a bloody Boston Southie who should know how to dodge pot holes."

"Sorry, sorry," Rashid called from the front seat. "My bad. Though I must point out that it is not my fault HQ picked a PZ without a decent road."

"Where the hell are we?" Kyle snarled. The pain building in his leg made him want to slug someone. "And turn off that damn siren!"

Rashid laughed. "No can do, partner. We've already made it through a couple of checkpoints thanks to the banshee and blinker. Just bear with it a little longer. We're almost there."

"There, that should help."

Kyle looked over to find Farrah putting away an empty syringe. He wrapped a hand around her wrist.

"What are you doing? I need to stay conscious."

She'd already lied to him once, promising he'd be awake when they left the clinic. Yet here he was, waking up hours and hours later, just minutes from their destination. The fact they were in a vehicle instead of on foot might have something to do with that, but he didn't really care. He hated the time he'd lost to oblivion. Not knowing if he'd missed another complication, maybe another fire fight, didn't sit well at all.

Farrah flexed her hand, but didn't try to pull out of his grip. The look she gave him held a mix of calm and fear. Nausea rolled through his stomach, forcing a rush of burning bile into his throat. Kyle swallowed hard and loosened his grip on her wrist. He'd scared her, damn it. Did she really think he'd hurt her?

"What I gave you won't put you out," she promised, her voice cool, but steady. "It's just to dull the pain. I'm sorry about keeping you under, but Joshua told me to, and I agreed with him."

His gaze bounced over to his best friend and locked. "You bastard, you told her to keep me out? How long have I been unconscious?"

"Don't use that tone with me, soldier. I'm the one in command here. Your doctor and I discussed it and decided your body needed the rest despite your stubborn hide. You're here and awake now, so what's your problem?"

Kyle tried to hold on to his anger, but it was hard to do. Whatever she'd shot him with was already taming

70

the gnawing pain so he could breathe evenly again. It also let his brain work through the last of the fog. What the hell was Farrah doing here? She was supposed to be safe back at the clinic. Being with them would only put her in more danger. She could be killed!

With an oath, he dropped her wrist like it was a live wire, not trusting himself as fear grew like a cancer in his gut. He wanted to pull her to him, hold her, and squeeze her until she would fit in his pocket, safe from the terrors of his violent world. He was such a stupid, love-sick fool.

"Get away from me," he growled. He strained, pushing himself up on an elbow so he could stare at Joshua. "She shouldn't be here. Why the hell is she here?"

Joshua pressed a hand to his shoulder, pushing him back down. "Easy, Kyle, easy. We've got it covered. Farrah's riding along to make sure you make it out in one piece. No one's going to hurt her. You have my word."

"To hell with your word. I don't need her here. I don't want her here. Send her back, damn it. Right now! Stop the car and send her back!"

"Kyle—"

"No, it's okay, Joshua." He caught a flash of something in Farrah's eyes, there and gone before he could figure out what it was. Those beautiful eyes settled on him with an expression that made him shiver. "It's not unusual for someone in a lot of pain to lash out. I'll be gone in a few more minutes, and he should calm down."

"Looks like another checkpoint ahead folks," Rashid called.

Kyle felt like screaming as he watched Farrah immediately move toward the front of the ambulance. She didn't understand. He wasn't arguing to hear the sound of his own voice. He honestly couldn't understand why she was here. Joshua should know better. That he didn't seem worried at all confused the hell out of Kyle. If Farrah was his, he'd never let her put herself in harm's way.

Farrah and Dell slid past one another, the soldier taking her place beside Kyle's stretcher. He was wearing a dark blue jacket with a white WHO patch on the front. A stethoscope was draped around his neck. "Hey buddy," he said.

"You change jobs?" Kyle asked.

He winked. "Nah, I'm just window dressing."

Around him, his fellow NightHawks shifted, flattening themselves on the van floor as much as possible. Gage and Dell draped dark blankets over the prone bodies, then pulled out some medical gear and set it on top of them. Kyle felt the cold butt of a pistol pressed into his hand. Joshua leaned close to his ear. "We've been getting through the road blocks fine, but just in case—"

Before Kyle could respond, Rashid called out again. "Damn it, looks like they're going to stop us this time. Show time, folks."

Chapter Five

The siren cut off abruptly. The van slowed, then jerked to a stop. Kyle gritted his teeth, but the expected stab of pain wasn't as sharp as before. Thank God for drugs. He checked the safety on the gun by feel. All they needed was for him to jerk the damn trigger by mistake. Kyle listened as Rashid spoke in a rush of Arabic to whoever was manning the checkpoint. He tried to pay attention, pick out words, but got distracted by Gage and Dell. The two men moved in quick, jerky motions, pulling out packages of gauze, tubes, and needles and slapping them on his stomach. Something wet trickled down his side. Kyle looked down to see a telfa pad soaked in blood lying on his chest. He jerked, trying to remember how he'd gotten wounded there, but caught Dell's wink before panic set in. Right, window dressing.

Dell began hurriedly inflating the BP cuff on Kyle's arm. On his other side, Gage was busy going through the motions of setting up another IV.

The conversation up front grew louder.

"Look," Farrah said, her studied Arabic coming out like starched linen compared to Rashid's smooth flow. "This man is a family member of the Commander of Cairo's police force. Detain us any longer, and you will have to answer for his death, not us."

Another spate of Arabic. The beam of a flashlight

swept into the van. On cue, Dell called out, "We're losing him."

Gage immediately rose on his knees and proceeded to press down on Kyle's chest, doing a great CPR imitation. Dell tipped Kyle's head back and leaned over, the wicked gleam in his eyes clearly visible. Kyle stiffened, but knew he dare not make a move to stop him. Damn, the guys would tease him about his for months.

The light vanished. The guard began another stream of Arabic that was lost in the roar of the ambulance's engine as it shot forward. Kyle shoved the muzzle of his pistol into Dell's stomach. "Bring that ugly mug of yours any closer and Gage is going to have another patient."

Dell froze, but smiled. The hand tilting Kyle's head back released him with a little pat. "Come on, Ghost, you telling me you'd rather die than let me give you the kiss of life? Damn, man, that's taking hetero to a new level."

"If I were actually dying, I probably wouldn't care. No offence to the gay populace, but put your mouth anywhere near mine any other time, and you'll find out just how hetero they raise us Clear Springs boys." Joshua rose up from his hiding place beside them. Kyle felt Joshua's hand slide against his, trying to reclaim the gun. He held onto it just on principle until Dell moved back, his hands raised in surrender, though his teasing smile remained in place. Bastard thought he was funny. The ambulance rocked as the other NightHawks crawled back into sitting positions.

"Looks like we're clear to the PZ," Rashid called.

"Roger that." Joshua tapped the com unit in his ear.

"Need a look see on P3, Capella. Any hostiles in the area?"

Kyle half-listened to Capella's response. He was waiting for Farrah to come back. He needed her to come back, to touch him again. Her touch was the best medicine. He opened his mouth to call for her, but Joshua reached out and lightly patted Kyle's leg. Just that slight touch made the dull pain flare into something that took the breath from Kyle's lungs. When he could breathe again, Joshua was staring down at him, his expression apologetic. "Sorry, bro. Did you catch that?"

Kyle rocked his head back and forth. He should have paid more attention, but between the pain, the drugs, and the worry over Farrah, his focus was shot.

"Our luck on this mission hasn't changed. Capella says he got word that the pickup point we're headed to might be compromised as well. Nothing concrete, but he talked Abe into stirring up a diversion on short notice just in case."

"What kind of a diversion?"

Joshua's expression shifted into a slight grin. "Beta unit's having a bar-b-que."

Besides being experts in urban warfare, Beta unit specialized in blowing things up. The half-mad group of explosive experts had tried to lure Brick away from the NightHawks ever since he joined up. Kyle tried to grin, too, but couldn't tell if he made it or not. "And they didn't invite us? I bet Brick is pissed." A non-committal grunt came from the back of the ambulance near the doors.

"Nah," Joshua said. "I promised him we'd throw a real bar-b-que of our own when we all get back safe and sound. He gets to blow out the pit."

Kyle clenched his fists. Home. The idea had damn fine merit. Safe would be good, too. A bit late for the sound part, though.

Reading his mood, Joshua said, "Hang in there, Kyle. Like Sam said, Farrah did good work. We both know you should be dead. Yet here you are, living, breathing, and you still have both legs. One's just a little messed up right now."

"A little messed up? Is that what you call this?" He waved one hand at the leg swathed in bandages and grabbed a handful of Joshua's shirt with the other, pulling him down until they were nose to nose. "I'll tell you what's messed up," he hissed. "Messed up is that woman up there being within a hundred miles of us right now. What happened to go in, get the leg stabilized, then get as far away from her as fast as possible? What happened to that plan, boss?"

Grim-faced, Joshua pried Kyle's hand loose. Instead of moving away, he settled on the floor next to the stretcher. He leaned close. The noise from the vehicle's engine and the wind rushing through the open windows up front allowed them a small bubble of privacy. He tilted his head in Farrah's direction. "She didn't want you moved. Said it would be too dangerous. Your knee was, still is, in pieces. Jogging you across town wasn't on the good doctor's list of approved activities." Joshua shrugged one shoulder. "When things got hot, I let her talk me into smuggling us out in the clinic's ambulance."

Kyle closed his eyes. God, had he heard right? Sweet, pacifist, Farrah Hastings voluntarily on the run with a bunch of special ops soldiers? If they weren't barely a step ahead of a well-armed, well-organized group of terrorists who'd do anything to get their hostage back, that might be funny.

"Kyle?"

Kyle opened one eye. "Quiet, you. I'm going back to sleep. I've obviously woken up in the wrong universe."

Joshua chuckled. Kyle closed his eye again. It was either the wrong universe or the whole world had gone insane while he was out. He couldn't believe Joshua let her do this. Especially considering the tender little scene Kyle's memory had no problem serving up in crystal clarity.

"You know, people keep asking me why I do things." Joshua sighed. "And I get tired of explaining that sometimes I have no damn choice. You know Farrah, Kyle. She's stubborn as hell. Woman wouldn't turn you loose."

And didn't those words send a warm fuzzy feeling through him. God, what he wouldn't give for them to be real.

"She insisted," Joshua continued, "on coming with us until she could turn you over to another MD. You have her worried, bro, and you know how she gets when something worries her. I would have had to tie her up to leave her behind."

Kyle opened his eyes and leaned his head back, trying to see the *she* in question. Farrah sat stiffly in the front passenger seat facing forward. He motioned Joshua closer. "You know you can't let her go back to that clinic. Not now. Not with the terrorists sniffing around. They're bound to figure out that she helped us."

Joshua glared at him. "Do I look stupid to you?"

"Lately? Yeah. Does she know?"

"That she's not going back? Not yet."

"Always living on the edge, aren't ya. If I didn't know better, I'd say you have a death wish."

"Just keeping life interesting."

He pursed his lips, then sighed. "You realize that if I lose this leg now, she's going to feel responsible." That was the reason he hadn't wanted her to operate on him. He knew Farrah. She'd take any loss personally. And occasionally, even the best physicians lost a battle. Why in hell she'd chosen to be a doctor, he'd never understand.

"Yeah," Joshua said, sounding as tired as Kyle felt. "Again, no choice, bro. I had to let her do it. It was that, or lose you." Joshua's hand landed heavy on Kyle's shoulder. "And let's face it, you'd have done the same."

Would he? Kyle felt ashamed he had to even ask himself that question. He might have a better shot at some kind of life with Farrah without Joshua around, but the two of them weren't blood brothers for nothing. Joshua would always be family. The last thing he wanted was to come between his brother and the woman he loved. "Yeah, well, I just hope Farrah sees it that way if something goes wrong."

Joshua dragged a hand over his face. "You and me both, bro. You and me both."

****

The pickup zone turned out to be a scraggly meadow behind a half-collapsed building outside a small village. Farrah eyed the run-down area as Rashid parked the ambulance in a copse of trees south of the crumbling structure. As soon as he turned off the lights, darkness closed in. Pale moonlight filtered through the sparsely leafed trees surrounding them, creating a sinister backdrop.

"Wouldn't it be better to wait by the building?" Farrah asked, trying to stifle a shiver.

Rashid shook his head as he peeled off the layer of civilian clothing. "Structures make good targets. Best to lay low in whatever natural cover we can find. Easier to see anyone coming and better chance of not getting blown up by booby-traps."

"Wonderful," Farrah said drily. She got out and moved to the back of the ambulance that was suddenly empty of all but Gage and Kyle. She glanced around, but the rest of Joshua's men, Jeff Waterhouse included, had already melted into the surrounding darkness. She turned back to the ambulance and climbed inside. "How's our patient?"

"He'll live." Gage flashed her a smile. "Just so we're clear, we have your permission to pack him as far as the chopper from here, right? I'm not the Harrier, so I don't want to get into trouble with a fellow medical professional."

"No, I'm the Harrier." Joshua stepped out of the dark, his voice so low she could barely make out the words. "And that means you take orders from me, not her."

Farrah welcomed the flash of outrage at his words. "He might take orders from you, but Kyle is still my patient."

"Only for the next five minutes. And keep your voice down. Sound travels pretty far at night." He placed a hand on Kyle's good leg. "Just a little longer, bro, and we're out of here."

"Good. Can't wait."

"How about another shot for the road," Farrah said.

She didn't mention it to Joshua or Gage, but she was worried about Kyle. His fever was definitely rising. "Just a small dose to take the edge off." She'd slip a little antibiotic in as well.

"Sounds like a plan, doc."

Farrah shot a glance at Joshua. No argument from Kyle wasn't a good sign. She didn't say anything, glad to see Gage taking another set of vitals without being asked. He looked at her and grimaced when he was done, wobbling his hand back and forth. She took it to mean that Kyle wasn't critical, but he wasn't good, either. She squirted the low-dose of morphine into the IV tube, followed by the antibiotic.

The muted sound of thunder rolled to them through the night. Despite being inside the ambulance and under some trees, Farrah couldn't help but glance up. A thunderstorm?

Joshua slapped a hand lightly against the floor of the ambulance, startling her. "That's our cue. Let's go. Farrah, can you take this end of the stretcher?" Farrah's heart began to pound. This was it. Another few minutes, and she would hand Kyle off to the military doctor on the helicopter. Kyle would fly off for a date with a first-class surgeon and she would return to the clinic. Hopefully things will have calmed down there and she could get back to learning what she'd need to know when she opened her own practice.

She hurriedly slipped the strap of her medical bag over her head and grabbed the end of the stretcher. Together, she and Gage pulled Kyle from the Ambulance. Joshua jogged ahead of them, his gun out and ready. She hoped he didn't expect her to keep up. Even though she had the light end of the stretcher, her arms and shoulders were already feeling the strain.

Brick appeared out of the night like a specter, making her stumble. "I'll take that, ma'am." She gladly relinquished her end of the stretcher, moving up to walk next to it instead. The sound of a helicopter grew louder, but she wasn't sure which direction it was coming from. All she could do was follow along and try not to trip on the uneven ground.

A shot broke the stillness of the night, followed by a yelp of pain.

"Sniper," Joshua shouted. "Take cover!"

Farrah dropped immediately to the ground near a bunch of tall weeds. She hugged the medical bag to her chest, wishing she knew who had been hit. More gunshots rang out. She pressed harder into the dry grass as several bullets whizzed by overhead. Twice the deadly hail landed so close she was sprayed by the sand kicked up by the impact. Farrah couldn't hold back a cry as she covered her head with her arms. Dear God, she didn't want to die here.

"Farrah? Farrah!"

Kyle's voice. Farrah peeked through her arms. She found his white face in the darkness, barely visible over a rise of ground a dozen feet away. It took her a moment to realize that Gage and Brick had followed Joshua's order a lot better than she had, taking cover in a shallow ditch.

"Here," Kyle called, waving her toward him. His wide-eyed gaze held a note of the same panic that coursed through her veins. "Crawl over here."

She started to obey, wanting more than anything to be beside him right then. Another shot rang out. Farrah jerked back to her scant cover. She didn't care if the sniper was aiming at her or not, she couldn't do it. She couldn't cross that few feet of bare ground. Stray bullets killed just as sure as well aimed ones.

"Farrah?"

She glanced over at Kyle again. Shock took her breath. The idiot had cut himself free of the stretcher and was crawling toward her, half-naked, a large knife in one hand. The light skin of his back stood out like a beacon in the night, a perfect target.

"What are you doing? Get back!" She waved him away frantically. "Kyle, stop, you have to stay still." If the sniper didn't get him, dragging his injured leg across the ground might. Her stiches would never hold up to the stress. Instead of listening to her, he seemed to crawl faster, reaching her in seconds.

"Don't worry," he said, panting hard as he pulled himself up beside her, "I'm here. I'm here. Are you hit?"

"No, I'm okay." But he wasn't. She could feel the heat coming off him in waves.

He shifted with a grunt, throwing his good leg over hers and covering her body with his. He placed his mouth near her ear. "Ty and Rashid are flanking the sniper. They'll take him out soon. Just stay down. I won't let anything happen to you."

Part of Farrah wanted to stay huddled under his big warm body forever. Just the weight of him made her feel safe, protected. His big bare chest and thickly muscled arms pressed tightly against her, shielding her. The other half of her felt like a coward. She was his doctor. She should be the one protecting her patient. She tried to wiggle out from under him.

"Stay still, Farrah. Please."

The pain in his voice froze her. "Kyle?" His body shuddered and suddenly went lax. "Kyle!" She wiggled harder, trying to get free of his limp weight. She stopped struggling when she heard someone else drop down beside them. Kyle's body was rolled off her.

"Damn, Fagan. You always know how to liven up a party," Dell said. "Check his leg, doc, but stay down. Ty took out one sniper, but he's after another. Don't want your pretty little brains splattered all over creation, now, do we."

"No, definitely not," Farrah agreed breathlessly. She pushed her hair back from her face. The heavy mass had come loose from the pony tail she usually kept it in, the long strands getting in the way as she bent over Kyle. She couldn't see much in the darkness, but felt the bandage wrapped around Kyle's leg. *Damp, but not soaked.* The skin above the bandage was warm, but not distended. No sign of blood pooling underneath.

"I think he's okay." Something small and fast zipped through the curtain of her hair, tugging several strands loose.

"Get down!" Dell shoved her to the side and followed her down, landing partly on top of her. His body jerked and jerked again as gunfire suddenly seemed to surround them. When the firing ceased, Dell rolled off her slowly. Worry over Kyle had her pushing past him. Not until she was sure Kyle hadn't been hit did she turn back to the soldier who had protected her.

"Sorry, Doc," Dell said hoarsely, blood staining his lips. "I think my wandering days are over."

Hands shaking like crazy, Farrah felt his body, quickly finding the bloody holes in his side. She shifted the bag of supplies she carried and pulled out a wad of gauze pads. She ripped his clothes where she could, and took a pair of scissors to them when she couldn't. Anything to get the pads pressed over the wounds. She knew controlling the bleeding was only a stop-gap measure at best. She could already hear the rattle in his chest that told her a lung was punctured. He needed surgery, now! Anything less was insufficient and useless in the long run.

Another body skid to a halt beside her, kicking up dust. Farrah whipped around, relief flooding her when she saw it was Joshua. His question and her answer came on top of each other.

"Are you okay?"

"He needs a surgeon."

Joshua glanced past her at Dell.

'Shit," he said. He tapped the com in his ear. "Eagle, Raptor, find that damn sniper and take him out now! Peregrine's down. Falcon, Brick, break off and get your asses over here. I want Ghost on that chopper two seconds after it lands!" He grabbed her arm. "Can you run?"

"Yes."

"Then follow me and stay low."

"But Kyle—"

"We got him," Gage said. He and Brick dropped the stretcher beside Kyle. "Stupid, Fagan. Heroic, but stupid." He shot a quick glance at Dell. "Whole damn unit's full of heroes today."

"Where's Waterhouse?" Joshua asked. "How bad was he hit?"

"Stitch has him," Gage said. "It's a through and through in the arm. He'll be okay."

Joshua nodded once. Reaching down, he pulled

Dell up and over his left shoulder. "Stay with me," he ordered her again. Then he ran.

Farrah swallowed hard and forced herself to follow. She didn't know how Joshua could move so fast carrying another man. She barely managed to keep a step behind him, staying low like he'd told her, trying to run and look over her shoulder at the same time. Then Gage and Brick were beside them. She could tell Kyle was conscious again from the set grimace of pain on his face. No help for it now.

Suddenly the downdraft from the helicopter was there, kicking up the sand around them. Farrah ducked her head and blinked rapidly as her hair whipped around her face. She saw the men flinch and knew another bullet must have hit close, though she couldn't hear it. She couldn't hear anything over the noise of the rotors spinning madly overhead as the helicopter set down. Joshua dumped Dell inside first, then reached for her as Gage and Brick lifted Kyle inside. She tried to back away.

"No. I have to get back to the clinic."

"Farrah, get in the damn copter!"

"The clinic—"

"You can't go back there. "He grabbed her and lifted her inside. "Besides, we need you."

He was right, she thought, crawling over to Dell. Blood from his multiple wounds already soaked the pads she'd slapped in place. She was trying to assess the injuries to see which one needed her attention first when Joshua pulled at her arm.

"Don't," she said urgently, "I have to stop the bleeding. Tell the other doctor I need him back here."

"There is no other doctor. He didn't make it

aboard." The anger in his voice was enough to make her flinch. "You need to help Kyle, Farrah. I'll see to Dell."

"Kyle? What—" She spun around, gasping when she saw Gage had a hand shoved down onto Kyle's leg while Kyle was swearing in a constant stream. She hadn't heard him over the noise.

"Something came loose," Gage shouted at her. "You have to fix it!"

Fear shot her heart into her throat. Where was the other doctor? There was supposed to be another doctor—one with a lot more experience than she had—one with the skill to save both Kyle and Dell. She watched in horror as the white bandage beneath Gage's hand turned a solid red.

"Farrah!" Joshua gave her a little shake. "Get your ass in gear! You can fall to pieces later! We need you. Kyle needs you!"

His harsh words, shouted over the heavy whine of the helicopter, finally penetrated Farrah's panic. She looked from one patient to the other. Who needed her more? How did she choose between them? If only she was one more person.

"Kyle first," Joshua said decisively, suddenly seeming very calm as the helicopter rose into the air. "You and Gage stabilize Kyle. I'll tape Dell up and stop the bleeding till you're done." Farrah met his gaze and let his unyielding calm center her. He was always like that in a crisis, she recalled. Always the cool one, the steady one. A solid rock in the midst of chaos. She leaned on that rock now by turning away from Dell and concentrating on Kyle. She began shouting her own orders. More light, betadine, plasma, sutures. The demands rolled off her tongue without thought.

Operating in the helicopter was not something she ever wanted to do again. Each time the big machine dropped dramatically as the wind got the best of the pilot, Farrah halted, afraid she'd nick something vital. Luckily, only a couple of stitches had come loose on the artery itself in a place that was easily repaired. She spent an hour replacing some of the inside stitching as well and most of the outside, before getting the bleeding under control. Twice she called over her shoulder to Joshua, wanting an update on Dell. Both times, he assured her the bleeding was slowing. By the time she wrapped the last bandage on Kyle's leg, the helicopter was dropping to land with enough speed to add to the nausea in her stomach. She sat back on her heels and shoved her hair away from her face with the backs of her bloody hands. "He'll do for now," she said to Gage. "Let's check Dell."

She turned around with a sigh and froze. Not simply because the look on Joshua's face was that of a man far beyond grief, but because of the tears tracking in a steady stream down his face. She'd never seen him cry before. Not once. One glance at Dell told her why. She lunged for the man Joshua held in his arms. He didn't try to stop her or hold her back. He just sat there as she confirmed her fear, the grief coming off him so palpable, she was surprised she hadn't noticed it before.

"Why didn't you say something?" she shouted. She balled a fist, wanting to hit him, but pounded her thigh instead. "Gage could have worked on him. We might have saved him." Tears choked her.

Joshua's voice was like a dead weight. "No. He was hurt too bad." He lifted a hand covered in dark blood that told her what it must have told him. "He was gone before you had Kyle's leg reopened," he confirmed. "You couldn't have saved him, Farrah. It was my decision to keep you working on Kyle. Mine. I take full responsibility."

Farrah scrubbed away tears with the back of her hand. "Why wasn't there a doctor on board? You said there would be another doctor."

His arms tightened around the dead soldier. "That's a very good question. One I intend to take up with Command as soon as we get settled. This mission has been a clusterfuck from beginning to end, and I'm not apologizing for the language this time."

For once, she didn't expect him to. She felt like cussing herself.

The helicopter touched down. Men rushed up to the door with stretchers. She noticed Kyle's eyes were open and scooted over to him. "Hey, you're going to be okay."

His hand fumbled for hers and she squeezed it tight. "Knew that," he said slowly, his words slurring a bit. "Love you."

"Love you, too," she said, the words coming automatically. As soon as they were out she froze, but quickly forced herself to relax. Of course, she cared for him; he was one of her best friends. "I'll check on you later."

She leaned over to kiss his forehead before releasing him so he could be moved. Soon Kyle and Dell both were being carried to a concrete building. Farrah crawled stiffly out of the helicopter and looked around. Not surprisingly, they were in some kind of military facility.

"You said Kyle would do for now," Joshua said, weariness and grief making his voice gruff. "Will he keep the leg?"

Farrah sighed. "I don't know. He's strong, but there's a lot of damage. I...I just don't know." Tears flooded her eyes again. Joshua drew her close and she collapsed against him. She felt wrung out, the flood of adrenaline and emotion she'd been riding as dried up as a desert well. There was nothing left to keep her going, not even hope. She'd done all she could to keep Kyle alive.

Whether it would be enough, whether he'd walk again on his own two feet, only time would tell.

Whether he would forgive her if he lost his leg?

Well, only time would tell that, too.

Chapter Six

Clear Springs, North Carolina: Eight months later.

"Did you say he was shot in the leg?" A shiver went through Farrah as she glanced up from washing her hands and arms. Her gaze swept over the man reflected in the mirror mounted over the sink, pausing on the sling cradling his left arm. Tidying up a through-and-through bullet wound wasn't something she did every day in quiet little Clear Springs. Farrah liked it that way. Gunshot wounds still had a tendency to hit her harder than any other injury, dredging up too many bad memories. Having just finished sewing up the holes in the man's arm, she wasn't in a hurry to do more. Still, as a doctor, she couldn't deny that even gunshot wounds came with the territory.

Standing behind her in the washroom's doorway, Sheriff Dan Penwell nodded. "Yep, I definitely winged him right after he got me. Not sure how bad." He cocked his head as if studying her. "You going to be able to patch him up when we catch him?"

Stifling a huff, Farrah grabbed a hand towel off a shelf. Everyone in Clear Springs seemed to know about the disastrous ending to her stint in Cairo. She squared her shoulders as she turned around to face the sheriff. At forty-something, he was still a handsome man, she thought absently. The few lines at the corners of his eyes and the gray hairs sprinkled at his temples made him look distinguished instead of old.

"Why wouldn't I be?" she said, trying to keep her irritation from showing. "I may not do surgery on a regular basis, but I did okay on your arm, didn't I?"

He touched the sling carefully. "You know that's not what I mean. Russell Craddoc's not like one of our local bad boys, Farrah. He's the real deal, a cold-blooded killer without a lick of conscience. Just being in the same room with him made the hairs on my neck stand on end, and I've been doing this job for almost twenty years. I'd rather ship him over to Asheville for treatment when we catch him, but I may not have that option."

Farrah tried not to grind her teeth. She'd been practicing medicine in her home town of Clear Springs for almost seven months now, and people still had a tendency to doubt her skills. Well, maybe not so much her skills as her fortitude. Everyone knew she abhorred violence of any kind. Becoming a doctor, someone trained to deal with the results of violence in its varied forms, seemed one of the last professions she'd choose. Only time would convince the local skeptics that she could handle whatever her career threw at her.

"I'll be available, Sheriff" she said, letting him hear the determination in her voice. "Just call me. You have my cell number."

He stepped back as she walked toward him, allowing her out of the washroom. "Fine, that's fine. Oh, and be careful when you go home tonight. I'm sending my deputies out to warn all the mountain residents to be sure and lock their doors and watch for Craddoc. With that bullet wound, he won't be able to make it far on foot. Might try to break in somewhere, maybe steal a vehicle."

"Good idea," Farrah said. "But aren't you forgetting that I don't live on the mountain anymore?" Not that she didn't like the mountains, but she'd bought a house on the flattest piece of ground she could find in the valley the moment she graduated medical school. The mountain terrain of North Carolina was heartbreakingly lovely. That didn't mean she wanted to brace herself to keep from rolling down into a gully every time she stepped outside her door. As far as she was concerned, a flat yard was a little slice of heaven.

His firm lips slid into a teasing smile. "That's right, you're practically a city girl now, aren't you."

She gave a soft laugh. If that were true, her office would be in Asheville or Charlotte instead of downtown Clear Springs. No, she had too many good memories here, too many good friends, to ever want to leave the small town she called home.

Her thoughts turned to the two friends she'd miss the most if she ever left Clear Springs for good. Not that she saw them that much anyway. Joshua and Kyle stayed on the go…or they had. The pair had taken to life in the military like she'd taken to medicine. The incident in Egypt proved they ate, drank, and breathed guns and violence, thriving on the dangerous missions that took them from home for weeks, often months, at a time. The few times she'd tried talking them into giving up such hazardous careers, they'd both laughed at her. Well, neither one was laughing now. She hadn't seen either man since that horrible night they'd all barely escaped with their lives.

"Heard anything from Kyle?"

Farrah didn't answer the sheriff right away, wondering how he knew what direction her thoughts had taken. Was she that transparent? Walking down the hall, she glanced into the treatment room she and Penwell had just left, noticing in approval that her assistant, Mary, had already cleaned up and readied it for their next patient. She entered her office at the end of the hall and sat at her desk before answering. "No, but I heard from Joshua. Kyle left the VA hospital in DC and is supposedly on his way home." She forced a smile before looking away from Penwell's sharp gaze. Kyle had left all right, as in walked out without saying a word to anyone. Stubborn man! That wouldn't have worried her, except he hadn't said anything to Joshua either. Nothing except for a two word note left on his hospital bed that said, "Going home."

When Joshua had called that morning to ask her to keep an eye open for Kyle, she'd heard the pain in his voice. Those two were like brothers. Arm-in-arm, they'd grown up doing everything together, their lives following the same path. Same hobbies, same classes in school, same branch of the military. Which was the problem, wasn't it? With Kyle's discharge due to his injury, he and Joshua were traveling separate roads for the first time in their lives. Hard not to wonder if Kyle's road would bring him home for good.

****

It wasn't until Farrah locked up her clinic for the night that she recalled she couldn't go straight home. Not that she was about to complain. She always drove up the mountain every Wednesday to check on Joshua's house when he was away. Usually her visits involved nothing more than a walk through the multi-level home to check for broken windows or leaking faucets, followed by a quick dusting of the furniture. Hardly an arduous task, but it did have its perks.

She slipped into her car, started the engine, and flipped the A/C to high. The weather for the past several weeks had been hot and dry. Rain was scarce this summer, the lack of moisture crisping grass and trees and causing the temperatures to hover on the edge of triple digits. Just thinking of Joshua's spring-fed pool caused Farrah to shiver with anticipation.

Half an hour later, she pulled to a stop in the small front yard of a quaint little cabin. She braced herself before opening the door and stepping out of the relatively cool car. Heat engulfed her. Despite the sun having set more than an hour ago, it was still uncomfortable. Sweat beaded her skin before she'd taken a dozen steps. Blotting her brow on her sleeve, Farrah forced herself to stick to her routine. She walked the exterior of the cabin first before heading to the steps carved into the cliff at the back. The luring gurgle of flowing water drew her down. She took the steps carefully, not wanting to risk a fall so close to her goal. As soon as her feet touched the wide stone balcony, she headed for the center point which overlooked the tear-drop shaped pool below.

Farrah gazed down at the shadow-laced patio area. She could barely make out the shape of the pool, but she could hear the gently lapping water. Even in the dry season, Joshua's spring flowed clear and clean, straight from the heart of the mountain.

She looked up. Clouds crept slowly across the sky, their dry husks still thick enough to block starlight and moonlight both. She'd have to turn the lights on before indulging in a swim. Animals sometimes wandered in for a drink, lured by the sound and smell of fresh water, like her. She didn't want to chance any surprises.

Anxious to feel the cool water on her skin, she turned, her steps taking her past a patio table on which sat a potted fern. Even in the shadowed night, she could tell the leaves were drooping. She'd given the lacy plant to Joshua the last time he was home. Something to make his manly refuge a little less austere. The look on his face as he had held the pot at arm's length made both her and Kyle laugh. Maybe she should just give up and take the poor thing home?

"Be right back with a drink," she said to the plant, moving to the sliding glass doors set into the two-story high wall of tinted glass. After punching in the security code, she tried to slide the door back. For a moment, she thought she'd gotten the code wrong, but the latch functioned just fine. It was the door that wouldn't budge. She pulled at it a couple more times. When it finally moved, the loud grating sound it made ran like chalk-board scratches down her spine. She winced. Something must have happened to knock the track out of line, though she couldn't imagine what. The darn thing had worked fine last week.

Gritting her teeth, she shoved a little more until the opening was wide enough for her to slip through. Instead of struggling with it again, she decided to leave the door open until she left. The extra heat would kick Joshua's air conditioner on that much faster, something else she liked to check each visit. With a sigh of appreciation, she stepped into the huge living area with its high, vaulted ceiling. The space was luxurious, or would be when it was finished. Right now, the wide marble fireplace built into the right wall lacked a mantel, and the floating staircase leading up to the second level looked like a scattering of wooden planks and metal bars frozen in mid-fall. A recliner and a pair of comfy couches in matching chocolate brown leather were the only signs someone lived here—that, and the faint glow of night lights coming from the kitchen and dining area to the left.

Farrah ran her hand over the back of one of the couches as she made her way to the kitchen. She usually overrode the lighting set by Joshua's automatic system, but tonight, the dimness suited her. She pulled a pitcher from under the sink, thinking, like she did every week, that she really needed to pick up a lighter, plastic model next time she was in town. The one Joshua had, reminded her of a thick ceramic coffee mug on steroids. Heavy steroids. After filling the pitcher with water, she lugged it back outside to water the fern. The dirt was so dry, the water just puddled on top, spilling over the edge of the pot. Instead of standing there waiting for it to soak in, she decided to get on with her routine and finish watering the plant later. She left the pitcher on the table and slipped back into the house. The sooner she finished, the sooner she could cool off in the spring-fed pool below.

****

Kyle paused his painful walk as soon as he caught the faint glow of light from Joshua's house through the trees. He leaned a hip against a convenient boulder to take the pressure off his leg while wiping the layer of sweat off his face. Not for the first time he cursed the piece-of-shit rental truck he'd grabbed on his way out of DC. Damn thing hadn't liked the mountain roads at all, deciding to overheat just a mile short of his goal. He could have walked that mile on the nice, fairly-level road, but the path through the woods was shorter, he reasoned. A little hike to stretch out leg muscles cramped tight from sitting too long had seemed like a good idea at the time. After all, it had worked before. Of course, those walks had been short trips up and down an air-conditioned hospital hallway, not almost a thousand yards of hot, uneven trail he could barely see. Uphill at that!

Easy to blame the bad judgment call on exhaustion. Seven hours of steady driving with only a couple of stops for gas was enough to mess with anyone's mental faculties. Add the aches and pains from his ruined leg and, well, maybe Joshua was right. He wasn't thinking straight. Hadn't been for the past eight months. But damn if he was going to admit it by turning around. Not with his goal in sight. Time to finish this hellish side trip.

He shifted his grip on the round top of his cane and pushed away from the tree. He'd fought against using the blasted walking stick when Joshua had first brought it to him. Now he was grateful for the extra stability. Especially since he could barely see where he was going. He stumbled and caught himself for the hundredth time just as the trail opened up. Damn it, even the weather was against him. Clouds blocked the moon and most of the stars, leaving him still feeling his way. You'd think with all those cumulous *whatevers* up there that there'd be a bit of cooling rain in the making. One sniff, however, told him he was shit-out-of-luck. Instead of the scent of rain, all Kyle could smell was dry, brittle earth.

The hot odor tightened like a band around his chest. Dry, hot air. Dust and sand all around.

Memories poured in, threatening to send his mind back to that damned doorway in Cairo.

The place where his life was altered beyond recognition.

Desperate to hold the depressing thoughts at bay, Kyle reached out and stripped some pine needles from a branch, ignoring the prickle against his palm when he crushed them in his hand. Lifting them to his nose, he closed his eyes and drew in a deep breath. The sharp tang grounded him, brought him to the here and now. He was home, not in Egypt. Home. Where thick green forests covered the mountains and rushing streams tumbled down hillsides.

Well, normally the streams would be rushing. Lately only the larger rivers were still rushing along, the smaller streams reduced to meandering. He opened his eyes and let the dry, broken needles fall to the ground. North Carolina wasn't the only state suffering from a dry spell. Several small forest fires had already broken out all through the south east, though thankfully none had been near Clear Springs. He hated the thought of one sweeping through the valley. The damage would be devastating.

Kyle limped on, crossing the last few steps to the wide slate patio surrounding Joshua's prized pool. He wasn't sure why he'd decided to stop by Joshua's house first instead of driving straight to his own place. His friend wasn't home. Wouldn't be home for a long while, based on Kyle's last glimpse of the Nighthawks' schedule. Maybe it was because Joshua's place had always been a rally point for the Hawks when they were in the area. A place where they ate, drank, and talked freely, reminiscing about old missions and planning new ones. A place where he belonged.

He slowly shifted his gaze from the patio and pool to the wall of dark glass rising above. Here he was, clutching at the last connection to a life he'd never belong to again. How pathetic.

****

It didn't take long to check the faucets and run a dust rag over the tables and counters. Still, by the time she was done, sweat had plastered Farrah's blouse to her skin and tiny trickles of moisture ran through her scalp, making it itch. She stripped in the downstairs bathroom, hanging her sweaty blouse and jeans on a towel bar to dry. Usually she brought a swim suit with her to Joshua's, but the Sheriff's early morning gunshot had scrambled her routine, and she'd rushed out of the house without one. Farrah eyed herself in the full length mirror. Her dark blue bra and panties would make a reasonable substitute for a suit. They were already soaked anyway. It was the thought of putting her clothes back on over wet underwear afterwards that made her pause.

No one was around to see. Why not go naked?

Farrah tapped a finger against her lips. The thought was definitely intriguing. *No one is here. There's no one to see if you decide to act a little out of character.*

She stared into the eyes of her reflection. Out of character was right. She'd never been one to take crazy chances. That was Josh and Kyle's forte, not hers. Back in school, she'd been the voice of reason in their little trio. The one always advocating caution and urging sanity—not that it helped much. When Josh and Kyle got together, there was usually no stopping them. Even now, she could almost hear them egging her on.

Come on, Farrah, loosen up a little. Life isn't all school and work, you know. Be spontaneous for a change!

A slow grin took possession of her lips. She snapped the waistband of her panties. They'd never believe she would take their advice like this.

Before she could talk herself out of it, Farrah hurriedly slipped off her clinging underwear. Truth was, swimming in the nude was something she'd always secretly wanted to do. Just the thought of how the water would feel sliding against her most intimate bare skin made her feel positively naughty.

Still grinning, she snagged a towel off a shelf, flipped off the light, and headed out of the bathroom. Halfway through the shadowy living area, she froze. Something moved outside on the balcony steps. Farrah strained to make out the shape in the flat darkness. Few animals explored farther than the patio below, though she'd startled a bear off the steps once. She clutched the towel tight to her chest as the shadow moved again, rising in a jerky motion. Farrah's heart jumped, its pace doubling as a head and limbs became discernible from the bulk of a large body. A human body. Male. Moving with a definite limp.

The sheriff's warning played in her head. *"With that bullet wound, Craddoc won't be able to make it far on foot. Might try to break in somewhere, maybe steal a vehicle."*

Farrah forced herself to stay still, to not run to the sliding glass door she'd stupidly left ajar. Craddoc was closer to it than she was. Even with his limp, he might reach it first. As it was, if he noticed the door was open…

Luck was with her. The dangerous man turned his back on the house and limped toward the edge of the balcony. She could see he'd picked up a stick from somewhere and was using it as a cane. Farrah moved cautiously to the door. She reached for the handle, then paused. Should she try to close it? He was sure to spin around at the first grating sound. The fact he was supposedly armed was the least of her worries. Joshua's wall of glass was bullet proof, including the sliding doors. The problem was getting the door to slide in the track. Could she get it to cooperate before he reached her? Before he shoved the gun through the opening and forced his way in?

The man took another limping step away from the house. Even with the lack of light, Farrah could tell he was right at the edge of the balcony. The plan that popped into her head was reckless, dangerous, and so not her. But if successful, she'd not only have time to close and lock the door, but grab her clothes and escape up the back stairs to the patch of yard above where her car waited.

Hardly daring to breathe, Farrah wrapped the towel around her, wishing with all her heart she hadn't chosen tonight to embrace her less responsible side. Then she eased out onto the balcony. A couple of tip-toe steps brought her to the patio table. She reached for the heavy pitcher and tried to pick it up without making a sound. The faint whisper of ceramic grating against glass might as well have been a siren. The man spun to face her, wobbling, favoring his injured leg. He raised his left hand. Something glinted duly in his clutched fist.

Farrah gasped. Oh, God! He was going to shoot her! She heaved the half-filled pitcher at the man with all her strength. He cursed as the heavy jug hit his shoulder, succeeding in knocking him further off balance. He staggered back near the edge, arms wind milling wildly. Afraid he'd catch his balance, Farrah ran forward, arms outstretched. She didn't get a chance to shove him. The harsh curse as he fell into the darkness below made her wince. Farrah waited for the satisfying sound of the big splash before turning to run back into the house. A shout drifted up from below.

"Damn you, Farrah Hastings! What the hell was that for?"

She whirled around. No! It couldn't be.

Cuss words, as blue as a mountain lake, floated up from the pool.

Yep, it was. She'd recognize that colorful vocabulary anywhere.

Hurrying to the balcony's edge, Farrah couldn't decide if she wanted to laugh or cover her ears. The quarter moon finally broke through the clouds as she gazed below. She could just make out Kyle's flailing form. He was churning up an awful lot of water to be such an excellent swimmer. But then, that had been before.

Farrah frowned. The memory of Joshua's phone call had her gasping. *Muscle weakness and constant pain despite the numerous surgeries.*

Even as she watched, the splashing stopped suddenly as Kyle sank beneath the water.

Oh, God, what had she done?

Knowing she had no time to turn on the lights much less go back for clothes, Farrah dove off the balcony. She hit the water in a clean dive, aiming deep. Blindly she pushed in the direction she thought she'd seen him last, arms out, sweeping the water. Once her fingers skimmed across something that felt like fabric, but it was gone before she could clutch it. Another few seconds of futile searching used up her air and she had no choice but to kick to the surface.

"Kyle!" she called as soon as she got a breath. "Kyle!"

No answer.

Farrah sucked in more air, folded her body, and headed for the bottom again. Why hadn't she turned the darn lights on as soon as she got here? It was next to impossible to see anyth—

Something touched her arm. A hand, she realized, relief flooding her as fingers curled, tightened, and pulled up. The strong grip reassured her. Thank God she wouldn't have to call Joshua and tell him she'd accidently drowned his best friend.

Water swirled around her from his kicks. Worried he'd do more damage to his leg from thrashing around, she got her own legs in motion, propelling them upward. His welcome cough was the first thing she heard after they broke the surface. Immediately she turned, trying to get behind him so she could get an arm around his shoulders and tow him to the edge. He shrugged her off with another hard curse.

"Damn it all, Farrah! You're not happy with shoving me in this damned spring, now you're trying to strangle me?" He hit the water with his fist, splashing her in the face.

She sputtered and shoved water back at him. "Strangle you? I'm trying to save you from downing, you idiot. And stop swearing at me. You know I don't like it."

They were close enough she could see his face. Anger glittered in his eyes. "Maybe you should have thought about that before knocking me in here in the first place."

"I thought you were someone else."

"Oh, yeah? Who?"

The question made her pause. "Never mind. I see you don't need my help after all." She struck out for one of the ladders.

"Damn it, Farrah, wait!"

She stopped at the ladder. Not because Kyle said so, but because she was suddenly, *acutely*, aware of her lack of clothes. The towel had come off shortly after she'd dived in, so she didn't even have that to cover her. Good Lord, this was embarrassing. Keeping her back to him, she looked over her shoulder. He'd almost reached her. "Stay there," she squeaked, thrusting out a hand.

"What the hell? Why?"

"Because." Lousy reason. She'd never accepted it herself, so what made her think he would.

The faint moonlight caught his narrowed eyes as he tread water merely feet away. "Because why?"

She licked her lips, turning reasons over in her mind one after the other. She couldn't think of a single one that didn't have her cheeks warming in embarrassment.

"You're not wearing a suit, are you?"

Her gaze flew to his face. The speculation in his eyes coupled with the way his lips spread into a slow grin caught her completely off guard. More than her face heated up.

He inched a little closer. "I'm right, aren't I? Miss Prim and Proper has finally slipped off her pedestal."

She shoved water into his face again.

"Hey!"

"You get back on the other side of the pool, Kyle Fagan. Right now! How dare you scare me half to death and then try to, to ogle me!" She winced a little at her choice of words. Had she really said ogle? How could she blame Kyle for his prim and proper remark when she sounded like a starched heroine from a Victorian novel?

"You're the one skinny dipping, Farrah Hastings, in case you haven't noticed. Me? I've got all my clothes on, thanks to you."

Farrah bit her lip, unable to deny either charge. At least he obeyed her order without more fuss. He leaned back, a few lazy back strokes taking him all the way to the other side of the pool. His gaze never left her.

"Turn around," she instructed when he did nothing further.

"What if I just close my eyes? I promise not to peek. Much." Teeth gleamed in the moonlight.

Wicked, wicked, man. She tried desperately to keep her face stern. He really hadn't changed a bit.

Chapter Seven

"Turn. Around. Now."

The exasperation in her voice had Kyle chuckling softly. Damn, the woman was a miracle worker. Not in her presence two minutes, and she had him laughing. He hadn't felt like doing that in months. But then, he'd always enjoyed teasing Farrah, watching the fire slowly build in her eyes, the way the color darkened her cheeks. He'd imagined more than once that was how she'd look when making love. Intense, passionate, focused only on her lover. He'd tease her some more, but kicking around in the cold water after that hike through the woods wasn't doing his leg any good.

"Kyle!"

He blew out a fake sigh. "All right, all right, I'm turning." What other choice did he have? He couldn't very well tell her that seeing her naked had been a secret desire of his almost from the day they'd met. A desire he'd never imagined satisfying. Now here she was, in all her bare glory, only a few feet away. How the hell was he going to keep from peeking?

He was still debating whether or not to give in to temptation when he heard the splash and drip of water. Damn, she was out of the pool. It was now or never.

No, this was Farrah. *Joshua's Farrah*. While she and Josh hadn't been together for years, to Kyle, she would always be Josh's girl. Lusting after her in his dreams was one thing. Ogling her in real life felt too much like a betrayal of Josh's friendship.

He heaved a real sigh this time and propped an arm on the side of the pool. Movement caught his attention from the corner of his eye. Now, this was interesting. Turned out the tinted glass forming the back wall of Joshua's house was a great reflector. Details were fuzzy, true, especially in the dark, but he could easily make out Farrah dashing quickly to the towel chest tucked next to the patio storage shed. A delightfully naked Farrah.

Kyle grinned and leaned on his arm to enjoy the show. He ignored the tiny bit of conscience that managed to stir before he squashed it. Not looking was out of the question. She was too damn beautiful. Despite the cold water and lack of details provided by the poor reflection, Kyle felt his body stir. He'd often wondered how those breasts peeking through the strands of her wet hair would fit into his hands. How they would feel as he cupped them, rubbing his thumbs over the pert nipples. No doubt they'd be as smooth as satin, just like the rest of her delectable body. The body he couldn't see well enough at all now, damn it. Even her face was turned away, though he didn't need the visual reminder of her features. Not with each detail engraved in his brain, clear hazel eyes tending toward a forest green, a small nose, high cheeks, and full, sensual, kiss-you-all-night lips.

Kyle swallowed hard. How many nights had he spent fantasizing about those lips and that body, knowing damn well she was off limits? "Glutton for punishment, Fagan," he muttered, watching as she struggled to open the chest. The weather tight seal had a tendency to stick. She bent over and strained to open it, her pert ass wiggling in the air.

The harsh cuss word slipped out before he could catch it.

Her head turned sharply. He didn't move as she checked to make sure he still had his back to her. If she didn't notice the whole reflection thing, damn if he'd call attention to it.

She worked on the lid a bit more before it popped open with a sucking sound. He watched her pull out a towel, shake it out, and wrap it around herself. The damn thing was huge, covering her from breasts to knees. Kyle took a deep breath and let it out slowly. Show over.

Damn it.

He reached up and laid his walking stick well back from the edge of the pool. The fine grain wood exterior was deceiving. Inside was a core of steel that made the cane, with its heavy knob handle, one hell of a club. The solid metal core also made the stupid stick sink like a rock. Unlike his knife, which he'd pulled the second he'd first heard a noise behind him, he'd lost hold of the cane when he hit the water. Diving for it in the dark hadn't been fun, but he needed the damn thing.

Palms flat against the smooth slate forming the pool's edge, he pushed, levering his body out with his arms. That was the easy part.

Kyle shifted his legs out of the water next—or tried to. His right one dragged, feeling like it, too, had a core of iron instead of just an outside skeleton of metal. He tried again, swearing when it refused to obey at all. He could feel a cramp starting, the tightening creeping inexorably up his leg. Soon his pitiful excuse for a limb would be nothing but one big knot of painful, useless flesh.

Anger flared, fueled by a heavy dose of frustration. The words "useless flesh" echoed over and over in his mind. He grabbed one of the brace's straps fastened just below his shitty excuse for a knee and jerked up, ignoring the multiple sharp pains the movement generated. Shifting around, he made room for the leg, all but throwing it down. The brace hit the slate with a dull ring.

For a second, he stared at the miss-matched pair of limbs. His left leg, so strong, so vibrantly alive, and his right one, weak, shriveled, dying day by day in its prison of metal bars and leather straps. Why the hell hadn't he let them just cut it off? Would it really have made a difference? At least he wouldn't have to put up with times like this. Times when, except for the pain, he felt as if he was dragging around a dead weight.

He thought about taking the rack of metal off before trying to stand, but knew from experience it wouldn't help much. He reached for the cane. The next minute wasn't going to be pretty. The VA doctor had said the cramping should get better over time, but Kyle wasn't holding his breath. The same doctor had said his movements should get smoother with time as well, that compensating for the new weakness would become second nature. Well, that time hadn't come either.

"All ri—"

Farrah's words broke off. Kyle tried ignoring her, still struggling to get his damned leg under him. Soft footfalls came closer, almost running. Despite the awkwardness of his position, he stopped mid-motion and snapped his head up. Her expression fired his simmering anger. "I don't need your help," he growled.

She stopped. As much as he hated the pity on her face, it was almost worse watching it drain away to be replaced by an expression he'd never seen on her before. An expression he didn't have a name for. After a few uncomfortable seconds, Kyle went back to his gymnastics, twisting and turning and heaving until he finally stood on both feet. Well, one foot and a cane, anyway. Only then did he meet her disturbing gaze again. She gestured.

"You need to get home and get off that leg."

Ah, yes, clinical detachment. That was the name of her expression. The good Dr. Hastings no longer saw him as an old friend. Not even as an equal. She saw him as a damned patient. He remembered getting a glimpse of that expression back in Cairo when he'd been flat on his back. He hadn't liked it then and liked it even less now. Damn if he'd let her reduce him to a stranger. A man who could barely stand up by himself.

Bitterness at the turn his life had taken welled up and spilled over. Kyle found himself gesturing right back at her. "And you need to get back inside and put some clothes on. What the hell are you doing running around Josh's house naked anyway? Are you waiting for a particular lover or just trying to get yourself raped?"

As soon as the words were out, he wished them back. Too late. Farrah's head jerked as if he'd slapped her. Shame joined the bitterness party, the rancid mixture flooding him till he felt physically sick. God, he was such a bastard. He had no right ripping into her like that. It wasn't her fault he was a cripple. She'd done her best to help him. He opened his mouth to say something, maybe apologize, but she held up her hand. Only then did he notice she was holding a second towel.

"I wanted to apologize for knocking you in the pool. I even brought a peace offering."

Kyle blew out a ragged breath. Now he really did feel like a maggot in a week-old carcass. No guessing who the adult was in this conversation. "Thanks." He held out a hand for the towel, more than willing for a return to peace between them.

Farrah's brows arched. "*Wanted* being the operative word." She swung her arm over the pool and spread her fingers wide. The towel landed in the water with a wet plop.

"Excuse me," she said, the words as sharp as his knife, "but I need to go get decent now. I wouldn't want to be accused of tempting one of my best friends into attacking me." She spun on her heel as neat as a recruit fresh out of boot camp, and headed for the balcony steps.

"Farrah…"

She didn't even slow down. Kyle watched as she marched up the steps to the balcony, feeling more helpless than when Joshua had broken the news to him about his leg.

Great job, Fagan, he told himself. Not home an hour and he'd alienated the last person on earth he ever wanted to hurt. Could his life suck any more?

****

Kyle finally walked out of Joshua's cabin over an hour later. Yes, his life could indeed suck more. Despite his earlier prediction, the weather had done a quick turnaround. Wind blew, sweeping down over the top of the ridge in an angry rush. Tall pines swayed, firs whipped, and oak limbs creaked like a chorus of bull frogs. All around him, dry leaves danced frantically, swirled by the frenzied currents. The scent of rain lay heavy in the air.

Great, more water. Just what he didn't need. His clothes weren't even completely dry yet from his unplanned dip in the pool. Kyle snatched up the plastic jug of water to feed to the rental truck's radiator and started the mile-long walk. He really shouldn't complain about the coming rain. The area needed the moisture. As for getting wet again, he had only himself to blame. Arrogant fool that he was, he'd sat by the pool, waiting for Farrah to come back down after she dressed so he could apologize. It had taken a good half hour for him to realize she not only wasn't coming back down, but she'd left.

"Didn't even bother to check on me," he muttered, stabbing the end of his cane into the ground with each limping stride. Not that he'd needed, or wanted, her to. It would have been nice, though, if she'd offered to give him a ride. She had to have noticed that hers was the only vehicle parked in Joshua's front yard. But had she come back down to ask how he'd gotten here?

No, she hadn't.

What kind of doctor did that make her? And what the hell was she doing running around without her clothes on in the first place? True, no one lived close by to see her, but hell, that just made it worse. Anyone could have walked up on her.

The more he thought about the whole episode, the angrier he got.

Thunder rumbled, the growling echoes rolling

around the valley. More followed. Soon the night was filled with a continuous cracking and booming. Kyle glanced at the dark sky. Lightning flashed almost constantly, sometimes lighting up the boiling clouds from inside, sometimes breaking free to skitter across the black background. The furious display matched his mood perfectly.

By the time he reached the truck, rain drops as big as dimes were coming down in sporadic showers. Kyle quickly topped off the radiator, thankful when the truck cranked on the third try. Tinkering with an engine in the middle of a thunderstorm was not on his list of things he liked to do. As the team's unofficial mechanic, he'd done it before, and it hadn't been fun then either.

He put the truck in gear and eased back onto the road just as the deluge hit. He'd walked the last of the cramp off, but the pain shooting up from his knee every time he had to switch between gas and brake pedal didn't help his mood. Cruise control had made the drive from DC bearable. Navigating the curves and inclines of a mountain road through gusting wind and driving rain quickly became a form of torture. By the time he pulled in next to his own truck inside his garage at home, Kyle was soaked again, this time by sweat.

He shoved the gear shift into park and turned off the engine with a sharp twist of his wrist. Instead of getting out, he closed his eyes and leaned his head back, listening to the storm rage. God, he was so tired. Tired of fighting, tired of hurting. Most of all, he was tired of thinking.

Despite his best efforts, his mind constantly returned to that alley in Cairo, going over his every move. What if he'd done this? What if he'd turned there? Why hadn't he noticed the sniper on the roof? Why hadn't Rash? It had been his job to take out roof problems, not Kyle's.

Why had life served him up such a shitty future?

Kyle heaved a sigh and rubbed a hand over his face. He didn't need a therapist to know such thoughts were destructive. He needed to snap the mental rubberband and change his thinking.

Snap!

Nope, didn't help. Never did.

Part of him hated thinking about the mission that had ruined his life. Another part seemed to crave the reminder of what he'd lost. Where were the Hawks now? Were his friends safe and dry, or were they lying in a similar storm, waiting for their prey? Damn, he wished he was with them right now. He'd take his life back—lying in mud and God only knew what else—over what he had now in a heartbeat.

With a shake of his head to dislodge that useless train of thought, Kyle opened the truck door and got out. He hobbled the few feet to the control panel on the wall and punched the button to close up the garage. Then he headed inside. He'd get his bag out of the truck tomorrow. Right now, he needed a hot shower and a glass of Jack.

****

Later, one glass of Jack turned into two, then three. Still searching for oblivion, Kyle tabled the rest of the whiskey in favor of a six-pack he found in the back of the fridge. Chasing good whiskey with stale beer wasn't the smartest thing he'd done, but hey, neither was getting shot.

Somewhere near the bottom of the fourth bottle, he

ceased to care about even that.

****

Farrah stared out her living room window, nibbling on her bottom lip. The glow from her outdoor security light was a dim shadow of itself, half-drowned by the cascade of a sudden burst of rain. Less than a minute passed, and the violent little squall was gone, pushed on its way by the whipping wind. She'd be a fool to go back out into that mess.

Still…

She leaned against the cool glass, wincing as another flash of lighting was followed almost immediately by a clap of thunder. She shouldn't have left him. No matter that Kyle was being, well, to put it crudely, an ass, she still shouldn't have left him. But he'd made her so mad! How dare he talk to her like that? She wasn't a child. Nor was she some stupid, helpless female. Just because she didn't approve of violence didn't mean she couldn't take care of herself. Hadn't she proved that in Cairo? Hadn't she proved it here by pushing him off the balcony?

Accusing her of trying to get herself raped by taking a naked swim in Joshua's pool? Really? She'd thought the idea preposterous at first. It wasn't until she recalled the Sheriff's warning again about half-way home that she admitted to herself that going to Joshua's alone hadn't been one of her best ideas. Not with Craddoc still supposedly in the valley. The Sheriff would think she'd lost her mind if he knew. But Kyle just got home. He probably didn't even know a dangerous criminal was on the loose. What was his excuse for ripping into her like that?

Pain, probably, guessed her professional side.

She'd seen enough of it on patients' faces to recognize that Kyle had been suffering. Her medical training had kicked in the moment she saw him out of the pool. She'd noted the sharpness of his features, the pale skin along his jaw denoting clenched teeth. She'd also noticed the way his soaked t-shirt clung to a chest and biceps that no longer resembled a granite boulder flanked by a pair of sturdy young pines.

Oh, he still had a body most men spent hours in a gym for, but she could tell he'd lost weight since she'd seen him last. The surgeries, the protracted hospital stay, neither would have been easy on someone normally so active and vibrant. So used to taking life at a dead run.

She drew in a sharp breath. Knowing Kyle, the injury was causing pain to more than just his physical body. Tough as he was, he couldn't hide all the signs. Not from her. She knew him too well, had watched him too closely over the years. Even before she and Joshua had split up, she'd watched Kyle Fagan. The man was just too darn sexy to ignore.

Farrah jerked as another bolt of lightning stabbed the night. Thunder cracked, shaking the whole house. Somewhere behind her, her cell phone rang. She pushed away from the window—with all that lightning, she really shouldn't be standing there anyway—and scooped her phone off the kitchen table. The number on the display made her smile.

"Hi, Joshua."

"Hi, sweetheart. You doing okay?"

"I'm fine, thanks." She walked into the living room and settled into a corner of the sofa. "I was going to call you."

"About Kyle?"

"Yes. He arrived a little after sunset."

She heard his relieved sigh even over the battering storm. "That's good. I'm glad he made it there safely. If he'd just waited another day, I could have driven him down. He's an impatient idiot, you know that, right?"

"Indeed I do," Farrah agreed dryly.

A slight pause. "Why do I get the feeling Kyle's already done something to reinforce his idiot status?"

Farrah bit back a laugh. Joshua had always been good at reading her tone of voice. She wasn't about to complain to him about Kyle, however.

"It's nothing, Joshua. Kyle's just being Kyle. And he's hurting. I thought the arterial graft would have helped by now. And I can't believe he hasn't had the knee replaced yet. Do you know what the prognosis is?"

"Nothing good. As you know, there was a lot of tissue and nerve damage. The kneecap was busted up pretty bad. The docs recommended a full knee replacement, but Kyle balked. Said he wanted to give it a chance to heal before going the artificial route. As for the artery, three surgeries and they still can't seem to get the grafts to work right."

She bit her lip. "Does he... Do you know if he blames me for that?" He would have to, wouldn't he? She'd done her best, but still...

"No, hell, no. He knows the problems with the graft have nothing to do with your work. According to the doctor, Kyle's lucky he still has a leg at all, not to mention being able to walk on it. That was thanks to you." A short pause. "We almost lost him, Farrah." The unspoken words, "we still might", hung heavy in the airwaves separating them.

Farrah's eyes burned. The pain in Joshua's voice touched a similar chord inside her. "He's strong, Joshua. You and I know that better than anyone.

Another deep sigh. "Yeah, I know. Problem is, I keep putting myself in his place, wondering how I'd handle the same situation. Being forced out of Special Ops. Having to give up a life I love to try and create a new one from scratch. The physical limitations. The constant pain. Don't get me wrong, I'm not saying I'd take the easy way out, just that the temptation would definitely be there. And you know how Kyle is about resisting temptation."

Yes, she knew. A two-year-old set down in the middle of a toy store and told not to touch anything could resist temptation longer than Kyle Fagan. She also knew she'd never allow him to take that deceptively easy way out. "You don't worry about Kyle. I'm not going to let him sit around and feel sorry for himself for long."

A soft chuckle. "That's my girl. Do me a favor and see if you can get him to agree to another consultation. Aberashoff rounded up a new pair of doctors before Kyle left," he said, referring to the head of Special Ops. "But our stubborn, idiot friend refused to see them. Private sector docs, too, top grade. One supposedly specializes in tough knee replacements and the other in some kind of popular artery surgery."

"You mean arterial popliteal surgery?"

"Yeah, that's the one. Something about restoring circulation to the starving muscles so Kyle can walk without that damn brace. Um…sorry 'bout that."

Farrah smiled. Joshua was always good about

curbing his harsher language around her. Kyle, on the other hand...

"That's okay. Listen, do you think you can get me a copy of Kyle's medical file? I know there will be privacy issues—"

"Say no more, sweetheart, I was hoping you would ask. I've already got our information specialist on it. You should have hard copy in a day, tops."

"Sounds good. In the meantime, I'll try and get him to let me examine his leg."

Joshua snorted. "Good luck with that. From what I gather at the VA hospital, he wasn't exactly cooperative the last few days he was there."

"Don't worry, I've dealt with difficult patients before." Not so much since she started her practice in the valley, but during her residency? Farrah stifled a shudder at the memory of some of the characters she'd had to treat. Difficult wasn't a strong enough word.

"Yeah, but this is Kyle Fagan we're talking about." The tone of Joshua's voice altered, became less kidding and more serious. "Don't let him get to you, Farrah. This injury has changed him. I hate to say it, but he's not the same person we grew up with. He's bitter, and I can't even blame him for it."

Neither could she. She'd already had a taste of Kyle's bitterness and let it push her away. Well, not anymore. She wouldn't let him curl into a ball and ignore the rest of the world. A little bitterness was to be expected when faced with a life altering experience you didn't want and had no control over. No doubt she'd be bitter, too, if her ability to practice medicine was suddenly ripped away from her. It was human nature. Getting Kyle past that bitterness would be the hard part.

She'd have to find a way to turn his vitriol into something positive, a way to channel his negative energy into something fulfilling.

Good thing she enjoyed a challenge.

Chapter Eight

The pounding in his head woke Kyle. He groaned as the throbbing seemed to pulse from the back of his skull to the front and back again. It wasn't fair. There should be a way to just stay drunk and oblivious without the pain of a hangover intruding. Damn if he'd ever found it, though.

The pounding intensified. It took him a moment to realize some of that pounding was centered in the area of his front door instead of inside his head.

"Kyle!"

Oh, crap. Farrah.

Kyle groaned again and opened his eyes. Yep, his brace still lay over against the wall. So did the walking stick. He vaguely remembered hurling them both over there at some point last night. It was going to be a bear to pull himself up and get to the damn things. He'd much rather stay where he was and go back to sleep. Maybe if he stayed quiet, Farrah would give up and go away.

More pounding.

"Kyle? I know you're in there."

Fuck.

He shifted his legs off the foot rest one at a time, ignoring the complaints from stiff muscles. Standing wasn't fun. The room spun. He stood still, one hand on the chair's arm, until things settled down a bit, then he took a limping step. Walking without the brace or aid of the cane was a losing fight between his determination and pure physics. Weak muscles just wouldn't hold weight no matter how much he willed it otherwise.

Kyle flung out a hand to break his fall as gravity took over. His fingers clipped the corner of the table next to the chair hard enough to tip it over. The table and everything on it joined him on the floor. The lamp made the biggest crash, but the empty beer bottles from last night's binge made the biggest mess. They hit the tile floor and shattered, a few pieces skittering half-way to the kitchen.

With a groan, Kyle rolled to his back. He'd only put on a pair of cotton shorts after his shower and the shock of the cold tiles against his bare skin kick-started a flow of cuss words. He was finishing up Rashid's list of favorites when he heard the front door open. The sound jolted him into action. He sat up, stretched out an arm, and managed to snag the light blanket he kept on the back of the recliner. He tossed the cloth over his legs—more specifically, his ruined leg—just as Farrah came into the room.

"Kyle? Oh, my goodness, are you all right?"

He threw a hand up to stop her. "Stay back, there's glass."

She made a huffing noise that might have made him laugh if his head didn't hurt so much.

"I see it. I'm not blind. Where's your broom?"

"Kitchen closet." He didn't bother trying to get up, but lay back down. This time he was braced for the cold, which was actually helping to clear his head. He listened to Farrah locate, then rummage in said closet. "How the hell did you get in, anyway?" he called. He couldn't recall ever giving her a key to his house.

She came back in the room and began sweeping. "Medicine wasn't all I studied in college. One of my roommates was from a family of locksmiths. She taught me how to pick locks."

Neat trick. Especially since the lock on his door wasn't just a simple tumbler model. It'd take a bit more than a casual skill with a hairpin. He eyed her through half-closed lids, wondering what other skills she'd picked up over the years that he didn't know about. She glanced at him a couple of times as she swept, but quickly looked away. With her thick, red-gold curls pulled back into a pony tail, he had no trouble seeing her face. No pity in her eyes this morning. That was good. No coldness either, which was even better. What was she—

Farrah bent over to place the dust pan on the floor, her jeans cupping every dip and curve of her ass like a second skin. Ah, hell.

Kyle quickly opened the blanket a little more so it would cover his lap. No sense advertising his frustration.

Settling back again, he put both hands behind his head, trying to look as if lying on the floor was something he did every morning. He cleared his throat. "What are you doing here? After the way you slinked off yesterday, I thought it'd be at least a month before I saw you again, if then."

Still sweeping, she shrugged one shoulder. "You thought wrong. And I didn't slink. I stomped. I was very angry with you."

"I had to walk back to my truck."

"What you said was rude."

"It was a mile away."

"I want an apology."

"Through a thunderstorm."

She huffed and turned around to face him. "Are you going to lay there and complain all day? Because if you are, I have better things to do than stand here and listen to a grown man whine like a three-year-old."

Kyle had been enjoying their banter, but her last words stung. He tightened his abdominals and sat straight up. "I do not whine like a three-year-old."

She arched her brow. For a second, he thought the dust pan full of glass in her hand was going to star in a repeat performance of the dropped towel from last night. Inside he cringed, preparing his aching head for the crash. Instead, those luscious lips of hers pursed provocatively, and she said, "Yes, you do."

She turned and headed for the kitchen, calling over her shoulder. "Do you need help getting up, or can you manage? I can call Bill Watson and have him bring his winch if need be."

A chuckle slipped out before Kyle knew what hit him. There she went again, making him laugh when he didn't want to. Winch, indeed. What did he need a winch for when he had a *wench* like her?

"You know, you're not a bit funny," he called back, raising his voice over the sound of broken glass going into the garbage can. Between bracing against the chair, and his determination not to play the part of a weak invalid in front of her, he was standing by the time she came back into the room. He held the blanket like a shield in front of him. Only his feet and ankles were visible from the waist down.

"Oh, I don't know," she said, her gaze shifting

from his face to his feet, before sweeping around the room. "I got a chuckle out of it." Her attention fastened on the brace and cane. She didn't say anything, but that damn eyebrow rose again.

"I can get those," he growled, damning all evidence to the contrary.

"I know," she said matter-of-factly. She crossed the room and picked up the brace, turning it over in her hands, examining it. "But like I said, I don't have all day."

Kyle shook his head, unable to get a handle on her mood. She wasn't exactly acting cold, but the brusqueness of her attitude, not to mention some of her frank comments, had his head spinning. Where was the compassionate angel he and Joshua had gone to school with? Was she still angry with him about yesterday or was it a hold-over from getting her involved in the Cairo mess? It was true his injury had essentially screwed up her time with the WHO, but that hadn't stopped her from opening her own clinic in Clear Springs. She was a full-fledged doctor, damn it. Didn't they teach bedside manner in medical school anymore?

He inched around and plopped his butt back in the recliner. Once seated, he carefully straightened out his leg under the blanket. He'd have to wait until she left to put the brace on. No way was he going to let her see what was left of his leg. True, she'd worked on it, but that was months ago. What was left wasn't pretty. Kyle held out his hand for the device when she approached him.

"No, let me," she said, kneeling in front of him. "I want to see how this fits and where it fastens." She reached for the blanket.

He slapped a hand down to hold the blanket in place. Leaning forward, he tried to snag the brace away from her. Damn wench scooted back just out of reach.

"What's wrong? You're not afraid to let me see your leg, are you?"

Kyle ground his teeth to keep from cursing. Afraid wasn't exactly the word he'd use. He just didn't want to see the revulsion on her face—or the pity. Just looking at the mish-mash of scars and twisted flesh made his own stomach roil, and he was a hardened veteran. He couldn't stand it if Farrah turned away from him in disgust.

She sighed heavily, fingers tapping the brace in her hands. "I thought you said you weren't a three-year-old. You know I'm a doctor, right? The only doctor in the valley? You're going to have to let me see your leg sooner or later." She reached out and placed her hand against the one he had anchoring the blanket in place. "Besides, this is me, Farrah. Your friend, remember? I've been sick with worry ever since the military made me leave Egypt and fly back home. Joshua kept in touch. He said you were doing as well as could be expected, but I still worried. Having you home helps, but it's not enough. Please, Kyle, let me see."

Kyle stared helplessly into her pleading eyes. Were those tears? Damn, he'd never been able to stand against Farrah's tears. Each one was like a knife in his chest.

With a forced shrug, he slipped his hand from beneath hers. "Fine. Knock yourself out." *And me too, while you're at it.*

He leaned back and closed his eyes. Maybe if he concentrated on his pounding headache he wouldn't notice her exclamation of disgust.

****

Farrah watched Kyle lean his head back and close his eyes. The relaxed pose didn't fool her. The slight wrinkles in his forehead and tension around his eyes told her he had a headache. Considering the empty bottles of alcohol she'd swept up, she wasn't surprised. But the headache wasn't the problem. Every muscle in his body was locked up, tense as bow strings. She was almost afraid to touch him.

Quickly, before either of them changed their mind, she reached down and flipped the end of the blanket aside. She almost gasped, but caught herself in time.

She'd seen worse, she told herself. Though at the moment, she couldn't remember when or where. So much damage. She didn't remember it being so bad. Whole sections of flesh were gone around the knee. Tendons stood out in stark relief, stretched tight beneath too thin skin. Other places were thick with scar tissue, the flesh so twisted, she couldn't imagine how the leg functioned. And this was only the damage she could see on the surface. That the limb bent and flexed at all had to come at a great price. No wonder he'd drowned himself in alcohol last night. Just bending his knee must be excruciating.

Guilt rose up and almost swallowed her. Not just because her skill hadn't been enough eight months ago. She'd pushed him into the pool last night and then left him to make his way back to his vehicle by himself. Could she be any more cold-hearted?

She was grateful when she glanced up and saw his eyes were still closed. Carefully, Farrah reached out and placed the tips of her fingers against the side of his knee. Not even a muscle twitched.

"Can you feel this?" Applying a light pressure, she ran a finger down his calf from knee to ankle. Some of the skin was smooth and tight, some rough with scars, and some normal, the hairs tickling as she passed over them. Kyle cleared his throat. The words still came out rough as sandpaper.

"Yeah. Some."

She started at the knee again, this time moving up along the outside of his thigh. "How about here?" Farrah noticed her own voice was a little uneven, not at all the crisp, professional tone she usually adopted when examining a patient.

"Yes," Kyle whispered.

Still watching his closed eyes, Farrah moved to the scars on the inside of his thigh over the femoral artery. Leather creaked. Farrah paused, her gaze shooting to where Kyle's hands tightened on the arms of the recliner. Was he watching her? She thought his eyes were closed, but was she wrong?

She let her finger make contact with his skin. His leg jerked.

"Sorry," he said.

She wet her lips. "Does this hurt?"

"No, it's just…your hand is cold."

"Oh." She stopped herself from automatically pulling away to rub her hands together. Her hands didn't feel cold. In fact, compared to the skin of Kyle's leg, she felt decidedly warm. And not just her hands. This examination was affecting her more than she thought it would. Having his bare chest at eye level didn't help. The only thing keeping her touch from drifting up into forbidden territory was the fact that in all their years of friendship, Kyle had never shown the slightest interest in her as anything but a friend. Unless she planned to make a complete fool of herself, prolonging the current situation would be a mistake.

Clearing her throat, Farrah gathered what was left of her professionalism. "Just bear with me another minute, I'm almost done." She took her eyes off his face and concentrated on his leg, forcing herself firmly into doctor mode. After checking for sensation in a few more key points, she examined the knee. She asked him to bend it several times to observe the contraction and expansion of the visible muscle. She also felt the joint as it moved, wincing a little at the slightly audible catch and grind. When she was done, Farrah concluded that Joshua was right. Kyle was lucky to still have his leg, much less be walking on it.

After slipping the brace into place and fastening the straps and buckles, Farrah found herself hesitant to stop touching him. Something in her wanted to soothe him, take away the hurt, and it wasn't her medical side. She ran a hand over his knee, the focus of his physical pain, fingers slipping between metal bars to caress the abused joint.

Yes, caress. She wasn't going to lie to herself.

His hand landed on hers. "Don't you have a clinic to run or something? I don't need you to sit here and babysit me."

The snarl in his voice sounded totally foreign. Kyle had always been the comedian to Joshua's straight man. Hearing him growl at her was a new experience. The buried anger and pain in his voice made her want to cry. She jerked her hand away and choked out a laugh instead.

"Is that what you think I'm doing? Heavens, Kyle, you still haven't realized the world doesn't revolve around you, have you? Oh, wait, I bet the last few months did little to abuse you of that notion."

She stood and waved a dismissing hand in the direction of his leg. Indifference and bluntness was the only approach she could think of that might break through that wall of anger he'd erected. Sympathy and compassion would only build it up, make it thicker.

"Bet that little injury got you a lot of notice from all the pretty nurses. Is that why you refused to see the new doctors Joshua told me your boss brought in? Why refuse, Kyle? Are you afraid if your leg gets fixed, you'll lose all the attention?"

For a second, she thought she'd pushed him too far. The frostiness on his face made her shiver inside. If he ever looked at her like that and meant it...

He leaned forward, very deliberately, and picked his cane up from where she laid it on the floor. Then he stood. No hesitation, no straining, no clumsy movements. Just a smooth rising to his feet.

"You," he said, never taking his gaze off her, "are an inch shy of stepping over the line. You and Joshua both. You can tell him for me, I am not going back to the VA. I'm through with that shit. No more doctors, no more hospitals, and definitely no more damn surgeries. If I lose my leg, so be it. It won't be anyone's fault but my own. Not Joshua's, not some nameless doctor's, and damn sure not yours."

Farrah swallowed, not daring to believe him. Of course he'd blame her. Why wouldn't he? Despite his aggression, she made herself stand her ground. The anger rolling off him washed over her in nauseating

130

waves. She wasn't about to let him bully her into going away before she was good and ready. If she left him alone, he'd have no reason to face his foolish decision to give up.

"In that case…" She reached around and snagged the folded paper from her back jeans pocket. "You need to sign this form giving me access to your medical records."

She couldn't believe it was possible, but his scowl darkened. "What the hell for?"

"Isn't it obvious? You may not want to go back to the VA, but you'll still need to see a doctor to tell you when that leg needs to come off to keep it from killing you. Infections can crop up overnight, you know. You don't want to let them get out of hand." She wrinkled her nose. "Gangrene is such a nasty condition to deal with. So many complications."

Some of the tension left his shoulders. He ran a hand through his hair. "Why you?"

"Don't be dense, Kyle. I'm the only doctor in the valley, remember?" She slapped the paper against his chest. For a second, she thought he wouldn't catch it as she lifted her hand away, but he did. He glared at her. Then, growling like a grumpy bear, he jerked into motion, limp-stomping around her to the desk in the corner. Since his back was to her, she let herself smile. Ah, the growl of a frustrated male.

She strolled over and propped a hip on a corner of the desk as he scratched his name on the paper, almost ripping it with the last flourish. He threw the pen down.

"There, you happy now?" Without waiting for her to answer, he stalked past her again, this time heading for the kitchen.

"It's a start," she said, folding the paper and putting it back in her pocket. She supposed with Joshua's connections, she really didn't need the signed release. Still, it wouldn't hurt as a backup in case problems cropped up. "It will take a day or two to get the files." He didn't need to know Joshua already had them on the way. "I'll call you after I've had time to study them."

"Fine. Whatever. Doesn't mean I'm coming to your precious clinic."

He'd snagged a beer from his refrigerator and popped off the cap. Farrah was about to launch into a lecture on drinking too much when a knock sounded at the door.

"Now what?" Kyle grumbled, shooting her an accusing glare, as if the person at his door was her fault.

This time when his back was to her, Farrah tapped into her own inner three-year-old and stuck her tongue out at him. Impossible man. He could give lessons to grouchy bears.

She heard the door open. There was a brief pause, then, "Kyle. Good to see you home."

Oh, dear, she knew that voice. Was she late? Farrah glanced at the clock on Kyle's kitchen wall. No, it wasn't quite time to meet the sheriff at her clinic to check his arm. Yet, here he was, tracking her down. Or was he?

"Shoot!" she muttered, heading for the front door. The sheriff was here to warn Kyle about Craddoc. Kyle Fagan wasn't dumb. He'd realize Craddoc was the one she'd mistaken him for last night. No doubt he'd launch into another scolding about her traipsing naked around Joshua's house with a felon on the loose. It wasn't the scold she minded so much as the fact she didn't want any audience participation. As soon as Penwell heard what she'd done, he'd add his own brand of chewing out. Two against one was lousy odds. It was time to leave.

****

Kyle opened the door at the same time he remembered his ruined leg was on full display. Damn woman. She had his mind so screwed up he couldn't think straight. "Sheriff," he said, knowing he could do nothing but tough it out. "What can I do for you?"

He had to give the man credit. Dan Penwell barely glanced at the leg encased in the brace before meeting Kyle's gaze again. His expression didn't change either, which really wasn't all that surprising. That inscrutable mask of his had been a part of Penwell's uniform for as long as Kyle remembered.

"Well—" the sheriff started.

"Excuse me."

Farrah's voice, sounding way too innocent and perky, preceded her arrival in the foyer. She eased past Kyle, not pausing or looking at him even when her breasts brushed against his arm. As if the slight touch didn't jolt through her like it did him.

"Sorry to run, Kyle," she said, giving him a quick glance and a quicker smile, "but I need to go open up the clinic. I'll see you tomorrow afternoon at three, okay? Hi, Pen. You going to make your eleven o'clock appointment today?"

Kyle eyed the sling cradling the sheriff's arm. He'd wondered about that. No cast, but there was a slight bulge around the biceps, straining the sleeve of the sheriff's uniform shirt. A bandage?

Penwell nodded. "I'll be there, Doc."

"Good, see you then. Bye, guys." She didn't look Kyle's way again, walking swiftly to her car. Only when she was inside and pulling away did she meet his gaze, her relief clearly apparent.

Kyle narrowed his eyes at her rapid departure, wondering what she was running from. Couldn't be him, since she'd already proven she could stand her ground no matter how much he growled at her. That didn't mean he'd just fall in with all her plans, however. He was in no mood to be poked and prodded. She'd eventually find out he had no intention of showing up at her clinic. As for checking his grafts, he'd seen enough festering wounds in his line of work that he could tell when one was going bad. He'd have plenty of time to find an MD in the next county if it came to that. Someone whose mere touch didn't set his body on fire and tempt him into the unthinkable. He might be only half a man, but that man desired Farrah Hastings with his whole heart. Always had. Not that he'd ever poach on Joshua's turf, but, damn, how much temptation was a man expected to resist?

"Did you say something?"

Kyle blinked. He was still standing with the door open, the sheriff waiting patiently on his stoop. He stepped back. "Sorry, Sheriff. Thinking too hard, I guess. Come on in."

The sheriff shot a glance at Farrah's retreating taillights. "Yeah, I can guess the direction of those hard thoughts. Have to say, I didn't know our Dr. Hastings made house calls."

Kyle pointedly ignored the remark. No sense giving the man more ammunition. He turned and led the way into living room, leaving the sheriff to close the door. Motioning to the couch, he said, "Have a seat."

"Thanks."

Kyle lowered himself into the recliner as the other man sat on the edge of the sofa. Not staying long, Kyle decided. Good. His headache hadn't gone away yet. Rubbing unobtrusively at his temple, he tried to remember where he'd left the bottle of aspirin.

"I'll get right to the point," Pen said, resting his elbows on his knees and leaning forward. "I don't know if Farrah told you yet, but we have a fugitive in the area."

Pen's words drove all thoughts of his aching head and misplaced aspirin from Kyle's mind. "No, she didn't mention anything about a fugitive." And he'd be having a little conversation with her about why not. The sheriff wouldn't have stopped by to talk about some guy dodging a traffic ticket. "Is he local?"

"No. Russell Craddoc's from the Nashville area. His rap sheet goes from petty theft all the way up to assault and battery. Last arrest included a charge of attempted murder. We picked him up on a traffic stop two days ago and found out he has an outstanding warrant for that one. Nashville wants him back, so we set up a transfer night before last."

Penwell paused, disgust creeping in and making his voice sharp. Kyle got the feeling that if they'd been outside, the sheriff would have spit.

"That's when Craddoc managed to snatch a gun from one of my new deputies."

He tapped the bandaged area on his arm. "Nicked me before he escaped, but I managed to pop him once, too."

A cold wave passed over Kyle. He was starting to

put the pieces together and didn't like the picture one bit.

"Where's he wounded?" As if he needed to ask. Farrah had more to explain than not sharing important information.

"Right leg. Not sure how bad it is. There was a blood trail to begin with, but we lost it right after he made the woods."

Damn!

"We've warned all the residents in the valley to keep an eye open," the sheriff continued, "but to leave the guy alone if they see him. With Craddoc armed, we don't want anyone taking chances trying to confront him."

"You think he's still in the valley?"

"Probably. We slapped check points on all the roads the first hour after he escaped. No one's seen him."

"That leaves a lot of real-estate unmonitored," Kyle reminded him. Several sections of forested mountain that weren't that hard to navigate on foot immediately came to mind.

Pen grunted. "True, but Craddoc's a city boy. Hiking out won't appeal to him, especially if he's injured. Sooner or later he's going to either knock on some unfortunate soul's door, or flag down a driver to steal their car." He pointed a finger at Kyle. "I'm telling you what I told everyone else. If he shows up here waving that gun around and demanding a ride, you give him the keys and smile while doing it. Even if it's that prized truck of yours. Your life's not worth a hunk of metal and rubber. No one's is. Understand?"

Kyle's fist tightened on the knob of his walking

stick. Not one to lie to an officer of the law unless he had to, he settled for a nod. Yeah, he understood. But would he turn his custom built Ford F150 over to some two-bit punk just because the guy had a gun? Not bloody likely.

He would, however, be paying a visit to the oh-so-practical Doctor Hastings. He remembered her saying she thought he was someone else last night. Someone with a limp—like a man who'd been shot in the leg. He couldn't believe she'd attacked him in nothing but a damned towel, all the while thinking he was an armed criminal. The little fool. Hadn't she got her fill of brushes with death eight months ago? Just the thought of what could have happened last night, what he might have found if Craddoc had shown up at Josh's before him, gave him a bad case of the shakes.

No, on second thought, he wouldn't be going to see the good doctor right away. Not until his temper cooled. If he went now, he'd do something stupid, like take her in his arms and kiss the living hell out of her. Yeah, that would teach her not to put her life in danger.

Chapter Nine

Farrah glanced at the clock on her office wall. The little hand was just past the four and the big hand was almost on top of the three. An hour and fifteen minutes past three o'clock. No doubt about it. Kyle wasn't coming.

She tapped her fingers on the thick stack of medical reports and x-rays on the corner of her desk. The two-inch file had arrived by courier that morning. It had taken her all day between appointments to sift through the mountain of information. Now she wasn't sure what to do next. She'd known Kyle might refuse to come, but it hadn't kept her from hoping. Evidently, the I-don't-care attitude she'd adopted hadn't worked. True, he'd signed the paper giving her legal access to his medical information but, apparently, that was as far as his cooperation went.

…Assuming she let him get away with it.

Pressing her lips together, Farrah pushed back her chair and stood. If Kyle Fagan thought he could just ignore her, he had another think coming. She removed her white doctor's coat and hung it up before going to the door.

"Mary?" she called down the hall.

The older woman appeared at the far end. "Yes, Dr. Hastings?"

"We don't have any other appointments today,

right?" She'd tried to keep this afternoon free so she wouldn't have to rush Kyle's visit. That didn't mean she'd turn away a mother with a sick child, or something equally urgent.

"No, ma'am. Your schedule's still clear." Mary's eyes widened slightly. The forty-something R.N. was a tall, stern looking woman. She had a kind heart but at the same time was quite capable of intimidating a difficult patient when necessary. Now, however, she looked almost playful. "You're going after your missing patient, aren't you."

A statement, not a question. Farrah responded anyway. "Yes, well, as his doctor, I can't very well allow him to ignore his health."

"Good," Mary said, lips spreading into a wide smile that warmed her face. "Without Joshua to keep him in line, no telling what mischief that boy will get into. I'd offer to go with you and help drag him in, but considering how he feels about you, I don't think that'll be necessary." She winked and disappeared back around the corner before Farrah could form a reply.

Farrah shook her head as she closed the door to her office. *Considering how he feels about you?* Now, what could she have meant by that?

She let the thought go as she retrieved her purse from her desk drawer and left the clinic by way of a private exit. Twenty minutes later, she turned the last curve and headed up a steeply slanted driveway. Kyle's neat little house was perched at the top on a tiny patch of ground gouged right out of the side of the mountain. Trees closed in on all sides. Their limbs and crowns hid the house from view right up until her car topped the rise and the driveway leveled out. Only then did Farrah release the breath she'd been holding. As much as she cared for Kyle, she absolutely hated the trip to his house. Even once here, there was barely enough yard to park, much less turn around.

Farrah made sure to set the parking brake before she got out. She wasted no time looking out at the magnificent view of the valley spread out behind the house, but marched right up to the front door.

She knocked. "Kyle?" And waited.

Nothing. No muffled sound of steps, no grouchy voice. And no un-nerving sounds of breaking glass this time, thank God.

Instead of knocking again, she walked around to the two-car garage and peeked in the window like she had yesterday. Rats! The shrouded shape that was Kyle's custom truck beneath a car cover sat all alone. The rental was gone.

Farrah turned around and stared out over the valley, the first whispers of worry edging into her mind. She hadn't given it much thought yesterday, but Kyle driving these roads with that injured leg suddenly seemed like a very bad idea. Worse case scenarios—images of him unable to switch his right foot from gas to brake in time, crowded her brain. Situations like a deer or bear wandering into the road and Kyle being unable to keep from hitting the animal. Impacts fast and hard enough could send the truck into a deadly spin. Or what if he was unable to slow down quick enough to make a hairpin turn and crashed into a tree? Or unable to stop at all and sailed off a cliff? Maybe that was why he hadn't shown up at the clinic. Not because he refused to come, but because he couldn't. Because he was injured…or worse.

She squeezed her eyes closed. No, no panic. She refused to give in to such a useless emotion. Panic solved nothing, benefited no one. Calm and methodical, that's what her instructors had drilled into her in medical school. Doctors had to be islands of calm in the midst of whatever chaos surrounded them. Only then could they be effective. She'd learned that was true back in Cairo, hadn't she?

But, darn it, this was Kyle.

She sucked in a deep breath through her nose, held it, and then slowly released the air through her mouth. All the more reason to stay calm. Find Kyle first, assess his situation, then take action. That's what she'd do.

****

Her first action would be to strangle him, Farrah decided, narrowing her eyes on the figure barely visible in the back corner of the dim, busy bar room.

It had taken her several hours of driving every scary road in the valley before she located Kyle—in town. Lounging in a corner booth of the local bar. Drinking. Again.

She was going to have to do something about that before it became a problem. As far as she knew, neither Kyle nor Joshua drank excessively as a rule. Both men had wills of iron and a tendency to avoid crutches of any kind. According to his records, Kyle had even refused the hard-core pain killers the doctors at the VA hospital had prescribed. Considering some of the other things she'd read today, however, she wasn't surprised by Kyle's need for a little extra artificial support. Constant pain had a way of wearing down even iron wills.

Farrah didn't march straight to Kyle's booth, but

made her way to the bar. It was nearly seven o'clock. She was tired, hungry, and the day was still hot. So was her temper. It wouldn't hurt to cool off a bit before tackling her recalcitrant patient. Not to mention, her throat was dry.

She caught the attention of the barkeeper, a pretty young girl who looked barely out of her teens much less old enough to serve alcohol. "A diet cola, please. Large, with lots of ice."

"Sure thing," the girl said.

Young, pretty, but efficient, Farrah decided. A tall, frosty mug of soda slid in front of her a handful of seconds later. She reached in her purse for her wallet. "How much?"

The girl grinned. "No charge. Compliments of the guy in the corner." She tipped her head to indicate direction.

Farrah didn't have to look to see who the girl meant. Without glancing at Kyle, she asked, "How do you know? I mean, he's way over there." And he certainly hadn't yelled out over the noise that Farrah's drink was on him.

The girl winked. "Barkeep's secret." She turned away, hands already reaching for empty glasses to fill another order.

Farrah stripped the plastic cover off her straw and took a long sip of soda. She hadn't even known Kyle was aware of her presence. The bar room wasn't huge, but it was crowded with Friday night patrons. Servers moved back and forth with their trays of glasses and bottles, slipping easily between occupied chairs. Canned music—a touch too loud in her opinion— blared from speakers in the ceiling, adding to the general din of dozens of conversations punctuated by the clink of glass and the crack of pool balls coming from the two tables off to the side. The whole atmosphere held a note of barely suppressed rowdiness that made Farrah a little uncomfortable.

She'd never been inside Harley's Bar before. Never been in any bar, for that matter. Not that she had anything against such establishments. It just didn't make sense for her to patronize a bar since she didn't drink alcohol. Farrah sighed, wishing for once that the term "liquid courage" actually meant what it said. She could use a little extra oomph to get through the impending battle with Kyle. It had been a long day and she was exhausted from treating patients and mentally wading through Kyle's file. Not to mention the emotional drain of searching for him while trying not to freak out. She just wanted the confrontation to be over so she could go home, get clean, and relax in her nice quiet house.

Wishing never got her anywhere, however, so she might as well get on with it.

Farrah grabbed a napkin from a stack on the counter and started for Kyle's booth. The short walk turned into a long trip as some of the bar's customers recognized her. She had to stop and exchange a few words with each person before easing again in Kyle's direction. She was almost to his table when a hand landed heavily on her shoulder and spun her around. Cold soda and ice sloshed out of her mug, splashing her hand and arm. Farrah sucked in a breath. She reached out to steady herself, her empty hand landing on a bare forearm marred by a long scar that looked vaguely familiar. A second hand grabbed her other shoulder.

"Whoa, doc, steady there," the man said.

"Let her go, Chet."

Farrah snapped her mouth closed on her own request for freedom. Was that growly voice, coming from over her shoulder, really Kyle's? She dared a glance to be sure. Yes, it was his. He stood so close she could feel the heat from his body. How had he gotten there so fast?

The man holding her shoulders sneered. She recognized him at once. Chet Wassile, the oldest of a trio of trouble-making brothers. She'd stitched him up several weeks ago, his arm a casualty of a fight in this very bar. All three Wassiles had a bad habit of starting fights they couldn't finish by themselves, the other two joining in to gang up on the unfortunate victim.

Chet's hands tightened a bit on her shoulders. "Back off, Fagan. I just want to talk to the doc here. Thought she might like to dance."

He leaned slightly to his left, looking around her, his gaze dropping down before slowly raising again. "I mean, it's not like she's going to be doing any dancing with you, now is it?"

Kyle's arm came around her waist. The action shocked her as much as the touch itself. The firm hold felt possessive, and far too intimate for the middle of a crowded bar room. Goose bumps broke into a party on her skin. "I said, let go of her."

Farrah could feel Kyle's muscles tensing up. Chet's were too, his grip on her tightening a fraction more, becoming almost painful. Behind him, she could see his brothers, Franklin and Arney, closing in. She had to do something. She had stop this before it got out of hand. Even with his weak leg, she didn't doubt Kyle could handle one brother. But all three?

She forced a smile. "Thank you, Chet, but I'm too tired to dance tonight. Maybe another time." She casually, but firmly, pushed at one of his arms, trying to get him to release her. His resistance lasted only a moment before both hands dropped away.

"No problem, Doc." His gaze stayed locked over her head. "I'll take that rain check."

Kyle shifted to the side, planting the tip of his cane almost on Chet's foot. Farrah moved, too, blocking him, leaning her body against his. His arm tightened, pressure from his hand trying to ease her aside. She put her own hand over his and leaned into him harder. He wasn't getting rid of her that easily.

Chet's gaze slid past them both. His hands came up in a calming gesture. "Nothing doin' here, Harley. Everything's cool."

The bar's owner, Harley Bentley, stepped up beside Kyle. He was a good looking, neatly dressed man in his mid-thirties who looked like he'd be more at home in a corporate office than running a bar. "I warned you, Chet. You or your brothers get into another fight in here again and you're all three banned for good."

"Shit, Harley, I remember. But this ain't on me. I was just asking Farrah here to dance and Fagan pops up like a jackass telling me to back off. Last I checked, she don't belong to him."

"That might be true," Harley said. "But she doesn't belong to you either. You know the rules, Chet. I run a clean establishment. No drunks, no fights, no drugs, and especially no unwanted groping. Keep your hands to yourself."

"Yeah, yeah, I know the damn rules. But come on Harley." Chet grinned, leaning closer to the bar owner as if sharing a secret. He pointed a thumb at Kyle. "Can you imagine any woman choosing a cripple like him over a hunk of a man like me?'

Farrah tensed. She could just imagine Kyle reaching around her to snatch Chet off his feet. When the man behind her didn't move, she glanced over her shoulder at him again. The expression on Kyle's face—or rather, lack thereof—chilled her to the bone. He looked like a figure carved from ice. No heat in his eyes, no softness. No emotion whatsoever. It was as if the playful, slightly cynical Kyle she'd known for years wasn't there anymore. In his place was a hard rock of a man, someone intimately familiar with violence in all its forms, someone who could kill without thinking twice.

Farrah shivered. For the first time, he actually scared her.

Harley's cultured voice, thick with disgust, snagged Farrah's attention. "That's it, Chet. Leave now. You're done for the day. I don't need you picking fights."

The idiot had the nerve to laugh. "All right, old man, I'm going. The boys and I were headed out anyway." Chet's smug gaze left Kyle and settled on her. Still angry at his deliberate insult to Kyle, Farrah found herself with the uncharacteristic urge to do violence.

"I'll see you around, Farrah." He winked at her and left with his brothers in tow.

Farrah decided she now had another reason for a nice long shower: washing off Chet Wassile's touch.

"Sorry about that," Harley said.

"Not your fault. Assholes are what they are," Kyle said, his arm leaving her as he turned back to his table. "Someone ought to cull them out of the gene pool."

Farrah shivered again, not sure if it was the coldness of his words or lack of his body heat that was the cause. Harley's eyes widened a little behind his wire-rimmed glasses. He shot her a worried glance.

"It's okay," she assured him, though she wasn't at all sure that was true. "He didn't mean it. He's just…well, he's in a lot of pain."

The bar owner cleared his throat. "Yes, well, any other drinks you two order tonight are on me. I don't like my customers being harassed."

"Thanks Harley," she said.

The man gave her a wave as he moved off. The noise level of the bar having lowered considerably during the tense exchange, returned to its previous level. Farrah reached the corner booth without further interference, though she felt speculative gazes on her the whole way. Inside, she cringed a little. She could just see the headline in tomorrow's town paper.

"Local Doctor's First Visit to Bar Results in Heated Confrontation"

Oh yes, that would do wonders for her practice.

And the real confrontation hadn't even started yet.

****

Kyle didn't give Farrah a chance to do more than set her drink down. "What are you doing here?"

She glanced at him, that annoyingly provocative eyebrow of hers arching up before she switched her attention to the napkin dispenser. "I thought that would be obvious," she said, pulling several paper napkins free and wiping at the spilled drink on her arm. "You missed your three o'clock appointment. I'm here to find out why. It's not my fault Chet chose tonight to be a jerk."

"I don't need you making excuses for me." Okay, that had slipped out. There were a lot of things he could have said besides that. *Do you always track down patients who don't make their appointments? Chet's always a jerk.* Or even the clichéd, *Do you come here often?* Though he was pretty sure he knew the answer to that one. He'd never known little Miss Straight-laced to step one foot inside a bar.

That's why he was here. Hiding like the scared three-year-old she'd called him yesterday.

Great, now he was insulting himself. His inner bastard needed to shut the hell up so he could concentrate. Getting Farrah to go away and leave him alone without hurting her feelings wasn't going to be easy. And damn him if he ever hurt her on purpose, emotionally or otherwise.

"I didn't."

Her terse reply jerked his attention back to her. "Didn't what?" What part of the conversation had he missed?

"I didn't make excuses for you."

Kyle ground his teeth. "You did. I heard what you said to Harley."

"What you heard," she said, sounding so prim and proper he wanted to reach across and kiss the prissiness right out of her, "was me explaining to Harley that you're in pain, thus your temper is short, thus your judgment is off, which explains your less than PC comment in a crowded room of people. You didn't hear me offer an explanation coupled with a request for forgiveness for your actions. That would have made it an excuse. Despite what some philosophers may think, there is a difference."

"Everything okay, Kyle?"

Kyle closed his mouth at the waitress' question. He wanted to argue with Farrah just for the sake of argument. Did she know her eyes darkened when her emotions ran hot, the hazel green a perfect match for the heart of a summer forest at twilight? Damn, but he could stare into those depths all day and all night. Forever.

He gave himself a mental shake, made himself look away from the tempting woman in the booth across from him to the waitress standing by their table. "Yeah, thanks, Tally. We're good."

"No problem." The girl turned to Farrah. "You can use this first if you like, before I use it on floor. It's clean and I wet it with hot water. Those napkins won't get the sticky off."

Farrah took the slightly steaming towel Tally offered her. "Thank you." She wiped the spilled soda off her skin and quickly handed the towel back. "Sorry about the mess."

"Not your fault, sweetie. Spills happen around here all the time."

As soon as Tally left, Farrah faced him head on. "You need to come in so I can do a full exam on your leg. I'll pick you up first thing in the morning. You shouldn't be driving."

Kyle bit back a growl. The woman was relentless. "I can drive just fine." He'd proved it this morning by driving the piece-of-shit truck down to the rental agency in Asheville. So what if the almost two-hour trip had triggered a round of muscle cramps that left him sweaty and shaking. He'd ground his teeth the whole ride back to Clear Springs with Seth Borden, and spent the rest of the afternoon sipping just enough beer to dull the pain.

"No, you can't. Especially when you've obviously been drinking."

He slammed his bottle on the table. "Don't start preaching that crap. You know I don't drink and drive."

"Maybe not," she conceded, "but you're still driving with your reflexes impaired. It's dangerous and irresponsible. I can't believe you made the trip all the way down from DC by yourself. What were you thinking, Kyle?"

Now that was an opening he couldn't resist. He sat forward. "I could ask you the same thing," he drawled. "Tell me, what's the thinking behind your own irresponsible behavior? Is it drugs, or did you develop more than just lock-picking skills the last few years?"

She blinked. "What are you talking about?"

"I'm talking about your death wish."

"My…? Are you crazy?"

"No, but apparently you are."

She sucked in a deep breath as if trying to calm herself. "I swear, Kyle Fagan, if you don't start making sense—"

"You'll what?" Kyle ground out, trying to keep a cap on his volume and rising temper, both. "What'll you do for an encore, Farrah? What could possibly top flinging your naked body at a desperate criminal supposedly armed with a gun? Huh? Tell me, 'cause I'd damn sure like to know."

Even in the dim light, he saw her cheeks darken as she realized what he was referring to. That didn't mean she was cowed. Oh, no, not her. Up came her adorable chin and back went her shoulders. "I wasn't completely naked. I had a towel wrapped around me. Besides, my plan worked, didn't it? You ended up in the pool as I remember."

He nodded once, letting the sarcasm flow freely. "Oh, right, you had a towel. That made it soooo much better." He couldn't keep from reaching across the table and wrapping a hand around one of her fragile wrists. Everything about her was fragile, breakable, a fact she seemed determined to ignore. "Come on, Farrah, you're smarter than this. You have to see how dangerous and stupid that stunt was. It worked on me, but it might not have worked on this Craddoc guy. What if he'd knocked you down instead? What then?"

He felt her body tremble. The blush on her cheeks faded in a rush. "That's right, honey, think about the 'what ifs'." He wasn't above using fear as a deterrent if it kept her from taking foolish risks in the future.

She held his gaze a long moment before slowly tilting her head forward, then back. "You're right. It was dangerous. I'll admit that. But it was the only thing I could think of at the time. The door was stuck. I had no way to keep him…you out of the house. What else was I supposed to do?"

He rubbed his thumb over her pulse, wanting to soothe her now that she'd agreed with him. "Hell, honey, there are always alternatives. You just have to avoid panicking and evaluate the situation from every angle. If Joshua and I've learned anything, it's once you look at a problem in the right light, a solutions is bound to present itself."

Her eyes widened slightly, then narrowed. She nodded again. "I agree. That's a very good philosophy. That's exactly why I want you to come in so I can examine your leg."

"God…" Kyle snapped his mouth closed as he released her and leaned back. He ran a hand over his face, counting to ten in his head. Surprisingly, Farrah remained quiet, not breaking the silence between them. Not even when he snagged his bottle off the table and took a good long swig of beer.

Feeling as if he had himself under control, Kyle met her gaze. "You examined my leg yesterday. You don't need to see it again."

Farrah's unladylike snort made him want to smile despite his irritation. "Please," she said, exasperation mixing with an excitement he could almost see building around her, "that was a cursory exam at the most. I want blood work. I want new x-rays and an MRI so I know what's going on beneath your stubborn epidermis. I want to see the current condition of that poor excuse of a joint you call a knee. I want proof your grafts aren't going septic." She leaned her arms on the table, her expression dead serious. "I've read your file, Kyle. Joshua sent it to me. I've also read the background on those two doctors your commander wants you to see. It's early yet, and I want to do some tests of my own to be sure, but I think there's a chance—"

"A chance for what, Farrah?" Kyle asked, his strained patience snapping like a dry twig. "To walk like I used to? To get my life back?" He matched her snort with one of his own. "Don't kid yourself, honey, we both know that's not happening. Not now, not ever."

He leaned back hard against the booth's cushion and finished off his beer in a gulp, struggling to get his temper under control. If anyone else tried nagging him like this, he'd already be out the door, daring them to follow.

It's not her fault, he repeated over and over in his head. The shitty turn his life had taken was no fault of Farrah's no matter how much she might think so. His decisions, his mistakes, his responsibility. He'd already accepted that. If she'd just leave him alone…

He set the empty beer bottle down carefully and gusted out a sigh. Reaching over, he covered her hand with his. "Look, Farrah, I'm through with getting poked and prodded, hear me? You might as well give up trying to get me to change my mind."

For a moment, she just stared at him without moving. Then she clamped her lips together and slipped out of the booth. She stared down at him, her expression harder than any he'd seen on her before.

"Does Joshua know you've given up?"

Shit! He kept his mouth shut and grabbed the empty bottle on the table, fighting the urge to fling it across the room. "Call it whatever you like."

"Huh," she said, tipping her head to one side. "I never took you for a coward."

Kyle snapped his head up, stunned by the insult—especially coming from her. She was already walking away. He narrowed his eyes on her retreating form.

Oh, no, sweetheart, you do not get to say something like that and just walk away.

He was out of his seat and after her in the next heartbeat, not even sure how he managed to clear the booth without tripping. Farrah didn't run, but she was damn quick. He caught up to her outside, almost to her vehicle. He clapped his hand on her shoulder, intending to swing her around to face him. At his first touch, however, she dropped her shoulder and spun away.

"Stop it!" she said sharply. "I've been manhandled quite enough tonight, thank you."

Kyle raised his free hand, palm open, trying not to make it obvious how hard he leaned on his cane with the other one. She was right. Grabbing her like that made him no better than Chet. At least she stood still instead of diving into her SUV and driving off.

The sun wasn't quite down yet, the last rays catching her face at just the right angle. Kyle frowned. Her lashes were wet and there was a lingering dampness on her cheeks.

"You're crying. Why the hell are you crying?"

She stabbed a finger at him. "Because of you, you idiot!" She swiped away another pair of tears before throwing her hands in the air. "Here I am trying to help you, and it's like you don't care about your own life. In all the years I've known you, I've never once seen you give up without a fight. Why in the world, when the stakes are so high, would you decide to give up now?"

He ran a hand over his face, feeling the frustration leak out of every pore along with his sweat. "Farrah...I'm not giving up. I just...I'm trying to be realistic here."

He sucked in a deep breath and looked away. The silence stretched between them, broken only by Farrah's quiet sniffles. It took all his strength to meet her wounded gaze again.

"Look, I understand you want to make things

better. I appreciate it. I really do. But you have to accept there are some things you can't fix. Trying to force the issue won't accomplish a damn thing. You don't know what I've been through, what I'm still—"

"I was there, remember? I'm a doctor, I know—"

Her words cut off as he moved into her personal space, forcing her to step back until she bumped against the fender of her car. He didn't stop until their bodies almost touched. Deliberately, he reached down and pressed a hand against her thigh, applying just a hint of pressure. The material of her gray dress pants kept him from touching skin, but the heat of her still seared him. He held her watery gaze as he slowly leaned to the side, moving his hand down, sliding his palm over her knee, then trailing searching fingers back up, up and around, until he stopped just shy of cupping her deliciously firm ass. Her heavy breathing matched his, their breaths mingling in the hot, August air.

"I don't feel a brace on your leg, Dr. Hastings," he said softly. "I don't feel any twisted muscles or hard scars. So how can you stand here and say you know what I'm going through? You can't."

Farrah drew in a deeper breath, the simple action causing her breasts to brush against his chest. Part of Kyle ordered him to step back, break the sweet contact. Another part of him begged to move closer, to press his whole body against hers the way she had earlier in the bar. The feel of her then had been a torture sweet enough to distract him from wiping the floor with Chet's face.

"Yes, you've been through a lot," Farrah said, her hands coming up to act as a barrier between them. "I get that. I even understand I have no personal experience to compare it to." Fingers curled, fisting the material of his shirt. "But, Kyle, I've seen people who have. People who've suffered traumatic injuries. People who have lost more than you. A lot more. And I've seen these people fight back. I've seen them grasp at every opportunity to better their situation. I've seen them beg for the help you're turning your back on."

Her voice had risen to almost a shout. She paused, glanced around quickly, and then met his gaze again.

"How can you just give up?" she asked, her tone soft and fierce. "Please, if nothing else, help me understand your reasoning behind that asinine decision."

Kyle couldn't speak. It wasn't so much her words as the pure desperation in them that silenced him. She was hurting, and he'd just gotten through promising himself he wouldn't hurt her.

"Farrah…" Kyle bent his head, unable to stop himself. All he wanted was to take away the pain. To kiss her until she didn't hurt anymore.

His lips brushed hers. He felt her shudder, but, thank God in heaven, she didn't pull away. He brushed her lips again with his, firming the touch. Her lips were soft as a snow flake, but warm, oh, so very warm. Fingers, strong and capable, flexed against his chest. He started to pull back, only to catch her needy whimper. Her body shifted against his, pressing closer in the most delicious way.

Oh, hell yes.

Putting both arms around her, Kyle pulled her closer. He deepened the kiss, running his tongue across her sweet lips. Her mouth opened on a little moan. He entered her gently, licking, tasting, sampling the flavor that was uniquely her. Sweet, sweet Farrah Hastings. His fantasy come to full and erotic life.

A car rolled by, horn honking, the occupants shouting and whistling. Like a pond in winter, Farrah froze. The hands on his chest flattened, pushed.

Kyle had to make himself let her go. She was right. The street was no place for this. They'd go to his place. No, hers. It was closer.

When he met her gaze, however, he knew there'd be no sweet climax in their future. Her beautiful eyes were stricken, shocked to the core, as if she couldn't believe what she'd done.

"I can't...I'm sorry. I can't do this right now."

She eased away from him, each step feeling like a thousand bullets to his chest. Kyle stood completely still and let her go, let her get in her car and drive away. Only when he lost sight of her vehicle's tail lights did he carefully bend down and pick up his walking stick. He'd dropped the damn thing when he'd put his arms around Farrah, reaching for the impossible, the unattainable. The forbidden.

Chet was right. What woman in her right mind would ever choose a cripple like him?

Chapter Ten

Bad news really did come in threes, Farrah decided, watching the ambulance drive away with the injured firefighter she'd stabilized.

First came the forest fire, sparked by lightning from the dry thunderstorm the previous night.

Farrah shielded her eyes and looked to the southwest. The dark stain just above the green peaks seemed bigger than it was this morning. She didn't know if that was just a case of the wind spreading the smudge of smoke across the sky, or if the inferno was spreading. So far, the firefighters had been able to limit the flames to an uninhabited area two valleys over. That didn't mean it would stay there. Fires were unpredictable, and not easily tamed. Hopefully, they'd have the thing under control soon, preferably, without any more casualties.

The second bad news came about mid-morning. According to the sheriff's deputy who'd stopped by, Russell Craddoc had evidently found himself some transportation. He'd broken into a house on the west ridge sometime late yesterday. Luckily, it was a vacation home, and the owners were hundreds of miles away. Craddoc had made a mess of the house and stolen a car housed in the attached garage. If not for the caretaker's weekly drive by, no one would know he was mobile. The only bright spot was the fact the gas tank was almost on empty.

The third bad news?

She realized about five o'clock this morning that she was in love with Kyle Fagan.

Farrah grimaced. Bad news? Good news? At this point, she wasn't really sure where that world-shaking epiphany fit in the grand scheme of things. She'd always imagined that when she found the one person she wanted to spend the rest of her life with, it would be a glorious time of celebration. But, Kyle Fagan? Really? Except for yesterday, the man had always held her at arm's length. Could she really mean something more to him?

Yes, apparently, if she went by that unexpected kiss yesterday. Though whether he still felt the same after her cowardly retreat was anyone's guess. Her cheeks still flushed when she thought of the way she'd panicked. She wasn't in the habit of running away from difficult situations. She'd much rather tough it out and get through her problems than put them off until later. Her body had known what was going on. It had just taken the rest of her a few sleepless hours to accept her new state. She was in love.

The realization that her feelings for Kyle were no longer lukewarm, but magma hot, had pumped so much adrenaline into her she'd gone numb. She'd thought she was done with the bad boys of the valley when she broke things off with Joshua years ago. He and Kyle were into violence, she wasn't. They couldn't wait to enter the military, and she hated the military for good reason. Her older brother had joined the Army straight out of high school. His death from a sniper's bullet six months into his stint in Afghanistan had nearly broken her. She'd sworn then that never again would she love someone whose job put them in danger.

Cue her Dear John letter to Joshua while he was in boot camp.

Not that Joshua, or Kyle either, had let her put that much emotional distance between them. She'd known for a long time that she was walking the edge of her vow with those two. She simply couldn't put them completely out of her life. Not when they'd both been so understanding and supportive after Mark died. As far as she was concerned, Joshua's platonic friendship after their breakup just proved he wasn't the one for her. Who would have thought his irreverent, foul-mouthed, hot tempered sidekick would stir things in her that she'd never felt before, not even with Joshua?

Farrah's hands balled into fists as she turned and marched back into the clinic. She wasn't the type to stand back and watch someone she cared about ruin his life by doing nothing. It was time to ramp things up. The challenge to shake Kyle Fagan out of his defeatist funk just got personal.

****

Kyle clenched his teeth as he forced his truck to a stop at the bottom of his steep driveway. He'd never thought twice about the sharp incline before, but damn if it wasn't on the top of his list of things to avoid now. Only problem being he couldn't avoid it forever. He needed to pick up his mail that had accumulated at the post office while he'd been gone. And, according to his stomach, he needed food—something more immediate in addition to the groceries on his list.

Post office, café, market. He had a plan.

Part of him had the nerve to wonder if he'd see

Farrah in town. He hadn't seen or heard from the aggravating woman since the disastrous kiss three nights ago. Not that he'd expected to. He knew he'd stepped over the line of their friendship.

She's leaving you alone. Isn't that what you wanted?

Well, yes, and no. He could do without the constant badgering about the sorry state of his leg, but he didn't want to do without Farrah's company. Her lovely face, her smile, the way she tilted her head up when she laughed, sending all those red-gold curls tumbling down her back. Hell, she was so beautiful, just looking at her had a way of lightening his heart. And when she spoke? Damn if it wasn't like listening to an angel, even when she was badgering him.

And, he was right back where he started, hoping he'd see her in town and knowing it would be better not to. Yeah, the situation sucked.

A growl of sheer frustration filled the cab. Why did life have to be so damn complicated?

There weren't any cars in the lot when Kyle stopped at the little post office on the edge of town. The flag flying from the pole off to the side snapped in the hot breeze, catching Kyle's attention as he got out of his truck. He looked up. The gray cast to the clouds scuttling across the sky wasn't a good sign. Firefighters were still battling the blaze started by the storm early Saturday morning. Unless this one had some heavy rain in it to go with the wind and lightning, it would only make things worse.

Kyle put his head down against the dust kicked up by the stiff breeze and limped inside. He went to the counter and rang the little bell for service.

"Hold your horses, I'll be right there," a voice called from the back. The older woman who appeared a few seconds later was as familiar to Kyle as his own reflection. Kay Downing had long, silvery gray hair she wore loose and flowing. A hold-over from her hippy days, she joked. She had sharp blue eyes that met you straight on, just as clear and canny as when she taught him in Sunday school years ago. Her pink-painted lips spread into a warm smile when she saw him.

"Kyle! There you are. I'd heard you were back." She held up a finger. "Give me just a minute. I knew you'd probably be in soon, so I've got your mail right here." She marched over to a line of cabinets along a wall, high heels clip-clopping on the linoleum. She opened a door and hauled out a canvas bag that had US MAIL stenciled on it. Even from where he stood, Kyle could see the thing looked heavy. He immediately felt guilty.

"Here, Ms. Downing. Let me in and I'll get that."

"That's all right, I got it." She wrapped the ends of the cords holding the bag closed around her hand and started dragging the accumulation of several months of hunting, fishing, and sports magazines across the floor. "Why do you think I put everything in this bag instead of a box? Easier for both of us to handle this way."

He met her at the locked door to the office.

"Here," she said, putting the cords in his hand. She flipped her long hair back over her shoulder with a practiced move. "You can drag it right out to your truck. It won't hurt it none."

Kyle wrapped the top of the bag around his hand, picked it up, and flipped it over his shoulder. The weight pulled him slightly off balance, but he compensated quickly. Mrs. Downing stared at him a second.

"Figures," she said, shaking her head a little.

Kyle grinned down at her. "Thanks Ms. Downing. I'll bring the bag back later in the week."

She waved a hand at him in a shooing motion. "You don't worry about that. I got more than one. Just get it back to me before you go gallivanting off again with that Colby boy."

And just like that, Kyle's good mood soured. "Yes, ma'am." He kept the smile pasted on his face as he left. No sense trying to explain to the kind woman that he wouldn't be going anywhere with Joshua any time soon. If ever.

He plopped the bag on the floor of the truck on the passenger side, cranked up, and headed for the café. He really didn't feel like eating anymore, but knew he had to. Besides, Marlee and Seth Borden served omelets 'til eleven, and it was just now ten. He hadn't had one of Seth's mouth-watering omelets in ages.

Kyle lucked out and found a parking spot on the street right in front of the café. As soon as he stepped inside the little restaurant, voices called out in greeting. He acknowledged them with a wave, his trained senses causing him to read each face, even though he didn't want to. The pity was easier to decipher on some faces than others. Pity, and curiosity. The two emotions seemed to be the driving force behind the friendly smiles. Word had gotten around that he was hurt, but not why or how.

Paybacks, he thought, hiding his grim smile behind a swipe of his hand across his mouth. Leaving them wondering about the cause of his injury was petty, but he'd take his satisfaction where he could get it.

Marlee Borden hurried around the counter, her gaze jumping from his leg to his face. Kyle did his own share of looking—at her rounded belly. She laughed, hardly any shadows at all hiding in her soft brown eyes. "Kyle, it's so good to see you." She wrapped him in a hug. Kyle carefully hugged her back. Marlee's husband, Seth, stuck his head out of the kitchen and waved a spatula in greeting. Kyle shot him a thumbs up. Seth grinned, gave a short bow with an exaggerated flourish of the spatula, and ducked back into the kitchen. Kyle had known the couple all his life, though they were a few years his senior. They'd always wanted a child.

"Congratulations, Marlee. You look like you're ready to pop," he said as he and Marlee both straightened.

She patted her curved stomach and sighed heavily. "Thanks. I wish that was the case. I've got three more weeks according to the doctor. Seth wants me to quit working, but I read somewhere that walking sometimes brings on early labor. At this point, I'll do anything to get this part over with." She touched his arm, some of the happiness warming her gaze replaced by concern. "How about you? Are you going to be okay?"

Sweet woman. She understood he wasn't okay now, but wanted to make sure he would be in the future. Damn if he didn't like that about her. He shrugged a shoulder. "They tell me it's like having a baby. You just have to learn to live with the consequences of all that fun you had getting there."

Marlee smiled slightly. She looked like she wanted to say more, but just nodded. "Come on," she said, stepping back. "Your favorite table is open. You sit down and I'll bring you a coffee. You want pancakes or an omelet this morning?"

"Omelet, please. Seth knows how I like it."

She grinned, already backing toward the kitchen. "Right. Everything under the sun and heavy on the jalapenos. I'll get him right on it."

Kyle made his way to the back booth. He sat with his back to the wall, giving him a good view of the entire café. The few patrons had gone back to their food and conversations for the most part. No doubt he was now a star topic.

"Here's your coffee." She set the steaming cup in front of him. "Food'll be up in a minute."

"Thanks Marlee." He glanced up before she turned completely away. Something about her smile, the way her eyes darted away from him, caught his attention. He watched her a moment, the tight muscles of her shoulders screaming a tension that hadn't been there before. She was nervous, he decided, but trying hard not to show it. Kyle continued to watch her retreat from the corner of his eye. Damn if she didn't glance back at him twice before she ducked into the kitchen. Definitely nervous. Maybe she was like the rest, wanting to ask him more about his injury, but afraid to. Yeah, that was probably it.

Kyle reached over to pull a packet of sugar from the little container on the table. He could drink black coffee, but enjoyed it more with a touch of sweet. He plucked up a white packet, his gaze automatically cataloguing the rest of the items sitting in a cluster: salt and pepper shakers, bottle of catsup, bottle of hot sauce—he'd need that shortly. Combination napkin and menu holder...

His gaze caught the word *knee* on the cover of the menu and stuck. He looked closer. No, not on the menu cover. There was something else tucked into the front of the holder. He jerked the folded paper free. What the hell?

Bold words on the front read: SAFE, EFFECTIVE KNEE REPLACEMENT

Beneath them were the words, Pain Free Walking Guaranteed.

The doctor's name and location was printed at the bottom, but Kyle didn't bother reading anymore. He ripped the pamphlet in two and tossed it on the table.

When Marlee arrived with his meal, her expression was wary. She glanced at the torn pieces on the table, but didn't say anything, just nibbled on her bottom lip. When she came back to top off his coffee, she still didn't mention the pamphlet. Kyle let it go. He already knew who was responsible, so grilling Marlee wouldn't do anything but upset the pregnant woman. She might be hoping for early labor, but he wasn't about to be the cause of it by distressing her.

He took another bite of the delicious omelet. Some of the juices from the chopped vegetables tucked inside escaped, trickling down his chin. Instead of going for the thin little paper napkins in the holder, he reached for the neatly folded cloth one Marlee had brought along with his plate. Kyle snapped open the pristine white napkin and mentally cursed as another pamphlet dropped onto the table. This piece of medical propaganda was different, touting the expertise of a Dr. Simon Gather, who had performed hundreds of successful popliteal artery bypass surgeries.

Restores   blood   flow.   Strengthens   starving

muscles…

Shit! Kyle muttered a few more choice words as he treated this pamphlet with the same care as he had the first one. He thought seriously about getting up and walking out without finishing his meal. But, no, that would only hurt Marlee's feelings. It was obvious, now, why she was so nervous. Farrah had somehow talked the sweet-natured Marlee into pestering him with the pamphlets. Damn stubborn woman!

Irritation had him bolting down the rest of his food. After draining his coffee cup, he left enough money on the table to cover the meal plus his usual big tip, and headed for the door. He made sure to smile and wave at Marlee on his way out. The woman waved back, still looking as stressed as a rabbit in a room full of wolves.

Kyle pushed all thoughts of Farrah and pamphlets and surgeries to the back of his mind as he shopped the little market down the street for a bachelor's necessary food stuffs. The chore didn't require much concentration. Frozen pizza, frozen dinners, chips, dip, and beer. Yeah, good, reliable staples. He grabbed a bag of baking potatoes, the makings for a salad, and a couple of steaks and chops for those days he craved something a little more substantial, and headed for the checkout stand.

Getting past the register seemed to take forever. The girl sliding his items past the scanner kept asking him questions about the military. Not a good subject for him right now. Soon enough, though, he paid his tab and claimed his purchases from the kid who'd bagged them up. When the skinny teenager offered to help Kyle carry the bags to his truck, Kyle let him, just because the offer came out sounding like a broken record, something the boy said to everyone.

When he got home and got the groceries inside, Kyle set about putting them away, starting with the cold stuff. The first frozen dinner he pulled out had a paper stuck to it from the condensation. Kyle thought it was a food advertisement until he peeled it off and stared. Another damn knee replacement pamphlet!

Growling, he wadded the thing up and tossed it in the trash. This was getting ridiculous. How many more of the damn things had Farrah handed out to people to give to him?

Turned out it was at least seven more. He pulled one from each grocery bag except the last, which held two. Apparently, the helpful young man bagging groceries had gotten carried away with his slight-of-hand at one point.

Kyle stared at the papers lined up on the counter. Three popliteals and four knees. He had to hand it to Farrah, she was persistent. Shaking his head, he swept the pamphlets into a stack and tossed them into the trash with the first one. If this kept up, he could fuel his own bonfire in the back yard.

An hour later, Kyle sat down at his small dining table, determined to go through his mail. Loosening the cords, he pulled the mouth of the mail bag open, reached inside, and pulled out a handful of magazines, a few envelopes, and—

"What the…!"

He slammed the mail on the table, scattering the legitimate post along with more of Farrah's quiet ammunition. Six, seven…there had to be at least ten pamphlets total in that one handful alone. Kyle stood up fast, knocking his chair over in the process. He grabbed the mail bag off the floor and turned it upside down, spilling its contents on the table. Magazines, circulars, envelopes, and yes, more pamphlets. A lot more.

Kyle stared. Holy shit. At least a third of the bag's contents were those damned medical leaflets. How the hell had Farrah talked Kay into putting those in his bag? Didn't the woman know she could get in trouble for tampering with the US mail? Hell, she was already in trouble. Way past in trouble. Badgering him herself was one thing. Enlisting the whole damned town was quite another.

He snatched up several pamphlets and headed for the door. It was time to put a stop to this nonsense right now.

****

Farrah came out of her office just as the clinic's front door slammed.

"Can I help you?" she heard Mary say.

"Where is she?"

Farrah stopped. Kyle was here. And from the sound of his voice, he wasn't a happy camper. Even knowing she was about to be confronted by an angry Kyle, she couldn't stop herself from smiling just a little. Operation Information Bomb must be working.

"Farrah! Get your butt out here!"

She glanced at her reflection in the glass of a picture hanging on the wall and smoothed every ounce of humor out of her expression. This was serious. In order to get him to agree to the new procedures, she had to, first, get him thinking about them. Hence, the information overload.

"There you are, you conniving wench."

Wench? She looked down the hall. Kyle stalked

169

toward her as only he could, jaw tight, lips pressed into a hard line, brows lowered over eyes the color of dark fire. That cane of his stabbed into the floor so hard with each step she was surprised it didn't crack the tile. Despite the whole grim thing he had going, a thrill shot through her at just seeing him again. Goodness, if he ever discovered how much he affected her, she wouldn't stand a chance at getting him to agree to anything.

She raised an eyebrow and pulled out her most professional doctor's voice. No sense waiting for him to start ranting at her. "Good afternoon. Shall we take this into my office?"

She didn't wait for him to agree, but spun around and headed down the hall, glad he couldn't hear how fast her heart was pounding. He didn't scare her, not exactly. But the knowledge that so much pent up energy and reined-in emotion followed hot on her heels sent her pulse racing.

He shoved the office door closed and slammed a handful of pamphlets on her desk before she even made it to her chair.

"I want you to stop this right now."

She sat carefully, getting completely comfortable before propping her elbows on the chair's arms and weaving her fingers together. "No."

He evidently didn't expect her calm, one-word reply, because he actually stared at her for a whole two seconds before leaning over her desk. "Yes, you will. Damn it, Farrah, I don't need the whole fucking town on my back. All I want is to be left alone. Is that too damn much to ask?"

Farrah made sure to keep her voice even and

professional. "Yes, as a matter of fact, it is. And cussing at me isn't going to get me to change my mind. I care about you, Kyle. We all do. You can't expect us to just sit back and watch you ruin your life."

He straightened sharply and slammed the cane on the top of her desk. The sharp report made her blink and jump in her seat. Reaching down, he grabbed one of the brace's straps and lifted his leg until his foot was propped on the corner of the desk. "In case you haven't noticed, my life is already ruined."

Anger bubbled up. She was tired of his sad sack routine. "Exactly why do you think your life is ruined, Kyle? Because you can't run with the big dogs anymore? Because you can't follow in Joshua's footsteps?"

The anger spilled over, forcing her to her feet. She reached out and shoved Kyle's foot off her desk, refusing to let his small wince of pain and the way he had to steady himself against her desk stall her. Somehow, she had to break through that blasted wall of his.

"Come on, Kyle," she said, putting as much derision into her tone as possible, "grow up. There's nothing that says you can't start over and do something else with your life besides killing the bad guys."

The line of his jaw turned white. "It's what I do—"

"Correction. It's what you did. It's time for you to suck it up and do something else."

"No, it's time for you to face facts, Farrah. This stupid campaign you've started isn't going to work. I told you, I'm not having any more surgeries. I'm done. Finished! Why can't you just accept that?"

"Why?" She rounded the desk, stopping just shy of

his personal space. "You really want to know why I'm not standing back and doing nothing? Then let me put it into perspective for you. You still know how to use your imagination, right? Of course you do, men fantasize all the time. So let's imagine, shall we, I'm you and you're me."

His brows lowered. "What are you—"

"Come on, Kyle, work with me here. I'm the one with the busted leg that's eventually going to turn gangrenous and have to be amputated so it doesn't kill me, and you're the one with the medical knowledge that can not only prevent it, but make it better. Tell me, are you going to just walk away whistling a tune while I risk my life because I'm too busy wallowing in self-pity to do anything about it? Or are you going to shake me up by getting in my face until I see reason? Don't lie, now, I want the truth."

Farrah let him have a couple seconds of silence. When she could almost hear his teeth grind together, she figured it was enough. She put a hand flat on his chest, over his heart.

"You'd save me, wouldn't you? You couldn't walk away from me any more than I can walk away from you."

She could tell he didn't want to admit it. Because if he did, he'd have to admit to it all—that his self-pity and bitterness was what was holding him back.

"Farrah…"

"Shhh," she said, putting a finger over his lips. She knew if she tried to force an admission from him now he could back up and shut down again. She had his brain pointed in the right direction, she just had to let him stew on it a while. Kyle wasn't a dense man, just stubborn. Once he admitted to himself that she was right, he'd admit it to her. Then they could move forward. She just needed to give him time to think things through.

"It's all right," she said, the torment and pain in his eyes made her want to hold him. So she did. She slipped her arms around his waist and put her cheek where her hand had been. The tightness of his muscles worried her. So did the pace of his heartbeat pounding away under her ear. "It's going to be all right," she repeated.

The tension didn't leave him. Farrah raised her head to look at him. If anything, the torment in his gaze was worse. One large hand slid around her waist while the other captured her chin. She met his stare, could tell he was searching her face for something.

"I thought you said you couldn't do this?"

His question confused her. Couldn't do what? Couldn't fight for him? Couldn't feel for him? Silly man. Farrah rose on her toes to show him how wrong he was. She pressed her lips to his. At first, she thought he wouldn't respond, that he'd reject her. But then he let out a soft groan of what she knew was surrender because his mouth opened. She licked inside. Kyle's arms locked around her, pulling her closer. She could feel his reaction as his body hardened against her, the ridge of his erection pressing into her lower belly with sudden urgency. Fire ignited inside her, low and hot, and spreading fast. His tongue stroked hers repeatedly, luring her in, inviting her to taste him, play with him. She indulged them both.

Farrah finally had to pull back to grab some air. Kyle was panting right along with her. She closed her eyes and pressed her forehead to his.

"I need you to trust me, Kyle. I'm not promising you everything will be rainbows and daisies. But I will promise to stand by you and help you get through this."

She felt him go still. Even his breathing stopped on a sharp inhale. His voice rough, he said, "Are you doing this just so I'll agree to the new surgeries?"

Not sure what he meant, Farrah leaned back so she could see his face. "You mean the pamphlets? Of course—"

"No," he said, his face almost void of expression as he made a back-and-forth motion between them. "This. Us. Are you trying to seduce me just so I'll fall in with your surgery plans?"

"What?" Surprise and hurt had her pushing out of his arms. Oh, the idiot. Did he think so little of her that he thought she would play with his emotions? "Of course not! My gosh, how could you even think—"

A sharp knock preceded the door opening. Sheriff Penwell stuck his head inside.

"Kyle. Farrah." His eyes widened slightly as he noticed how close they were standing to one another. "Um, sorry to interrupt, but we need the doc."

Farrah straightened her white medical coat, grateful beyond words for the interruption. "What is it? Another injury?"

"Several," Pen said. "There was a backdraft that forced a group of firemen off a cliff. We got broken bones, concussions, and God only knows what else. County's asking for medical volunteers. I volunteered you."

Farrah nodded. "Give me a minute to grab supplies." She stopped mid-step when Kyle's hand shot out in front of her, barring her way. "Kyle—"

"Just a second." He turned to look at the sheriff. "What cliff are we talking about here?"

"The one on the east face of Breakers Ridge, about fifteen miles north of Fontana Lake. Don't worry, we've got a trained rescue crew extracting the victims. Paramedics are on scene, but county big-wigs want some MDs if they can get them. This fire has already generated more injuries than normal. They don't want to compound the problem by adding fatalities."

"Fine," Kyle said, nodding slowly. "As long as she's not expected to climb down into that canyon, she can go."

Farrah shoved Kyle's arm out of her way, unable to believe her ears. Less than a minute ago, he was accusing her of seducing him. Now he was treating her like a child?

"Hold on. First of all, *she* is standing right here. I can darn well speak for myself, thank you. Secondly," she poked him in the chest, "I don't need your permission to do anything. You aren't my boss."

"Well, someone should take charge of you," Kyle said, his movements sharp with anger as he pushed past her and the sheriff and into the hall. "Considering your decisions lately, you're obviously having difficulty making the right ones by yourself," he called over his shoulder.

Farrah narrowed her eyes, his words sparking her own anger. She stalked after him, Pen wisely stepping aside to give her an open path. "My decisions are just fine. I've been making my own for years."

Kyle swung around in the thankfully empty lobby. It was bad enough that Mary and the sheriff were witness to this argument.

"So have I, honey," Kyle snapped. "But that's something else you seem to have trouble with."

"That's different, and you know it. I'm trying to help you."

"I. Don't. Need. Your. Help."

The slow, quiet way he said the words struck Farrah harder than if he'd shouted them. She fought back sudden tears. No crying. She didn't have time for a bunch of useless wet works. She had patients waiting. Darn Kyle for being so stubborn!

Farrah propped her hands on her hips. "Well, know what? You're in luck. I'm too busy right now to bother with you." She waved a hand in his direction. "Go! Hide in your house. Or Joshua's house or Harley's bar, or whatever hole you feel the need to crawl into. But trust me, we will finish this discussion when I get back."

She spun around, already going over the list in her head of things she'd need to take with her. Kyle's voice followed her down the hall.

"No, Farrah, that's where you're wrong. This discussion is already over. I'm telling you for the last time, stop meddling in my life!"

She made another shooing motion in his direction as she opened the door to the supply room, not bothering to reply. The man made her furious, simply furious. No matter how loud he yelled or how much he cursed, she would not let him accept things as they were. She couldn't, even if she weren't a doctor. She cared about him too damn much.

Darn much!

Good grief, now he had her doing it!

****

Kyle slammed out of the clinic. The woman was too stubborn for her own good. And what did Penwell mean by dragging her into a fire zone? It was too dangerous. She had no business up there with no one to keep an eye on her. Farrah didn't think things through, that was her problem. When a situation cropped up, she jumped on the first thought that popped into her head and ran with it. Shit, what if she got caught in a backdraft like those men she was going up to help? An image of her broken body, bloody and motionless at the base of a cliff, flashed into his mind.

Kyle threw a punch into the nearest solid object.

"Damn, Kyle, I thought you loved that truck."

Ignoring both the dent in his beloved truck and the pain in his hand, Kyle turned on the sheriff. He pointed at the clinic with a throbbing finger.

"Go back in there and tell her she isn't needed."

Despite the open regret on his face, Pen shook his head. "I can't do that. She is needed. Like I said before, there've been too many injuries fighting this fire. Resources are stretched thin trying to keep it out of populated areas. People are making mistakes. The more doctors we have at the on-site medical triage stations, the better."

"Shit!" Kyle limped to the front of his truck. The sky in the south west was a nasty mix of brown, black, and gray. Ominous.

"Speaking of resources…"

Kyle faced the sheriff. The man had moved close enough to lean his tall body on the hood of Kyle's truck.

"I've been told they're having trouble keeping

some of the equipment running." He patted the hood. "You know how it is. The county's been meaning to replace the older models, but hasn't gotten around to it. Gene Anderson wanted to come," he said, mentioning the mechanic who'd taught Kyle everything he knew about cars, "but you know he's got asthma. A few other mechanics are up there trying to keep things repaired, but frankly, they're run ragged. They could use some help?"

The last sentence came out sounding like a question. Kyle met the sheriff's patient gaze. "Funny you should say run," Kyle said, rapping the brace cinched tight around his leg with his cane.

The sheriff didn't even bat an eye. "Last I checked, you held tools in your hands, not your feet. And there's no running required when you've got those hands in the guts of an engine. This isn't Bedrock, you know."

Kyle snorted a laugh.

"What do you say, Kyle? Tinkering with a bunch of reluctant engines beats crawling into a hole any day, right? Besides..." A slyness slipped into Penwell's shrewd gaze. "I can probably get you assigned to the same station as Farrah."

A mountain of tension avalanched off Kyle's shoulders. The chuckle that escaped his lips was a combination of relief and admiration. "Damn, Pen, I'd forgotten what a canny bastard you are."

The sheriff shrugged. "What can I say? Canny is part of the job description."

The door to the clinic popped open. Farrah appeared, a heavy duffel bag hanging off one shoulder, her arms loaded with boxes. Her nurse, Mary, came out behind her carrying several stuffed-to-bursting plastic bags.

"I'm ready." She stopped and glared at Kyle. "You're still here? I thought you'd have the dirt pulled in behind you by now."

Kyle wiped the grin off his face with effort and replaced it with what he hoped was a black scowl. "Don't worry, honey, I'm leaving." He must not have been completely successful because Farrah's expression turned suspicious.

"You're not going to try talking me out of going again?"

He widened his eyes as he opened the dented door of his truck. "Who, me? Nothin' doin'. I'm a firm believer in the old saying, if you can't beat 'em, join 'em."

He closed the door, cranked the truck, and lowered the window. "Send a map to my cell," he murmured, just loud enough for Pen to hear. "Oh, and don't tell her."

The sheriff nodded once. Kyle glanced at Farrah, took in her puzzled frown, and almost burst into laughter. No, that would keep. He'd wait to see her face when he showed up at the outpost, then he'd laugh. Shifting into gear, he backed up and pulled out of the clinic's small parking lot. Oh, yeah. Proving Miss Proper wasn't always right about him was going to be a hoot.

Chapter Eleven

"Dr. Hastings? We got another one coming in!"

Farrah jerked awake. She could already hear the thumping of the helicopter as it circled to land on the stretch of bare beach between the medical tent and the winding mountain stream. Biting back a groan, she rolled to her side and sat up. She blinked at her watch. Two whole hours of sleep. That was almost more than she'd gotten altogether over the past two days. Maybe that meant things were slowing down.

"Dr. Hastings?"

"Yes, I'm coming." She shoved back her hair as she stood, quickly tying the unruly mass into a messy pony tail with the band she kept around her wrist. She hurried to the sink set up in the corner to begin washing up. "How many?"

"Just one, I think." Crissy, the young RN volunteer assigned to Farrah stood by the tent flap, ready to pull it back.

"Rose getting some rest?" Farrah asked. She'd sent the other volunteer nurse to bed hours ago. Rose had been manning the triage station by herself until Farrah and Crissy had arrived.

"Far as I know," Crissy said. "Though I bet she'll wake up when that helicopter lands."

Probably. Nothing she could do about that though. Farrah dried her hands and stepped past Crissy through the tent opening. She looked up, squinting, but could see nothing beyond the bright emergency lights illuminating the night. She scanned the rest of the busy camp. Things were only slightly less frantic in the false daylight than they were during the day. The fire gobbling up acre after acre of water-hungry forest didn't care what time it was. It burned constantly, regardless of the harried and exhausted humans.

The helicopter dropped out of the darkness. As soon as it settled in the designated landing area, men rushed forward to the door and pulled out her next patient.

Farrah stepped out of the tent an hour later. The helicopter carrying her latest patient to the nearest hospital was already out of sight. She'd immobilized his broken leg, making sure the compound fracture did no more damage to fragile vessels and veins. She'd also packed the ragged wound to slow the bleeding, and given the man something for the pain. She'd wanted to finish the job, set the bone and sew the torn tissue closed, and had to remind herself that was someone else's job. She was triage, her focus was minimizing trauma to the wounded, making sure they were stable enough to make the longer trip to the hospital. She lifted her arms over her head and stretched, wincing as joints popped and tight muscles loosened. "How long has it been?"

Crissy and Rose exited the tent behind her, both of them looking as bleary-eyed as Farrah felt. Rose yawned and waved at Crissy. "Your turn."

Crissy looked at her watch. "Two days, twenty-two hours, and…" Her lips moved, counting. "Thirteen minutes."

"They lied," Rose said flatly. "When I volunteered, they said the fire would be under control within twenty-four to thirty-six hours."

"Oh, come on, Rose," Crissy said. "You didn't really believe them, did you? I'm usually the naive one and *I* didn't believe them."

"I'm just saying they shouldn't have lied, that's all. I can have an opinion, can't I?"

"Yes, but your opinions usually involve a lot of yelling and rude gestures."

Rose smirked. "You know what they say. A rude gesture a day—"

"Keeps the fools away," Crissy finished quickly. "Yeah, Rose, I know."

"Not fools. The word's as—"

"I know, Rose! Just leave it alone, will you? Geeze."

Rose laughed and pointed at Crissy. "Geeze is right. You should see your face. You'd think you never heard the word ass—"

"Rose! I swear, if you don't stop…"

Rose just laughed more and gave the other woman a brief hug. "Darn, woman, you get so cranky when you're tired."

Farrah smiled. The two longtime friends liked to argue back and forth. She didn't mind their bantering or even the occasional cuss word from the more outspoken Rose. Truth was, she was too tired to care about much of anything. What she wouldn't give for a nice long shower and an even longer nap in a nice soft bed. She sighed. Neither was in her immediate future, however.

Then her gaze rested on the fast stream of water flowing nearby. Nice, cool, refreshing water. Farrah looked over her shoulder at Rose. "Where did you say that little pool with the waterfall was?"

****

The sound of feminine laughter drew Kyle from beneath the hood of the pickup. He squinted across the clearing to the medical side of the station. It was the first time he'd seen Farrah outside the triage tent in almost twenty-four hours. He'd lost count of the times he had to stop himself from going in there and dragging her out so she could get some proper rest.

"Hey, Kyle, almost done?"

He turned back to the truck to face its driver. "Give me a second," he said. After tightening a couple of hard-to-reach bolts, he straightened and slammed the hood. "Okay, try it now."

The truck's engine turned over on the first try. The driver whooped and jumped out of the cab. He held a hand out to Kyle. "Thanks, man. I can already tell it's the best this old clunker has run in years."

Kyle wiped his hands on a rag before taking the man's hand. "You're welcome." The man popped back into his truck and backed up to turn around, headed once again to one of the fire lines with a load of supplies. Finding a clean patch on the rag, Kyle wiped the sweat from his face, then turned back to the medical tent. The two nurses were seated at a picnic table beneath a lighted canopy, talking and drinking from bottles of water. Farrah was nowhere to be seen.

He grabbed his cane from where it lay across an open tool chest, leaving the wadded up rag in its place. He limped over to the table.

"Ladies." He nodded his head.

"Hey, Kyle," Rose said, her voice a husky

invitation. She scooted a little on the bench seat. "You can sit over here by me if you like. I promise not to bite."

"Rose!" Crissy hissed. "Leave the man alone." The pretty blond looked over her shoulder at Kyle. "You'll have to excuse her, Kyle. She's been breathing too much thin air."

Kyle smiled. Both women had started flirting with him as soon as he arrived, Rose more so than her friend. He didn't mind. Not after he found out both ladies were happily married. Then he realized the little come-ons were nothing more than a harmless stress reliever. Kind of like the bantering he and the other Hawks engaged in right before a battle. Well, used to engage in.

He paused. Funny how the pain of that thought didn't seem quite so sharp this time.

"Are you looking for Dr. Hastings?" Crissy asked, pulling his attention back to the two women.

"What makes you ask that?"

Rose snorted softly. "Please. You're always looking for Dr. Hastings."

No he wasn't. Except for when he'd first arrived, he'd made a point of not seeking her out. And hadn't that meeting been fun? The split second of dumbfounded disbelief on her face had been worth every painful step since then. And there'd been a lot of painful steps. As soon as he'd arrived, he'd been up to his elbows in engines. Trucks, tractors, even generators, he'd worked on them all. The sense of accomplishment he felt after each engine started and ran without sputtering had surprised him. He hadn't thought he'd ever feel that again; the satisfaction of knowing he'd not only completed an assignment, but done it well.

"She went that way." Crissy pointed upstream. "Said she wanted to cool off."

"Cool off?"

"Yeah," Rose said. "There's a small pool with a little waterfall up that way. Just stay by the stream, you can't miss it."

"Has she eaten?"

"Awwww," Rose said, "are you going to take her a picnic lunch? That's so sweet."

"Hush," Crissy admonished. "You're just jealous." She jumped up from the table. "Hang on, Kyle. Ham sandwich and bottled water okay?"

"That'll be fine."

She was back within a minute. He took the plastic bag she handed him and started off into the woods. The dark night closed in as soon as he passed the ring of lights. Kyle pulled out the mini flashlight he kept in his pocket and shown it down the path. When he caught sight of the dim glow of a lantern, he switched off his flashlight. Moving with a fraction of his old stealth, Kyle eased up to the small pool fed by a waterfall no more than a dozen feet high. In the center of the pool, floating on her back, was Farrah.

Air caught in Kyle's throat. The thin t-shirt she had on was plastered to her skin, outlining every feature of her beautiful breasts, including the very taut nipples. He forgot about the bag of food in his hand, the pain in his leg. Forgot everything but watching Farrah.

She rolled over and dove under the rippling dark water as graceful as an otter. When she rose, she pushed her thick mane of hair off her face. The normally light, red-gold waves glinted like wet, dark honey in the steady glow of the lantern, her skin turned to burnished gold. She waded to the waterfall and stood under the spray.

Time stood still for Kyle as the woman he craved tilted her head back, arms reaching up, breasts jutting forward. He could have stood there forever watching her. The forest could have burned down around him and he didn't think he would notice. He couldn't look away, couldn't give her the privacy he knew she'd come here for.

Time started again when she stepped out of the flow, ran her hands over her face, and spoke. "Are you going to just stand there ogling, or are you coming in?"

Kyle pried his gaze from her luscious body up to her face. He wasn't surprised to see her staring straight at him. The confidence and strength he saw in her dark hazel eyes made his already hard body throb in anticipation. "Is that an invitation?"

She flicked a finger in his direction. "Only if you leave that sorry attitude of yours on the bank with your clothes. This pool is too small for giant-sized pity parties."

He let the dig go, not about to waste time arguing. A chance like this only came once in a lifetime. Instead, he hung the bag of food on a tree branch and leaned his cane against the trunk. He wanted to take his time stripping for her, raising her temperature as hot as she'd raised his, but that wasn't happening. He couldn't go slow if he tried. He found a bare rock near the water's edge that held Farrah's clothes and a towel. He scooted them aside and sat. His leg brace came off first, followed by boots and socks. Kyle held Farrah's gaze as he removed his shirt next. The heat in her eyes had sweat breaking out on his bare skin. Still sitting down, he unfastened his belt, fingers hesitating over the snap of his jeans. He knew if he got into that pool without any clothes on, he wouldn't stop himself from taking her. He'd make her his and to hell with any prior claim Joshua might have. Betrayal, outright betrayal. Man, was he really going to do this?

Hell, yes! He might carry a load of guilt around with him for the rest of his life, but it would be worth it. Oh, so worth it. Much better than the load of regret he'd carry if he didn't take advantage of what she was offering, whatever that might be.

At his hesitation, Farrah slipped lower into the rippling water without breaking eye contact with him. A few strokes brought her within arm's reach.

"Let me help."

She crawled out, placing her knees on the moss-covered ground in front of him. The t-shirt clung to every curve of her body, making him want to drool. Cool wet hands urged him to his feet. Kyle rose, keeping most of his weight on his good leg. The feel of her fingers on his zipper sent a jolt through him. Blood flooded his already aching penis, making it strain against the fabric of his black briefs as she pushed his jeans down. With her beautiful mouth only inches away, it was all he could do to stand still.

"Here," she said, taking one of his hands and leading it to the top of her head. "Use me to balance."

Kyle tried to suck in air as he let her lift his damaged right leg and remove his jeans. When she tapped his left leg, however, he knew that wouldn't work. He removed his hand from her head and half-sat, half-fell back on the rock.

"I've got this."

She didn't say a word, just watched as he finished removing his jeans. Her gaze dropped to his crotch. Damn if she look didn't turn hungrier by the second.

"Get in the water." He had to get some space between them.

She leaned back a little, her gaze speculative, then gave a small shrug. Without a word, she scooted back until she reached the water, arched her back, and slipped completely under the gentle ripples.

Kyle let out the breath he'd been holding and ran a hand over his face. Damn woman could start a forest fire all on her own. Before his more honorable side could come up with any more excuses, he stripped his briefs off, releasing his shaft and every lock he'd ever placed on himself when it came to her. Then he levered himself to the water's edge and dove in.

Blessedly cool water surrounded him, sucking the heat of the night straight off his skin. He appreciated the fact his body also settled down a bit. He didn't think just grabbing Farrah and having his way with her would work, though the possibility made him feel like a horny teenager.

The pond was shallow enough that he could walk across it if he wanted to, and still keep his head above water. Instead, he let the buoyant water support him and swam to where Farrah waited. The unaccustomed exercise made his leg protest, but he didn't mind. He moved close to Farrah, accepting the hand she held out to him, letting her pull him in. Slim arms came up to encircle his neck while below, her legs opened to cradle him. Kyle shivered.

"Cold?"

He snorted softly. "Not even close."

She smiled knowingly. "The water feels good, doesn't it?"

"Among other things."

It was easier to move around on his bum leg in the water. Even holding Farrah close, he managed to maneuver until they were almost under the little waterfall. Leaning his head back, he let the flow drench him. Farrah's laughter followed him, the delightful sound pulling his lips into a grin when he ducked out of the spray and shook the water from his eyes.

"What's so funny?"

"Nothing," she said, still chuckling. She pushed his wet hair back from his face. "I was just remembering a bunch of other times we've gone swimming together. Used to, Joshua and I would have to sneak up on you and throw you under a waterfall."

Her mention of Joshua sobered him. The question popped out before he could think better of it. "Do you wish he was here?"

Her eyes grew wide in surprise. "Joshua? Goodness, no." Her lids dropped, and the smile she gave him made his blood run hot. "Don't you want to be alone with me?"

He held her gaze while he turned his head to plant a kiss against her wrist. "More than anything."

"Good," she said. "Because I've wanted to be alone with you for a while now."

That statement took him by surprise. He didn't have time to wonder at it, however. Not with her rising up to brush her lips against his. Kyle closed his eyes and took her kiss, letting the heat of her mouth awaken things in him he'd kept long buried. God, how he wanted this woman.

Her mouth opened beneath his. He accepted the invitation, unable to keep from rushing in and taking what was offered. He kissed her deep, sliding his tongue against hers, pulling out slowly, temptingly, urging her to follow his lead. It seemed like the kiss went on forever, until she finally pulled back, panting. Her breath warmed his face as she ran her soft lips along his cheek and neck. He gave back to her, licking a path along her jaw to her ear where he suckled a drop of water from its lobe.

She moaned and arched her back. Kyle tightened his grip on her. He eased them both down into the water, still licking and kissing her sensitive neck as he moved them back to the edge of the pond. When they were close enough, he lifted her slightly and leaned forward to press her back against a water-smoothed boulder. He kissed her mouth again, demanding, claiming. Then, he trailed his lips down her throat to her breasts, her nipples tight and hard behind the thin barrier of her wet t-shirt. He sucked one nub into his mouth, his slight erection jerking when she moaned and arched into his touch.

Talk about dreams come true.

Kyle released his hold on her to allow his hands to roam. He caressed her hips, moving up to push her shirt up and up, all the way, until he could strip it off her. Then he slowly trailed his hands down her bare body, down her arms and shoulders, over her breasts, her waist, down her thighs into the water to smooth his hands over her strong calves. The path he took back up was far more intimate. He paused when he reached the apex of her thighs, drawing out the moment. She wiggled beneath him.

"Touch me," she whispered.

His erection jerked again, growing despite the cool water lapping at his legs He wanted to do more than just touch her. He wanted to lick her, taste her, devour her like a starving man. He wanted, more than anything, to be inside her making them one, but now wasn't the time. Now was for her, for Farrah.

His heart pounding away, he did as she asked, bringing his hand up to cup her through her wet panties. The thin silk proved to be no barrier at all. A flick of his finger, and the fabric was pushed aside. At last, he was skin to hot skin, stroking her, making love to her. He raised his head to capture her mouth again. He wanted to tell her how much he wanted her, how long he'd waited for this moment. He wanted to claim her in a way she would know she belonged to him, and no other, especially not Joshua Colby.

Slowly, he increased the pressure, moving past the outer lips to the slick wetness deeper inside. He let the evidence of her desire coat his fingers, first one, then another, all the while mimicking each slow movement with his tongue. He pushed deeper.

She was so tight. And hot. Like a wild fire burning out of control.

"More."

The sultry, drawn-out command slid through him like warm honey. Oh, yes, he'd give her more. First, he pulled his fingers out slowly, then pushed back inside, just as slowly. He did it again, and again, building the pace, stoking the flames. He started rubbing his thumb around her hard little nub. She liked that. She moaned and lifted to him, her breathing as rapid as a bird's.

"Kyle, my Kyle."

Oh, hell yes! That's what he wanted to hear!

Her hand came down, reaching for something, for him. He threaded his fingers with hers and held on as her muscles tightened. Then she exploded beneath him, his name on her lips as she came. The contractions around his fingers buried deep inside her felt glorious. He kept moving, kept the pressure on her clit as her body shook with tiny aftershocks. Once they slowed and she started to relax, he freed both hands to reach for his jeans. He had to be inside her. He was about to bust, and when the dam broke, he *had* to be inside her.

He fumbled in the pockets, finally finding the condom he kept on him out of habit. Thank God for habits, he thought as he rolled the latex over his engorged shaft. He placed his hands on her hips, positioning her just right for his thrust…and paused.

She'd let him touch her. She'd let him bring her to climax. But would she take more from him? Did she want more? Did she want *him*?

Kyle looked up to find her watching him from beneath languid lashes.

"Don't stop," she said softly, her voice blending with the splashing water behind them. "I want you too much."

Thank you, God!

He pushed inside her. Slowly, inch by inch, he fed himself into her until he was fully seated. She felt like heaven, like home. The urge to come right then hit him like a concussion blast. Instead of letting go, he locked his jaw, closed his eyes, and simply savored the moment. Her husky laugh zinged through every cell of his body.

"Are you just going to stand there?"

He managed a smile with his eyes closed. "Give me a few more seconds. I've waited a long damn time for this moment. I'd like to prolong it if I can."

She pushed herself up on one elbow and reached for him, her hand caressing his face. He opened his eyes and met her gaze.

"There'll be other moments," she promised.

Like that, all restraint vanished. He drew back and surged forward. When she moaned, throwing her head back and closing her eyes, he knew he was lost to her. He kept moving as he shackled her wrists and led her hands to his neck. Then he cupped her ass and held her, pounding into her. The words "I love you" hovered on his lips, but he bit them back. She might not be ready for that level of commitment, and he definitely wanted more of those moments she'd just promised him. Hell if he'd scare her off now.

With her holding him and writhing in his arms, it wasn't long before he reached his limit. He shifted and began rubbing her clit with every stroke, determined to bring her with him. Tears of pure joy wet his eyes by the time she came, shuddering around him. He threw himself into his own climax, keenly aware it was Farrah who had taken him to this moment of euphoria.

When he could breathe again, see again, he slowly, ever so gently, leaned her back against the smooth rock. It shook him when he brushed back her hair to find her eyes closed and her cheeks wet.

"Farrah, honey, are you all right? Did I hurt you?"

She shook her head. "No, you didn't hurt me. Quite the opposite in fact."

Her eyes opened. The deep hazel orbs gazed at him in what he could only describe as complete satisfaction.

He felt his chest swell with pride. *He* had put that look there. Him, Kyle Fagan. The knowledge made him feel like he could walk on water. She stroked his face from temple to chin, touching him in places her fingers could never reach without a scalpel.

"I'd tell you how amazing you are, but I can see your ego inflate by the second."

He sent a command to his shaft, forcing it to move inside her. "That's not my ego."

She chuckled softly. "Oh, isn't it?"

"No. That's me showing you how much I want you." *How much I'll always want you.*

Chapter Twelve

"Dr. Hastings? Kyle?"

"Where are they?"

"How am I supposed to know? Keep going. We're not at the waterfall, yet."

Noisy footsteps drew nearer.

Beneath him, Farrah tensed. Kyle lifted his head to look down at her. Beautiful wide eyes stared at him in panic.

"Get off," she mouthed, wiggling her delicious body and pushing at his chest.

Kyle knew there was no time for them to dress. He grabbed up her shirt and thrust it at her, tightening his arms around her and rolling them both into the pool at the same time. When he came up, he made sure to put a couple of feet between them. Rose and Crissy skid to a halt at the water's edge.

"There you are!" Crissy said.

"Whoa." Rose grinned. "Are you guys skinny dipping?"

Crissy huffed. "Rose! Honestly, can't you stay focused for two seconds? Dr. Hastings, we've been ordered to pack up."

Farrah swam closer, her t-shirt back in place. "We're leaving?"

Kyle felt her warm hand wrap around his arm as she came up beside him. The touch surprised him. He'd thought she would want to maintain a discreet distance between them for appearance sake.

"Yeah," Rose said. "You were right, Kyle. The wind shifted. The fire is coming this way now. We have to be out of here in thirty minutes."

"Okay," Farrah said, still not moving away from him. "You two start packing. You know the protocol. I'll be there in a minute."

Crissy grabbed Rose's hand. "Right. Come on, Rose."

"But Kyle might need me. I'm a trained nurse, you know. I should help him get his brace back on. After I help him with his underwear and jeans, of course." Kyle bit back a laugh. From her broad wink, he knew the teasing was for Crissy's benefit more than his.

"Rose, I swear, if you don't come on right now, I'm telling Rob."

"All right, all right, you don't have to get mean." Letting Crissy pull her along, Rose threw a grin over her shoulder. "Bye Kyle."

Kyle shook his head. He pitied the playful woman's husband. A woman like that would drive him crazy, shoving his possessive streak into overdrive.

Farrah was already out of the pool and drying off with the towel by the time he pulled himself onto the bank. He couldn't even blame his leg for moving slow this time. She whipped the wet t-shirt off without turning her back to him and all he could do was stare like a starving man at her bare breasts. He shifted from the wet ground to the rock again, stifling a groan as he watched her wiggle into dry underwear.

"Damn, woman, you're cruel."

She flashed him a smile that warmed his blood to

near boiling. "Here," she said, tossing him the towel. "Hurry up. We've got moving orders."

Kyle ran the damp cloth over his arms and legs, watching as Farrah finished dressing. Every once in a while her face would catch the glow of the lantern, highlighting drawn brows and worried eyes. Was it the fire? Or was she afraid he'd read more into what just happened between them then she did? He wanted it to be more. More than a one-time deal. More than a pity-fuck between friends. He wanted the right to take her in his arms anytime, anywhere. The right to hold her close and just breathe in her scent. The right to kiss her senseless anytime he felt the urge. The right to love her.

Fingers snapped in front of his face. "Earth to Kyle."

He looked up and met her worried gaze.

"You all right?" she asked. "Need any help?"

He gave himself a mental shake. "No, I'm fine. You go on ahead. I'll be there in a minute."

"Okay, but don't be long. We've got less than thirty minutes now."

Then she leaned down, her mouth settling over his in a kiss that was in no way gentle. In fact, it was close to bruising, definitely demanding, and hot enough to scramble his brains. It was also too damn short. She pulled back and stepped away just as he reached for her. At least her breathing sounded as ragged as his. Small comfort.

Kyle stretched his arm in her direction, fingers brushing her bare skin. "Come back here, woman."

She skipped away another step, shook her head, a small smile tugging at her lips. "Call it incentive to hurry and come back to camp." Then she spun around and was gone.

Kyle swore. Incentive, was it? He'd show her incentive.

****

The camp was in an uproar by the time Kyle made it back to the clearing. Ordered chaos, the Hawks would call it. One of the young mechanics who'd been helping him the last two days already had Kyle's toolbox packed and closed up. It only took a minute to wheel it around and lift it into the back of Kyle's truck. He thanked the guy and waved away further help. Climbing into the bed was a little awkward, but not, he realized, as bad as it would have been a few weeks ago. He was learning to compensate, and so was his body. He guided the toolbox to the front of the truck's bed, then leaned down and locked the wheels. A thick bungee tie secured it in place for good measure. No telling how rough the drive down the mountain was going to get.

Kyle sat on the side of the truck and paused, glancing over at the medical tent. Things were busy there as well. Two men exited, carrying a heavy-looking crate between them. Thinking he might give Farrah and her ladies a hand, he flung his other leg over the side and slid to the ground, surprising himself when he stuck the landing on his good leg without even thinking about it. Damn if the doctor at the VA hospital might be right. Maybe with time he'd learn to get around without feeling like half a man.

He wasn't quite at the tent when he caught the familiar thump of a helicopter.

"Kyle!"

He turned to see one of the coordinators looking

his way, hands cupped around his mouth. "Hey," he yelled. "Let the doc know we got an injury coming in, will ya? Tell her to hurry it up."

Kyle raised a hand to signal he'd heard, then headed for the tent again. Inside was even more chaos, though again, chaos with purpose. Each woman had a plastic box clearly labeled, and was filling it as fast as hands could fly.

"Farrah."

She looked up from clearing a shelf, frowning when she saw him. "Kyle, is something wrong?"

"You got incoming."

"Now?" Crissy squeaked, jerking her head up to look at him, her eyes wide.

Everyone looked past him to the helicopter just setting down. Farrah tossed her box on the ground. "Dig out the usual supplies, ladies. I'll go see what we have."

Kyle moved back to let her pass him. He waited by the tent opening, pulling back the flap as the injured man was brought in. From the look on Farrah's face, he knew it was bad.

"Crissy, I need a unit of plasma and a surgery tray, stat. Rose, unpack the anesthesia. You," she pointed at one of the men leaving the tent. "Let command know we're not going anywhere for a while. This man needs surgery now, or he'll bleed out."

The man glanced outside the tent then turned back, wiping his soot covered face on his sleeve. "I'll tell command, but you realize that fire's coming over the ridge in less than two hours."

"I hear you," she said with a wave of a hand, her attention already on the man on the table. Kyle watched her. The tender, almost shy lover of a few minutes ago was gone, replaced by a competent doctor sure of her skills. He would have been content to stay in his corner of the tent observing her work, but she glanced up and pinned him with her sharp gaze.

"Don't you need to go pack up your stuff?"

"No, I'm done."

"Good." She lifted her chin in the direction of some half-packed boxes. "Do you mind finishing up those boxes so the girls can help me? That way, we'll be ready to move when we're done here."

"Sure."

****

Farrah worked as fast as her fingers could find something to fix. Twice, someone stuck their head into the tent, asking for an update. She let the others answer for her, too caught up in what she was doing to pause even for a second. The branch that had impaled the man had torn a ragged path through muscle and soft tissue, including a bad gash to the liver. She had only one shot at saving the damaged organ and the man's life.

Images of another man, dead from a liver shredded by a bullet meant for her, worked their way into her thoughts. Fighting back a shudder, she called for more suction and continued setting stitches. After Cairo, she'd read everything she could get her hands on about artery and liver repairs, from minor nicks to major reconstruction. She'd assisted with numerous surgeries, observed many others, and gone to several conferences on both subjects. Arterial work was still tricky. She wasn't comfortable with that level of difficulty even now. But liver repair? Never again would someone bleed out right in front of her from a damaged liver. Not if she could help it.

"Dr. Hastings!"

"Farrah!"

"What?" She was almost finished. If they'd just leave her alone for a couple more minutes…

"Farrah, we have to go," Kyle insisted.

"Give me a second." She whipped the thread around and pulled, setting the last knot.

"Farrah, tie it off. The chopper's here. We have to go, now!"

She snipped the thread, held up her hands, and stepped back. "All right, I'm done. Pack the wound, Crissy. Let's get him ready to move. Rose, what're his vitals looking like?"

"He's stable."

"Good enough." She pulled off her bloody gloves and tugged down her mask. Only then, did she glance around, surprised to see the nearly empty tent was hazy with smoke. Surprised, too, to see Kyle, bare-handed, helping Crissy pack the wound.

"Wait, that's not—"

"No time to wait, Farrah, that fire is almost on top of us. Let's move it, ladies."

Rose and Crissy quickly piled anesthesia and IV equipment on the stretcher with the unconscious patient. The wheels were unlocked and they were moving. Farrah gave the few items left behind one glance, then ran after them. Outside, she paused and looked to the west. Dense smoke blanketed the sky, boiling up in angry-looking layers. So close.

"Farrah!"

She turned back around to see Kyle standing by the helicopter, waving to her. Reaching him, she grabbed his arm, suddenly afraid of letting go. She let him help her up inside, but still didn't release him. The copter was small, the space inside cramped. In addition to the stretcher-bound patient and the two nurses, two EMTs were aboard. There was barely enough room for her. Kyle's bulk was going to make it a tight fit. She felt him try to pull away.

"Let go, Farrah,"

Turning to him, she pushed hair out of her face so she could meet his gaze. Kyle, her Kyle. Strong and stubborn, and full of so much love. Why hadn't she seen it before?

"Come on," she said trying to pull him inside. "Kyle, come on, climb in."

****

"I'm not coming."

"What do you mean you're not coming?" Farrah yelled at him. "There's room. We'll make room."

Kyle shook his head. "No need, the road should still be clear. I'll drive my truck down."

He tried to pull out of her hold again, but she held on like a leach, just staring at him. Then, in a move that both amazed and annoyed the hell out of him, she climbed out of the helicopter. "What do you think you're doing? Damn it, Farrah, get back in the damn chopper."

"No, I'm not leaving you to drive down off this mountain alone. You might need help."

"I'll be fine—"

"No! I'm staying. We'll drive down together." She released him then, darting around him before he could stop her, her head lowered against the wind from the spinning blades overhead. Kyle swore.

"Fagan!" The chopper's pilot called, clearly anxious to be in the air.

Knowing he didn't have time to wrestle her back on board, Kyle waved a hand at the man. "Go," he yelled. He took several steps back. "Just go. I've got her."

He turned his back on the easy way out of what was soon to be a hell hole, finding Farrah waiting a dozen yards away. Kyle didn't bother watching the helicopter she should have been on rise into the air. He marched up to Farrah and took possession of her arm. Then he began dragging her in the direction of his truck. "Damn fool, stubborn woman. One-day-be-the-death-of-me woman!"

Her arm jerked in his hold. "Stop man-handling me. You know I don't like it. And I don't need you swearing at me, either. Cuss words don't solve anything."

"They make me feel better."

"No, they don't. Yelling makes you feel better. It releases endorphins—"

"Farrah, really, I don't need a damn science lesson right now. I just need you to come along with me quietly. If you don't like that, too bad. Hell, woman, you made the asinine decision not to get on the chopper, now you have to live with it."

She tried to jerk out of his hold again, this time digging in her heels. "I know that, you idiot, stop pulling on me. I'm perfectly capable of walking by myself."

Kyle stopped all right. He planted the tip of his cane in the ground and spun Farrah around in his arms. Gripping her shoulders, he pulled her until they were nose to nose. "Yes, you're capable. You are, without doubt, the most capable woman I know. Hell, you're as clever as a raccoon and twice as devious. But did it never occur to you that the *smart* thing to do would have been to get on that helicopter? In case you haven't noticed, we're about to be over-run by a damn forest fire!"

More smoke wafted into the clearing, driven by the ever-changing winds. The acrid smell burned his nose and Kyle's eyes watered. He blinked, but didn't look away from Farrah's determined stare. Even as he damned her stubbornness, he couldn't help but admire her strength. The woman simply didn't know how to back down.

To prove his point, she said, "No, it didn't. Not for an instant. Not without you."

"I can take care of myself."

Her hand suddenly cupped his cheek. Kyle froze. A forest fire was bearing down on them and he couldn't seem to move a damn muscle.

"I know you can," she said. "You're a strong man, Kyle Fagan, just like I'm a strong woman. But together, we're more than just strong. We're unbeatable."

Kyle pulled her into his arms. He couldn't speak for the emotion choking him. Never, not in all the years of his life, had he dared to dream that Farrah would say those words to him. He felt blessed and scared shitless both at the same time. How the hell could a man hope to live up to something like that?

Another cloud of smoke swirled around them, thicker, darker, hotter. A stab of fear shot through him. He had to get her to safety.

"Come on." He set her back and took her hand in

his. "Let's get off this mountain."

"Let me drive," Farrah said, holding out her hand for the keys. "You can navigate." When he hesitated, she heaved a sigh. "Come on, we're a team, remember? You can save your leg for walking."

He reluctantly handed her the keys. A whooshing and crackling sound came from behind them. Kyle turned to see the tops of some pine trees, about fifty yards away, burst into full blaze.

"Time to go." He gave her a push toward the truck. They both dived into the cab. Farrah cranked it up and had them out of the clearing in five seconds flat.

The road down was clear of everything but smoke, and thankfully, that wasn't as bad as it could have been. They could still see the road. Kyle estimated they'd traveled only about a mile when Farrah brought them smoothly around the first of several tight curves. She braked. Ahead of them, the road was blocked by a large tree limb. To the left, the thickly brushed hillside rose steep enough that the truck wouldn't make it. To the right, the narrow shoulder of the road dropped off sharply into another steep hillside. No way could they go around the makeshift barrier.

Farrah put the truck into park. For a few seconds, neither of them said a word. Things fell into the roads that thread through the mountains all the time. Rocks and boulders were common, as were trees and old limbs. He'd seen enough fallen branches to know when one had been dragged into place.

He opened his door. "Stay here."

"Kyle—"

"I know." He met her gaze. "It didn't get there by itself. But turning around isn't an option. We have to get past this. Just keep your eyes open."

Farrah bit her bottom lip and nodded. Kyle closed his door and approached the dead limb someone had pulled into the road. He stopped and looked around. Nothing moved. No one jumped out to take credit for the poorly planned prank—if that's what it was. Maybe the fire service thought everyone had evacuated and had the limb put there to discourage anyone from driving up to see the fire? Yeah, maybe, but he didn't think so.

Kyle gripped the limb with one hand and lifted. Using the other end as a pivot, he limped around until at least half of the road was clear. As soon as he dropped the limb, he caught movement from the corner of his eye.

"Kyle," Farrah called, no doubt trying to warn him about the threat limping out of the brush. The man was bedraggled, his shirt and jeans filthy, his bushy hair tangled. The look in his dark-eyed gaze was wild. He swung the gun he was holding in Farrah's direction, then back at Kyle. Good, he'd rather that danger was aimed at him instead of her. Kyle shifted forward a little. He needed to get a lot closer.

"Don't move." The man pointed the gun back at Farrah, but kept his eyes on Kyle. "You move and she's dead."

Damn it! Kyle wanted to yell out his frustration. This was Craddoc. He recognized him from the picture on the flyers Penwell was handing out all over the valley. What was he doing up here? He was supposed to be long gone, wasn't he? Yet here he was on foot, and apparently well-armed. Instead of the .38 revolver Penwell had said Craddoc had taken from the deputy, he carried a stainless .45. And it was pointed back at

Farrah. The man was jumpy and desperate, not a good combination. He had to get the man's attention.

Kyle waved a hand at Farrah, hoping she'd stay calm and stay in the truck. He didn't want her to draw the criminal's fire. "Good morning," Kyle said. He lowered his gaze to the bloody rag tied around the man's right leg. "Looks like we have something in common."

Craddoc didn't answer, just motioned with the barrel of the gun. "You, lady, out of the truck."

Kyle took a step forward. "Do you need a ride? We'd be happy to give you a lift down the mountain."

"Shut up! Lady, out of the truck, now!" he yelled when she didn't move right away.

Kyle ground his teeth as Farrah shut off the truck, opened the door, and climbed out. She moved slowly around the front of the vehicle until she stood between him and Craddoc. He silently let the cuss words flow.

Brave, but stupid, Farrah.

Did she really think being a woman would slow a man like Craddoc for an instant? He'd shoot her in a heartbeat. He probably planned to shoot both of them.

He glanced at the drop off at the edge of the road. Only one way out, and it was three feet away. Now if Farrah would just move back a couple more steps…

His muscles tightened as she did just that. Launching an attack at Craddoc was no longer an option, not with Farrah standing in plain sight. She had nothing between her and a possible bullet. The only escape was down.

"Stop right there," Craddoc ordered. He licked his lips. Kyle saw him dart a quick glance up at the smoke darkening the sky. The fire was bearing down on them fast. Shit if this situation wasn't getting worse by the second.

"Now here's the thing," Craddoc said. "I've been having a devil of a time getting out of this damn state. You," he motioned to Farrah with the gun, "are going to be my ticket out of here."

"And me?" Kyle asked. He shifted forward a little, trying to get closer to Farrah and out from behind her at the same time. He wanted to be able to grab her before he flung them both off the road, but if Craddoc decided to take a shot at him, he didn't want her in the line of fire.

Craddoc raised his gun. "Stop right there, hero. I need her. I don't need you. I could shoot you right now."

"I'll do whatever you want if you let him go," Farrah said.

"You'll do what I want regardless." He leered at her. "Though maybe if you ask real nice, I might just leave him here bullet free. Like me, he's not going anywhere fast under his own power."

"If you leave him, it's the same as killing him. The fire is moving too fast."

She took a step away from Kyle and toward Craddock. "Please, let him ride in the back of the truck until we get further down the mountain." She took another small step. He had to get her to stop.

"Farrah."

She held out a hand to Craddoc. "I promise I'll get you out of the state if you just let him ride with us."

Craddoc shook his head. "Can't do that. We might run up on someone, and he'll be in the back, free to holler for help."

"No, he won't," she assured him quickly. "Think about it. You'll have your gun on me, right? He won't risk you shooting me. He'll be quiet."

Kyle groaned quietly. Giving the bad guy ideas was not a good thing.

"I'd like to, lady, I would, but I just can't take the chance." Craddoc straightened his arm, bringing the gun up so he could sight down the barrel at Kyle.

"No!" Farrah screamed and spun around, trying to put herself between them at the same time. Knowing he had no choice, Kyle dived to the side, giving Craddoc a clear target. He hit the edge of the road just as the gun barked. Heat brushed his shoulder as he threw himself into a roll. He heard Farrah scream again. Rocks and limbs dug into him as he barreled down the steep hillside. Pain shot through him as his body flipped and rolled, coming to a stop with a bruising jolt.

"Kyle! Kyle!"

Her screams tore through him. He wanted to answer her more than anything, but knew he didn't dare. If he moved or made a sound, Craddoc might decide to finish him off. If he stayed down, the chances were good he might walk away from his alive. And staying alive was plan A. Getting Farrah away from Craddoc? That was everything else.

Above him, he could hear Farrah's sobs. "No, let me go. He could still be alive. I have to—"

The crack of a slap against flesh almost made him sit up. A second slap. Kyle bit his tongue to keep from roaring out his rage. Craddoc was a dead man, he just didn't know it yet. Kyle took a chance and cracked one eye open, searching for the top of the hillside through his lashes. He saw Craddock and Farrah outlined against a dirty sky. Craddoc had the barrel of his gun shoved under Farrah's chin.

"Now you listen to me, bitch. I'm you're new boyfriend. I could shoot your old one again or not, makes no difference to me. Either way, you're going to drive me down this mountain and right into the next state, you hear me. We get stopped, you're going to be convincing as hell. If not..." His arm jerked, shoving the gun into the soft spot under her chin. "You understand me?"

Silence.

"Answer me," he said harshly. "I want to be sure you understand. Wouldn't want you meeting St. Peter by mistake, now would we?"

Kyle didn't hear her answer. He hoped she said yes. He hoped she wouldn't do anything foolish.

Then they were gone.

Kyle lay still. He wasn't a religious man by any stretch of the imagination. What he was, was a man who had been raised in a God-fearing household. A man who had been on a first name basis with Jesus Christ since he was ten, though they seldom spoke nowadays. Now, all he could do was hope that long-distance relationship didn't get in the way of his prayers.

God, please watch over Farrah. Please, please*, don't let me be too late.*

And please, by all that's Holy, let my leg hold out long enough to save her.

Said leg throbbed like a son-of-a-bitch, and the rest of him wasn't far behind. The idea of moving didn't thrill him. Yet, he couldn't stay motionless for long. Craddoc had Farrah. He'd heard the truck start up and drive off. That meant he didn't have much time. He knew this road, knew it went on for another couple of miles before hitting a switchback that took it back in this direction. That was the nature of mountain roads. They wound their way like a snake. Right now, he was grateful it took thirty horizontal miles of asphalt to traverse ten vertical miles of mountain. His only problem was getting down to the next coil of road before Farrah and Craddoc.

Slowly, limb by limb, he moved, wincing as muscles protested and branches dug into his back and side. When he was sure nothing was broken, Kyle pushed himself up and looked around. Rough terrain surrounded him. Rocks and boulders sprinkled the hillside along with pines and a few oaks and evergreens. Bushes, like the one he'd landed on, grew in profusion, filling in spaces.

He looked around closer until he caught sight of the shiny knob of his cane. He leaned over and snagged it, then used it to push himself to his feet. He took a step on the uneven ground. Pain shot up his leg, worse than usual, but still bearable. Now all he had to do was keep putting one foot in front of the other. What was he going to do once he reached the road? Well, the old limb across the road trick had worked once, hadn't it? Maybe it would work again.

Chapter Thirteen

Getting down the hillside was a nightmare. To make matters worse, Kyle kept having stupid flashbacks of missions. The damn memories popped up in full blood and gore color; images of men he'd killed, of men, *and women*, he'd seen killed. Farrah's face kept superimposing over the female bodies, blood turning her burnished gold hair a nauseating red. Kyle swore and jumped, landing hard enough that the pain wiped his mind clean for a moment. He had to save her. Somehow, he had to trick Craddoc into letting her go without hurting her.

The woods suddenly ended. Kyle stumbled onto flat road, leaning heavily on his cane, not sure how he'd gotten there. It didn't matter. He shoved the throbbing ache of his leg back and looked around. No handy dead limb presented itself. He cursed a blue streak, glancing up and down the road, running a hand through his hair in frustration. There had to be some way to stop the truck. Some way...

His gaze lit on a pile of scree blanketing the downhill side a few yards to his left. The pile began at the edge of the road and flowed down in a static cascade. Nothing there. On the uphill side, however, was the other half of the slide. The tight jumble of rocks looked promising. One good-sized boulder, about five feet in diameter, sat perched on several smaller rocks, the larger one acting as a dam for a pile of rubble just begging for a nudge. Why it hadn't already been cleared, he didn't know or care. All that mattered was that it was there. Kyle limped over, eyeing the rocks through years of mountain experience. He'd seen slide traps like this before. If he could just shift that one boulder enough, the whole thing would give way, sending it all tumbling into the road. He looked around and spotted the stub of a pine sticking out of the dirt nearby, probably a victim of the original slide. He stuck the end of his cane into the ground and tugged, pulled, and twisted until at last, what remained of the broken off tree came free in a spray of dirt. He hefted the small trunk, thankful it still felt solid. The sturdy young pine made the perfect lever.

Kyle jammed the end not encased in old roots beneath the keystones and leaned hard. Wood creaked and popped. The boulder sitting on the keystones shifted slightly. Kyle leaned harder, putting his whole weight into it. The bullet burn across his shoulder stung as sweat rolled into the wound, but he ignored it. Rocks above shifted. Dirt, shale, and small pebbles rained down. He'd have to be careful not to get caught in the slide when it happened. Another good shove. The keystones moved. One popped out and landed on the road. More rocks swiftly followed. With a muted rumble, the boulder broke free and started to roll.

Kyle threw himself back, stumbling and landing on his ass as the miniature rockslide tumbled past him. The large boulder rolled ponderously into the road, coming to a weighty stop almost in the middle. Other rocks slid down in a dusty torrent, rolling and bouncing into the road like happy children, creating a half-decent roadblock. Not perfect, but it would have to do. Kyle picked up his cane and levered to his feet. Brush was thicker on the downhill side, and he quickly made his way to cover, making sure to wipe out his tracks as he went. Now, he just had to wait. Wait and pray that he'd made it to the road in time.

The wait wasn't long. The dust hadn't even settled good when he caught sight of the truck a few seconds later. Relief flooded him. He had a chance, one chance. Damn if he wouldn't make it count. He didn't move an inch as the truck slowed and came to a stop opposite him. He could just see Farrah through the driver's side window. She looked scared, her eyes red. She'd been crying. Still was, he realized as he watched her wipe away tears. He heard Craddoc's voice. Farrah shook her head and said something in reply, motioning to the rockslide. Craddoc barked again. Farrah winced, as if she'd been struck. Kyle bit back a growl. Damn Craddoc. He'd kill the bastard for touching Farrah.

The truck shifted into park and turned off. The driver's door opened. Kyle had hoped Craddoc would get out and move the rocks himself. Should have known better. He thought about grabbing Farrah and making a run for it, but that would be too dangerous. Craddoc still had that pistol. He watched Farrah survey the mess in the road. If the big boulder could be moved to the right a couple of feet, the truck would be able to go around it, over the smaller rocks.

Craddoc rolled down his window. He hit the side of the truck with something, probably the gun, breaking the quiet of the mountainside. Farrah jumped.

"Hurry up," Craddoc shouted. "We ain't got all damn day."

"Ignore the pine, Farrah," Kyle whispered urgently. "Pretend you can't move the great big rock." He needed Craddoc out of that truck.

As if hearing him, Farrah walked past the tree Kyle had used, placed both hands against the boulder and pushed. The thing barely rocked back and forth. She pushed again, still with no results.

The truck door opened. Kyle tensed when he saw Craddoc crawl from the cab. The scumbag spewed insults. "You stupid bitch. You're worthless." He limped angrily to Farrah and gave her a shove. "Stand over there and don't move." He waved the gun at her. "If you run, I'll shoot you."

Farrah nodded and backed away. She glanced around, her gaze darting from side to side as if looking for a way out. *Don't run. Not yet, honey, not yet.* If she ran now, Craddoc would shoot her down in cold blood. Under the felon's harsh gaze, she shifted her feet, crossed her arms, and stood stiffly, muscles tight, ready to run. Kyle watched Craddoc stuff the gun into the front of his pants, then use both hands to pick up the pine. As soon as he had it wedged under the rock, Kyle moved.

If he'd had the full use of his right leg, he could have cleared the distance before Craddoc could turn. He knew, because he'd done this kind of ambush before. As it was, he barely made the road before Craddoc swung around, one hand going for the butt of the pistol. Farrah screamed. Kyle swung his cane, hitting Craddoc's arm a glancing blow. The gun fell to the ground. Kyle plowed into Craddoc, shoving him back against the boulder. He hammered a punch at the criminal's face. Craddoc grunted and shoved him back.

They rolled off the boulder and onto the ground. Stones ground into Kyle's back as Craddoc landed on top of him. Craddoc closed a hand around Kyle's throat and squeezed. Kyle gasped for air. He tried to get leverage, ignoring the screaming pain from his leg and shoulder. His hand found the bandage around Craddock's thigh and he squeezed.

Craddoc screamed. He punched wildly at Kyle. "I'll kill you! I'll kill you!"

One of the punches caught Kyle a glancing blow to the temple. Black dots danced through his vision. He shook his head and jabbed his straightened hand into Craddoc's throat. The man choked and coughed then pulled away. Kyle tried to hold on to him, but Craddoc's shirt slipped through his fingers. Kyle pushed himself up, diving for Craddoc. He had to put the guy out. Craddoc kicked and scrambled away, almost running into Farrah in his frenzy to evade Kyle. Craddoc saw her and made a grab for her ankle. She skipped away.

"Get back! Run!" Kyle shouted.

Then he saw it. The gun lay not two feet from Craddoc's hand. The criminal saw it, too. He shot Kyle a satisfied smirk and dived for the pistol.

"Run Farrah!" Kyle pushed himself up, stumbled, then caught his footing. He cursed when he saw Farrah running toward him instead of away. The gun went off just as they collided at the edge of the road. Somehow, the shot went wide. Kyle wrapped his arms around Farrah and threw his weight toward the downhill side of the rockslide. He twisted to take the brunt of the fall, stones cutting into his back and shoulders as they hit. The scree exploded in a spray of rock and dirt, sending them both sliding down.

Another gunshot sounded, this one kicking up bits of rock where the bullet hit.

Kyle rolled, taking Farrah with him, trying to protect her. They needed to get out of Craddoc's sight. They needed to…

The ground disappeared. Farrah screamed. Kyle had time to take a deep breath before the landslide dumped them both into a little river still fast enough to give them trouble. Cold water closed over them, taking their breath. He tried to hold on to Farrah, tried to push them both to the surface. The current whipped them around like a couple of twigs, tumbling them, slamming them into rocks, dragging them along the bottom.

At last, he was able to kick them both up with his good leg. They broke the surface, both of them coughing and sucking in air.

The third gunshot echoed through the mountainside just as they were swept around a bend in the river. Kyle's heart stopped when he saw Farrah's head jerk back. Her limp body sank into the water. He lunged forward, barely managing to snag a handful of her shirt before the swift water swept her out of reach. He kicked hard, damning his useless leg as he tried to get them into calmer water. He grabbed her and turned her over. Terror surged as he took in the bright red blood welling from a wound at her hairline. Her eyes were closed.

"Oh God," he murmured, praying twice in one day. "Dear God, please, no. Farrah? Farrah, baby, come on, wake up." He gently slapped her cheek. "Wake up for me, honey. God, Farrah, please, please be all right."

He shook her, relieved when she suddenly sucked in a ragged breath and began coughing. "Thank you, thank you, God," he whispered over and over as he pulled her to him and set out for shore. She remained limp once they reached the shallows. Kyle set her back so he could see her face. No haunting hazel gaze met his. He scooped up some water to wash away the blood and examined the wound on her scalp. Shallow, thank God it was only shallow, and not even an inch long. Just a kiss by a bullet, his old team would say. She should be awake soon. He wanted to stay there and hold her until she woke up, but knew better. He had to get her out of the cold water. And as long as Craddoc had bullets left, they weren't safe out in the open.

He gently propped Farrah against a half-submerged rock and quickly tore a strip from the bottom of his shirt. Working fast, he wrapped the wet cloth around her head to try and stop the bleeding. Carrying her over his shoulder wouldn't be good for that wound, but he didn't have a choice. He couldn't carry her in his arms like he wanted to. Walking without his cane was going to be hard enough. He'd have to find a sturdy limb as a substitute. Damn, why hadn't he listened to the doctors and had his damn knee replaced? Why put it off? It wasn't like waiting was going to change anything.

He continued to berate himself as he worked to get himself and Farrah out of sight of the river. He knew he wouldn't be able to stay ahead of Craddoc for long if he came after them. Even with his own injury, the criminal would catch up to them long before Kyle could carry Farrah to safety. He had to find a place to hide her. And soon.

****

Farrah came awake slowly. The first thing her memory served up was the sight of Kyle lying still and broken halfway down the slope of the mountain. Fresh tears seeped from under her lids, painting warm trails down to her hairline and ears. She didn't care. Her Kyle was gone. If not dead from Craddoc's bullet, then the fire…

No, that wasn't right. Another memory surged up. Kyle, alive and well and fighting Craddoc. He was alive. Her heart began to pound with joy. *He was alive!*

She opened her eyes. Kyle, her Kyle, leaned over her. She tried to sit up, throw her arms around him, but slumped back down when her head began to throb in agony. She lifted a hand to touch her forehead, only to have Kyle stop her.

"You have a head wound. Don't worry, it's just a graze."

"Hurts."

"I don't doubt it. Bullets are a bit—sorry, bullets have a tendency to do that."

Farrah blinked up at him. She had to kiss him. Dear Lord, she had to. She reached up and buried a shaky hand in his hair. "Come here."

The kiss was nothing long and luscious, just a sweet press of lips and a quick lick of her tongue against his. Still, she couldn't stop the shiver that went through her as she let him go.

"What was that for?" he asked, his voice sounding husky, as if his throat was tight.

She kept it light, not letting him know how much that simple kiss had meant to her. She still couldn't believe he was alive. "Call it a reward for remembering not to cuss."

His body relaxed and he grinned. "Positive reinforcement. I can work with that."

Farrah smiled back, then winced as pain stabbed through her head.

"Easy there," Kyle said. "Try not to move your head."

"Where are we?"

Kyle looked around. "An old bear's den, I think. Probably abandoned this spring when the river rose. Don't worry, it's been empty a while from the looks of it."

Farrah froze. They were in a hole in the ground? How could she not have noticed?

"Easy," he said again. Warm hands rubbed her arms. "Don't freak out on me, honey. It's okay, there's a nice big opening at your feet. Plenty of air getting in." He moved a little to the side. "See."

Despite the pain, Farrah leaned her head up so she could see the patch of forest through the opening. The air stirred, bringing with it the smell of dirt and growing things. And smoke.

"Where's Craddoc?"

"Not sure. If we're lucky, he'll finish moving the damn boulder and be on his way."

"I don't think we're that lucky." She slipped a hand into the pocket of her scrubs and pulled out the key to Kyle's truck. "Unless he knows how to hotwire a vehicle, he's probably coming after us."

Kyle took the key from her then brushed back her hair with a gentle hand. "I want you to stay here while I go check. If he's out there, I can lead him away—"

"No. Not without me."

"Farrah, you can't run right now. Head wounds are serious business. You're a doctor. You know that. You have to rest. I'll lead him away and circle back to you before the fire gets here, I promise."

She grabbed his hand. "I don't want you to go." Large opening or not, she couldn't stay in the bear den without him.

"Honey—"

"I'm cold." She didn't even have to fake the shiver that shook her body. Her wet clothes clung to her, leeching away what little warmth her body generated. "I have to keep moving, Kyle. We have to keep moving. Craddoc won't stop, and neither will the fire." Kyle stared down at her for a long moment. Then he blew out a breath.

"All right, but we've got a few minutes. You stay here and rest."

She grabbed his arm. "Where are you going?"

"Easy," he said, taking her hand in his. He kissed her knuckles. "I'm not going far. I don't know how wood-wise Craddoc is, but I don't feel like taking chances. I just need to make sure our tracks are covered outside."

She started to nod, but stopped herself in time. "Okay." A few minutes rest would be good. She could last a few minutes. She lay quietly, her eyes closed, listening for his movements. She hadn't been kidding about being cold. As a doctor, she knew the dangers of lying on the ground in soaked clothes. Unfortunately, she also knew there was nothing to be done about it right now. She couldn't undress, that was for sure. No telling when they would have to run again. She thought of Kyle, of his big, warm body, and hoped he would return soon. A few minutes lying in his arms would be heaven…

"Farrah!"

The urgency in that far away whisper made her heart speed up.

"Farrah, come on. Wake up, honey. I need you to wake up!"

Something shook her. Something tapped her cheeks. Farrah tried to open her eyes.

****

Kyle felt relief wash over him when Farrah's eyelids fluttered open. He'd come back from covering their tracks and found her still and unresponsive. Panic had almost sent him over the edge until he realized she'd simply fallen asleep. He carefully pulled her into his arms.

"Damn, sweetheart, don't do that to me again. You have to stay awake." He forced a chuckle. "You know Joshua is going to kill me for getting you into this mess. And I won't blame him. Guess we'll be even when it comes to screw ups."

"You...you didn't screw up. C-Craddoc's fault." She pushed deeper into his embrace. Kyle obligingly tightened his hold on her, pulling her closer. "Joshua has no say in the matter," she continued. "I don't belong to him."

She leaned her head back until he could see her face. The red-stained bandage around her head made his heart ache. His gaze dropped to her eyes, full of determination and wet with un-shed tears.

"I don't belong to Joshua," she repeated clearly.

Her chin tilted up in that stubborn gesture he loved so much.

"I haven't been his since high school. Even then, there was someone else I was interested in, but he never gave the slightest indication he thought of me that way."

Kyle stilled, feeling like he'd just been punched. She couldn't mean what he thought she meant.

She touched his face. She seemed to like doing that. He liked it, too, leaning into the press of her fingers like a shameless kitten begging for more.

"Oh, Kyle, you silly man. How could you not know I liked you back then."

"Ummm." He cleared his throat. "As a friend, right? Just as a friend." If it was more, if she cared about him even half as much as he cared about her…he didn't want to think of the time wasted.

"That, too."

Damn. He let her stroke his cheek, not trusting himself to put anything more into words. Not now, when they were in danger. He wanted her safe when they had this conversation. Safe and warm and well. Not dizzy with cold and a head wound that might be making her say things she normally wouldn't.

"I believe in you," she whispered. "I know you'll get us out of this."

Oh, God, could he take any more?

She leaned forward, her lips an inch from his when he heard what sounded like the crackle of brush outside. He tightened his arms, whispering a quiet, "Shhh."

He reached down with one hand and checked the buckles on his leg brace. The water had allowed the straps to stretch a bit and he'd had to tighten them while he was covering their tracks. They felt fine now, but he knew he still couldn't trust the thing to hold him up for long. Not by itself. He'd saved the limb he scavenged to use in place of his cane which he'd lost somewhere on the road in his fight with Craddoc.

Moving as quietly as possible, he eased away from Farrah and inched his way toward the opening. She tried to hold on to him for a few seconds, but released him when he kissed the back of one of her hands and put it firmly away from him. She sat up, and he let her, knowing he didn't have a choice. The noise could be only a passing animal, though he didn't trust their luck. They might still have to make a run for it, but he hoped not. Dodging sniper fire was not on his list of favorite things to do, especially with Farrah.

At the opening, he paused to listen. The noise came from the left. More limbs snapped. As dry as the forest was, even a sniper would have trouble walking without being heard. Male muttering drifted on the breeze. Kyle tensed and closed his hand around the sturdy limb he'd left outside. Craddoc. Had to be. Though how he'd gotten on this side of the river was a good question.

Kyle eased out, peeking through the brush that hid the den. Yeah, it was Craddoc. He could just see the man's red shirt through the brush about twenty yards away. He was bumbling through the woods like an idiot, that gun of his in one hand and, damn it, Kyle's cane in the other. Kyle ducked back inside. If the criminal kept coming in the same direction, he'd stumble right onto their hiding place. There was nothing to conceal the opening any better, not without making too much noise. He glanced back at Farrah. She was looking at him in question. He appraised her, not liking how pale she was or the way her body swayed as she knelt. Change of plans. He couldn't ask her to run in her condition. That left only one option.

Somehow, he had to get close enough to take Craddoc out.

Kyle waved Farrah to the back of the den and followed her. "It's Craddoc," he confirmed. "He's coming this way."

Fear widened her eyes. "We have to go."

"No. *I* have to go. You have to stay here."

"Kyle—"

"This is not up for discussion, Farrah. You're staying hidden back here and that's final."

"Says who?"

He carefully wrapped a hand around the back of her head to hold her still and kissed her. Hard. When he was done, he closed his eyes and leaned his forehead against hers. "I say so. Because if something happens to you, I might as well be dead."

"Don't say that."

"It's true. I love you, Farrah Hastings. Always have, always will. Now you get back in that far corner and stay there. If you scrunch really tight, he won't be able to see you if he looks inside."

Then he let her go and scrambled back to the opening before she could reply. If she didn't feel the same, he didn't want to know right now. All he wanted was to kill Craddoc and take Farrah home. A good plan. Simply. Easy.

Kyle grimaced. Yeah, and next to impossible. Who was he trying to kid? With his bum leg, they'd be lucky to make it off this mountain alive.

Chapter Fourteen

Farrah waited until Kyle left before making her way to the opening of the den. No way could she stay tucked in the back of that hole. And not just because of her claustrophobia. No, she was far too worried about Kyle to stay put. What if something happened to him? What if she never got the chance to tell him she loved him, too? The infuriating man hadn't even given her a chance. He'd just darted out, right into danger. Just like the soldier he was.

She sighed quietly, barely keeping it from turning into a sob. A soldier. Dear Lord, she never thought she'd end up with one of those in a million years. But that's what Kyle was, with or without the uniform. A soldier, a fighter, a protector. Someone she could always depend on.

A spate of loud cussing echoed off the mountain. Farrah peeked out in time to see Craddoc wrestling with a blackberry bush. The sight almost made her smile until she saw Kyle rising up from his hiding place a few feet away. He had a sturdy limb in his hand and used it as a crutch until he was within reach of Craddoc. Farrah's heart stuttered when the felon swung in Kyle's direction, gun in his hand. Kyle whacked the limb against Craddoc's arm in an underhand swing, forcing it up just as the gun went off. Farrah jammed her fist in her mouth to keep from screaming. She wanted to run out and help, but knew she'd only be in the way. Still, she couldn't take her eyes away as Kyle tackled the other man, taking him to the ground.

They wrestled, rolling back and forth over the uneven ground, both men trying to take possession of the gun. Kyle's fist rose, once, twice, catching Craddoc with solid blows.

Suddenly the gun was gone, lost somewhere in the dry leaves of the forest floor. Craddoc shoved Kyle away and surged to his feet. He lifted a stick above his head like a bat and swung. Farrah did cry out then. The stick was Kyle's cane, and she knew how heavy it was. Kyle rolled, dodging the first blow, and came up with the limb he'd charged in with to block the second. The limb broke in two with an echoing crack on impact. Kyle used the smaller half to fend off a third blow while shoving the longer piece between Craddoc's ankles. He twisted the limb, trying to trip Craddoc. The felon stumbled, did a little hopping dance, but managed to keep his feet with the help of the cane. Kyle used the time to pull himself up. He lunged at Craddoc before he could bring the cane to bear again. With a hard left punch, he slammed his fist into the other man's stomach. Craddoc coughed and doubled over, dropping the cane.

Kyle hesitated. Farrah didn't understand why until he moved again. With a wordless cry, she reached out to stop him, but there was nothing she could do. Kyle planted his good leg on the ground and brought his injured leg up, his whole weight behind his bent knee. Farrah cringed as Kyle's weakened joint connected with Craddoc's face, the crack of bone louder than the limb breaking. Craddoc went down in a spray of blood.

Kyle went down, too, roaring in pain.

Farrah dashed out, needing to reach Kyle. Before she could get there, Craddoc rolled unsteadily to his knees, blood streaming from his broken nose. Silver gleamed in his hand. Somehow, he'd found the gun and was aiming it at Kyle. Farrah didn't think. She scooped up Kyle's cane and swung it with all her strength. The impact of the silver knob handle against Craddoc's temple vibrated up her arm. The dull sound of crunching bone was all but drowned out by the last gunshot, the bullet going wide into the trees. Craddoc flopped over and didn't move.

Time seemed to slow to a crawl for Farrah as she stared down at the man she was afraid she'd just killed. She'd never struck anyone before in her life. Not for real, not in fear or desperation. Not in anger. She'd felt all of that and more when she thought she was about to lose Kyle. It only took her a single glace at him to realize she'd do it again in a heartbeat. Her fist tightened on the cane. If Craddoc moved, she'd definitely hit him again to protect the man she loved. She held onto the cane as she hurried to Kyle, trying not to look at the blood on the silvery round end.

"Is he out? Is he dead?" Kyle yelled, still rocking on the ground, both hands squeezing his thigh just above the brace, as if trying to hold the pain at bay. Farrah glanced at Craddoc. She didn't want to go near him. If he wasn't dead, she knew a part of her would feel some kind of obligation to try and save him, and right now, she didn't want to do that. He'd tried to take Kyle's life…and hers. He didn't deserve her mercy.

"He's dead," she told him, hoping it was true.

"Good," Kyle gasped.

"Here, let me see." She moved his hands enough to get a good look at his rapidly swelling knee. "You can't walk on this."

He gave a rusty chuckle. "Tell me something I don't already know." He reached over and took her hand. "We'll take the river. It's the only way." He tried to sit up and groaned. Farrah eased him back down. Carefully, afraid of hurting him, she examined his leg more closely. Immediately she started loosening the buckles of his brace. He batted at her hands. "Leave it on."

"Trust me, I'm not taking it off. You can't see it, Kyle, but you're knee is swelling by the second. I'm just loosening the straps so they don't cut into your flesh. We need to find a way to lock the brace in place to keep your leg straight."

Lips pressed tight together, he draped an arm over his eyes. "You know what this means, right? You have to go for help by yourself, Farrah. You can do that, right? I'll wait in the bear den while you go get us some help. I can drag myself that far."

"Uh-huh. And my nose is as good as yours, Kyle Fagan. I can smell that fire getting closer." Worse yet, she could see it. She looked up and across the river. The flames weren't actually in sight, but judging by the thickness of the smoke rolling down the slope, they weren't far behind. She looked back at Kyle. "You're just trying to get me to run to safety without you. Even if I weren't a doctor, that's not going to happen."

"Farrah—"

"Don't *Farrah*, me." She carefully refastened the buckles of the brace, wincing in sympathy at the pained noises he made in the back of his throat when she snugged them down. When she was done, she moved his arm and brushed the sweat off his forehead, picking a few leaves out of his dark hair. "I'm not leaving you here to die. We'll take the river, just like you said. I'll help you get there. You and I have things to talk about and I'm not letting you off that easy. Besides, I can't see you leaving me here if the situation was reversed."

"Not a chance in hell."

"See, I knew you were my hero."

He shook his head. "Don't try hanging a halo on me, honey, it'll just fall off."

She met his gaze, the pain in his eyes making her ache to make him better. All she had to give him was a smile. "You saved me from Craddoc, Kyle. That makes you a hero whether you like it or not. A hero's halo might slip a little now and then, but it's always there."

He tried to move again, wincing as the pain hit him. "Well, I'd trade that halo, my cane, and one used brace for a nice ATV right now."

"Hello!" "Anyone there?"

The shouts had them both looking up. Coming through the woods at a trot were three men dressed in fire-fighting gear.

"Hello," one of the men said again. "We thought we heard a gunshot."

Kyle pointed a hand a Craddoc. "Escaped criminal. Carjacked us."

The fireman bent down to examine Craddoc. "Huh. Dead escaped criminal. I recognize him from the flyer they've been passing around." He stood and held a hand out to Farrah. "I'm Phil Webster, by the way." He looked around. "There's no road around here that I'm aware of. Where's your vehicle?"

Farrah pointed this time. "His truck is still up there somewhere, I guess."

"Damn, man, that's tough," one of the other firemen said. "It's gone for sure. That fire is moving fast."

"Right," Phil said. "We need to get you folks out of here."

Farrah pointed at Kyle's leg. "He can't walk. His knee is busted. Can you help me apply a splint over the brace to make it more stable?"

One of the men slipped a huge pack off his back and began rummaging inside.

"Tyler here will fix him right up," Phil assured them. He motioned to her scrubs. "Are you medical?"

"Yes, sorry. I'm Dr. Farrah Hastings."

His eyes widened. "Great! We were told to keep an eye out for you. And this must be Kyle Fagan. Sheriff Penwell will be glad to hear from you guys. He was worried. Soon as Tyler has your friend's leg splinted we'll get you both over to our truck." He pointed at the third man. "Carp, hike on back to the truck for the stretcher. Radio in while you're there and tell them we found the doc and Fagan. We need a chopper for a medical evac. And make it snappy. I don't feel like getting singed today."

"Will do." Carp left at a dead run.

"Don't worry," Phil said, coming to stand by Kyle as Tyler helped Farrah apply the splint. "Carp runs cross-country marathons. He'll be back before you know it."

Hardly a minute later, a wave of hot smoke rolled over them. Farrah coughed and looked back up the mountain. Flames could be seen now, licking the tops of trees. The crackle of the fire was loud enough to be heard. Even as she watched, the fire flared and jumped, pushed along by a self-generating wind. Phil swore.

"Sorry, Mr. Fagan, looks like you'll have to go out the old fashioned way. No time to wait for the stretcher."

Farrah coughed again as she hurriedly finished tying off the splint. As soon as she was finished, Phil squatted down next to Kyle. "All right, up you go."

Kyle bit off a yell as Phil hauled him up over his shoulder.

Farrah put out a hand. "Wait, what about Craddoc's body?"

"We'll have to leave it."

Kyle grunted. "Justice. He was going to do the same to me, only I was still alive."

Justice indeed, Farrah thought, walking past Craddoc's body without a second glance.

They met up with Carp after only a few dozen yards and transferred Kyle to the stretcher. Even then, she could tell the pain was getting to him. By the time they reached the truck, he was unconscious. Farrah was glad. The ride in the helicopter to the hospital was nearly as bad as the one she remembered in Egypt. Turbulence kept them bouncing like a truck over a washboard road. She breathed a sigh of relief when they finally touched down on the helipad.

Now all she had to do was get her man back on his feet. Both of them.

Chapter Fifteen

Kyle blinked his eyes open. Hospital room. That was good. That meant he and Farrah had made it back. He tried wiggling his toes. Left ones worked fine. Right ones worked, but damn if he wanted to wiggle them again anytime soon. He looked down where his right leg lay under the covers. The bulk under the sheet was actually re-assuring even though it was half again as big as the left one. Damn, he'd really done it this time. At least he still had a leg, though. Half way to the firemen's truck, he'd expected to wake up to nothing but empty space on that side.

"Hey, good to see you awake." The gruff voice drew his gaze to the other side of the bed. Sheriff Dan Penwell sat slouched in a chair, looking decidedly rough around the edges. There were dark circles under his eyes and at least three days growth of whiskers on his face. His uniform was rumpled, though the Sheriff badge still shone a bright silver.

Kyle cleared his throat. "What are you doing here?"

"Waiting to take your statement."

"About?"

"Craddoc."

"Oh, that." Kyle closed his eyes and heaved a sigh. Might as well get it over with. "Craddoc ambushed us. Kidnapped Farrah. Shot me." He could feel the dull throb beneath the bandage across his shoulders. "I ambushed him back. Took Farrah back. He shot Farrah." His body still went cold at how close he'd come to losing her. "He chased us. We fought. He's dead and we're not." He opened his eyes again, his suddenly racing heart giving the monitor attached to him fits. He looked over to find the Sheriff with a pen in one hand and a little notebook in the other. "Farrah's okay, right? She was only grazed."

The Sheriff waved the hand holding the pen. "She's fine, she's fine. Said to tell you she had to go back to her clinic." He scribbled a bit more in the notebook before looking up. "I noticed you didn't say who actually killed Craddoc."

"Does it matter? He tried to kill us both." Kyle forced himself to relax back against the pillow, willing his heart to slow down. Farrah was okay. Apparently okay enough to go back to work. He tried to ignore the little stab of hurt that caused. Couldn't she even bother to wait around 'til he woke up?

"'fraid it does. There's a reward, you know."

He glanced at Pen who was suddenly standing by his bed. "What?"

"A reward for Craddoc. Nashville PD posted it two days ago. Now personally I don't care who ended the scumbag." He tapped his left arm. "He shot me, too, if you'll recall. NPD isn't going to be so apathetic."

"Apathetic?"

"Indifferent, then. They're going to want specifics."

"What did Farrah say?" Would she have admitted to killing the criminal? Damn, it was probably going to give her nightmares for months to come.

"Oh, she admits to killing him all right. If anyone were to ask me, I'd say she's almost proud of it."

"What?" That didn't make sense. Not for Farrah.

Penwell grinned. "She said Craddoc was going to shoot you and she wasn't having that. Said it with a straight face, too. Can you imagine?"

No, he couldn't. Not at the moment. And especially not without seeing her for himself. Damn it, where the hell was she?

"So, you corroborating her story?"

"Yeah," Kyle said. He waved a hand in the direction of his knee. "I'd just cracked my knee to pieces on Craddoc's face and was on the ground. Craddoc found his gun and would have shot me if not for Farrah." He literally owed her his life.

"Good," Penwell said, patting his shoulder. "Now I can go home and get some rest." He started to turn away, then paused. "Oh, by the way. You have any idea what you're going to do when you get out of here?"

"What do you mean?"

"You know, work. Have you given any thought to what you might do?"

"Work?" What kind of work would a one-legged man be good at?

Penwell chuckled and shook his head. "Guess you're still a little doped up. Doc said you might not be tracking real good when you woke up. Yes, I'm talking about work. Doing something with your hands and brain besides twiddling your thumbs all day. Cause if you're looking for something to do, Gene Anderson is retiring next week and moving to Kentucky. His garage is up for sale if you're interested. Only reason I mention it is because I got real good reports on you from the firefighters. They said they never worked with a better mechanic. Don't be surprised if you start getting calls from people wanting you to work on their cars. Anyway, you might want to think about it. I can tell Gene you're interested if you want. Sure he'll wait till you get out to close the deal. We definitely need that garage to stay open, it's the only one in town. You get some rest, now, okay? Doc'll be by later to check on you." With that, he was gone.

Kyle blinked, still a bit stunned by Pen's suggestion. He'd always loved working on cars. A bum leg wouldn't be that much of a hindrance for a mechanic, would it? He was already starting to compensate some, too, just like the doctor's had said.

He laid a hand carefully on his leg. If he had that knee replacement surgery and that popular whatever artery surgery, he might could get around even better. At least enough to run his own garage. The idea brought a smile to his lips. His own garage. *Fagan's Garage.* Damn if that didn't have a nice ring to it. He'd need to talk it over with Farrah…

Or would he?

Farrah had left him. Did that mean she was done with him? True, he'd told her he loved her, but he hadn't given her a chance to reply. Had he scared her away? The possibility made him physically ill. He fumbled around on the bed for the nurse call button. The pain was growing, too, getting worse. He couldn't think straight. Didn't want to think at all. Not if it meant Farrah had decided he wasn't worth her trouble. God, she'd killed a man for him. Could she ever forgive him for that?

A nurse pushed her way into the room, smiled at

him, and started taking his vitals. She chatted while she did so, but he barely paid her any attention. Not until she also pointed out the neat morphine button that he immediately took advantage of. When the drug kicked in, he didn't fight it. The pain of his body eased off, but the one in his heart remained. Still, he drifted off, wondering what life would have been like if Farrah cared for him half as much as he did for her.

****

The room was bathed in shadows when Kyle woke up again. The machine next to his bed beeped softly, small lights winking at him. More light came from the hall beyond the door, which was partially closed. He could hear the murmur of voices outside. Another noise came from nearby, sounding suspiciously like a soft snore. Kyle turned his head. A mass of red-gold hair lay next to him on the bed, cradled by a pale arm decorated with several small adhesive bandages.

Kyle stilled. Was it really her?

Slowly, half-afraid she'd disappear, he lifted a hand to touch her to be sure. He jerked back in surprise when the wealth of hair popped up at his first touch, revealing Farrah's gorgeous, sleep-wrinkled face.

"Oh, you're awake finally. Thank God!" She leaned over and brushed her lips against his forehead. She smiled. Kyle found himself smiling back at her, relief making him feel strong and weak both at the same time.

"You're here."

She ran her fingers through his hair. "Where else would I be?"

"Penwell said you'd gone back to work."

"Only for an hour. I needed to arrange for someone

237

to take my patients for the next couple of weeks."

He tried to hold back the frown, but didn't have the strength. "You going somewhere?"

She snorted softly. "Not hardly. You see, I have this one particular patient who's so cranky, he demands all my attention."

A warm glow began deep in his chest. "Does he, now?"

"Oh yes."

"Maybe you should put the son of a—"

She pressed a finger against his lips. "You know, we're really going to have to work on your vocabulary."

He pursed his lips to kiss her finger. "Sorry, I'll try to keep the swearing to a minimum. I might not always remember, though."

"Hmmm, maybe all you need is the right incentive. What if, when you catch yourself and use something a little less colorful, I promise to..." She bent and whispered in his ear. Her erotic suggestion sent a surge of blood straight to his groin. The machine monitoring his heart stuttered and jumped into overtime as his erection swelled like it was connected to an air compressor. He cleared his throat.

"Um, sounds great, but I think we might need a license for some of that to be legal."

Farrah cocked her head. "Why Mr. Fagan, if I didn't know better, I might think that was a proposal."

He swallowed hard. Please, God, don't let him mess this up now. He took her hand, caressing her soft skin with his thumb. He met her gaze and held it. "What if it was?"

She stared at him. For a long moment, she didn't

say a word. He waited, saying nothing, almost afraid she wouldn't answer. Then, "Well, in that case, I guess I'd have to say yes."

Relief drenched him like a bucket of water. He grinned. "For real?"

She stroked his cheek. "Yes, for real and always."

The blast of euphoria that blew through him was better than a ton of morphine. Pain? What pain?

He pulled her to him. "Come 'ere, woman." Their lips met. Kyle wasted no time in rushing in to taste her again. She was even better than he remembered. The sweetness of her sent a rush of desire through him. Damn, how he wanted her. Their tongues met and dueled, happiness pouring into him each second like a spring shower. He tugged a little harder, pulling Farrah onto the bed with him. She snuggled in, careful of his leg, her lips trailing kisses along his jaw and down his throat. He felt her hands on his chest and wished desperately that the damn hospital gown was gone. He wanted her hands on him. He wanted his hands on her. Skin to bare skin, just like back at the pond—

A knock sounded on the door.

He wanted some damn-it-to-hell privacy!

"Oh! I guess I can come back a little later to check your vitals." The male nurse at the door chuckled. "They'd be all over the place right now anyway." He left, pulling the door closed behind him.

Farrah giggled and tried to sit up.

"Where do you think you're going," Kyle growled. "I'm not done yet."

She smiled and snuggled next to him again, running her fingers down his chest and stomach, making his muscles jump. "And what might you have in mind that could possibly be safe to do in a hospital room?"

Kyle grimaced. Time to surrender. "Talk, I guess. You know those pamphlets you were passing around?"

Her wandering fingers stilled. He could see the hope in her eyes, guarded though it was. "Yes?"

"Well, if I'm going to stand up in front of a church full of people, I should probably go ahead with those operations you were pushing at me."

Her slow smile reminded him of a rainbow after a thunderstorm, too beautiful for words and full of promise. "I think that sounds like a wonderful idea. Not to mention you'll be able to get around your new garage better."

He fell back on the pillow and groaned. "You've been talking to Penwell."

The smug look she gave him would have done a cat justice. "Of course, who do you think gave him the idea in the first place?" She raised an eyebrow and reached down to pat the thick bandage around his leg gently. "I hate to break it to you, but you're already scheduled for one of those operations."

He gave her a mock scowl. She'd surprised him. That she could do that to him so easily didn't bode well for his future peace of mind. "I am?"

"Yes." Her expression sobered. "You tore things up pretty bad when you kneed Craddoc. Bad move, by the way. Gutsy, but still bad for you."

"I was hoping to hit him with the brace."

"You missed."

"Still took him down though, didn't I? And don't you need my permission for an operation?"

"Not necessarily," she said airily. "Next of kin

works just fine when you're unconscious, and you were still out when we arrived. I have your mother's phone number and she was more than happy to fax me a signed release form."

"What about the doctor? Wasn't he supposed to be some kind of specialist?"

"He is." The look she gave him now started out pensive, but quickly morphed into mutinous. "I called Dr. Powell four days ago and asked if he could fly in for a consultation. Considering you're such a decorated veteran, he agreed. He'll be here tomorrow."

Kyle tried to hold on to his scowl, but failed miserably. He leaned forward and kissed her on the nose. "Are you always going to be such a pushy female?"

"Probably." Her body relaxed in a way that told him she'd been worried over his reaction to her high-handedness. She curled into his embrace, all but purring. "Are you always going to be such a stubborn male?"

"Da—I mean, darn right."

Farrah looked up at him, her eyes narrowing seductively. She leaned forward to brush her lips against his. "See, that wasn't so hard."

"Do I have to wait until after the wedding for my reward?"

Her hand slipped under the sheet and drifted down, caressing that part of him that was not only silky hard, but hot and throbbing. "Not at all," she said. "I believe in *instant* positive reinforcement."

"Thank God."

Epilogue

Farrah relaxed back into the water, closing her eyes against the late October sunset. The cold water felt wonderful, buoying her, caressing her skin, every wonderful bare inch of it.

"I can see your gooseflesh from here. Not to mention you're starting to shrivel up like a prune."

She smiled without opening her eyes. "Will you still love me if I'm all bumpy and wrinkly?"

"Yes, but that's not the point. The sun's going down."

"So the point is?"

"It's going to get a lot colder and I don't want you catching a chill. Not good for you in your condition. Come on, time to get out."

She opened one eye. Her soon to be husband stood at the edge of Joshua's pool, hands on his hips and gloriously naked. She opened both eyes to get a better look. Kyle's body had filled out some over the last few weeks. His right leg, bare of any mechanical brace, would never have the muscle it used to, but it was better. He could stand, and even walk, albeit with a decided limp. And there would always be some pain when he over-worked the muscles that were left.

"Like what you see?"

She waved her arms through the water a little, moving herself in his direction. "I could ask you the same thing."

She watched as his gaze roamed hungrily over her body. He started at her feet and worked his way up, pausing at the juncture of her thighs and again at her still flat stomach, before lingering on her bare breasts.

"Mmmm, da—darn right I do."

She grinned and crooked a finger at him. "That calls for a reward, I think."

"Yes, ma'am." He stepped off, into the pool and came up beside her. Farrah curled her body around his, her arms going around his neck, legs around his waist. The center of her settled over the center of him and she rubbed against him blatantly. "That feels good," he said groaning and leaning in to kiss her.

Farrah kissed him back, loving the way he tasted, the heat of him, the way he took control of the kiss. Kyle would always be all male to her. Even if the arterial bypass someday failed and he lost his leg, he would always be her alpha male. He pulled back, his grin warning her before he took them both under water.

They came up near one of the ladders.

"You're serious about making me get out?"

Still grinning, he nodded. "I've got plans."

She took one of his hands in hers and put it over her stomach. She batted her lashes. "But the baby loves swimming and we might not get to do it much longer. Winter's coming."

"I'll build her an indoor pool," he said, pushing her toward the ladder. "You first."

Farrah huffed, not really upset by his demand. That naked eyeful of him had warmed more than just her cheeks. Rubbing against him hadn't hurt matters either. "You just want the rest of your reward for not cussing."

"*Instant* positive reinforcement, isn't that your plan to reform me?" He looked down at himself sadly. "How can it be instant in a freezing spring?"

She laugh then, feeling the joy and love warm her far more than the weak October sun. Besides, he was right about the water being cold. She was starting to shiver.

She'd propped one foot on a lounge chair and was bent over, drying it off when Kyle came up behind her. The silky hardness that nestled between her butt cheeks sent a rush of wetness between her legs.

"Ah, this is more like it," Kyle said, leaning over her and tugging the towel away from her. He tossed it aside and led her hands to the arms of the chair. Then he nudged her feet with his until she widened her stance. "See," he said, nuzzling her neck, "isn't this better?"

She felt him pull back, the thick hardness of his shaft sliding across her sensitive flesh. She could feel her wetness on his skin when he slid back, pushing forward slowly. He took his time, gliding back and forth teasingly, nibbling on her neck and ears, fondling her breasts. He tweaked both nipples, pulling a gasp from her and making her arch back into him. "Are you ready for my positive reinforcement," he asked, his voice a harsh whisper.

"Yes, oh, yes."

"Good." He shifted, sliding forward and into her with one swift move. Her breath caught. He was big, but she was so wet there wasn't the slightest pain. Only pleasure, so much pleasure. He pulled out, almost all the way, and slid home again. She let him get away with it a few more times, let him have his way. When she couldn't take it any longer, she arched into his next thrust.

"More, Kyle. I need more."

"You want it faster?"

"Yes."

"Harder?"

"Yes!"

He gripped her hips and gave it to her, building the pace slowly, steadily until he was pounding into her. The slap of flesh against flesh was loud in the twilight of the evening. A staccato beat against the backdrop of their moans and gasps. Farrah felt the pressure building, the tingling in her clit a teasing sensation that begged to be fulfilled.

"Go ahead," Kyle ordered, his breath hot in her ear. "Touch yourself, Farrah. Please," he begged, "touch yourself for me."

She obeyed him, reaching down to press a finger against her throbbing nub. She could feel Kyle moving inside her, his every thrust making her quiver, making her tingle, making her…come.

Farrah cried out and flung her head back. Her body jerked in Kyle's careful hold, her insides clenching on him, pulling, milking, until he was coming, too. He cried out her name and she smiled.

****

Kyle was still hunched over Farrah and panting when he heard the glass door to Joshua's living room slide open. He pulled out of her, scooped up the loaded Glock off the chair, and snagged the towel to cover Farrah all in the space of one breath. He was facing the house and aiming at the figure on the balcony in the next. Around them, light blossomed.

"What the...Kyle is that you?" Joshua said. "What the hell are you doing down there? Are you naked? Damn, man, you've got no sense of...Wait, is that Farrah? Aw, honey, not you, too. I thought the plan was for you to influence him, not the other way around." The laughter in his voice was unmistakable.

Kyle swore, for once foregoing the lure of Farrah's positive reinforcement. Behind him, her throaty chuckle sent a shot of fresh need through him. Too bad he couldn't do anything about it right now. He lowered his gun. "Shut your mouth and go back inside," he yelled to Joshua. "We'll be up in a minute." He turned to Farrah. "Damn fool. I thought he wasn't supposed to be here until Saturday."

Still chuckling, Farrah wrapped the towel around herself. "Just be glad he's here. Now there's nothing to stop the wedding."

He pulled her into his arms and kissed her. "He's the one who should be glad." He placed a hand over her abdomen. "My Katrina has waited quite long enough for her parents to marry."

She locked her arms around his neck. "And whose idea was it to try for a baby *before* the wedding?"

"Hell, woman, I just didn't want to fool with waiting to put on all those condoms. How was I to know you were so damn fertile?"

She pressed a finger to his lips. "See, I knew Joshua would be bad for your vocabulary."

He nipped her finger. "Only because I know there won't be any positive reinforcement going on for a while. I'll go back to being good when we're alone, promise."

The sliding glass door slid open again. "Hey,"

Joshua called. "You two coming up here, or do we have to come down there?"

"We?" Kyle said over his shoulder. "Who's we?"

"Sam and Gage just got here. They want to see their new sister again sometime before the year is out."

Kyle started to swear, but found himself kissed instead. He smiled and kissed her back. "That's one way to shut me up."

"I can think of others," Farrah said. "Just give me time."

"We've got all the time in the world now, sweetheart. All the time in the world."

A word about the author...

Kathy is a central Florida native who devours books on a regular basis. Fiction is her favorite because it allows her to exercise her ever-active imagination.

She started writing short stories and poems in high school, continuing to dabble in science fiction and fantasy off and on until 2006, when her spunky niece, Darelle, dragged her to a writers' conference. There her desire to write morphed into the dream to write well enough to be published. Four years, three manuscripts, and numerous edits and revisions later, the dream became a reality with her Bloodsworn series.

Now Kathy writes for her fans, inviting them to join her, not only in the fantasy world of Avalyr, but in the dangerous world of covert ops.

~*~

Other Kathy Lane titles
available from The Wild Rose Press, Inc.
SNIPER SHOTS
BLOODSWORN: BOUND BY MAGIC
(2011 Prism - FF&P Best Fantasy)
(2011 Prism - FF&P Best First Book)
BLOODSWORN 2: LINKED BY BLOOD
REBORN IN AMBER, A BLOODSWORN TALE

Thank you for purchasing
this publication of The Wild Rose Press, Inc.

If you enjoyed the story, we would appreciate
your letting others know by leaving a review.

For other wonderful stories,
please visit our on-line bookstore at
www.thewildrosepress.com.

For questions or more information
contact us at
info@thewildrosepress.com.

The Wild Rose Press, Inc.
www.thewildrosepress.com

Stay current with The Wild Rose Press, Inc.

Like us on Facebook
https://www.facebook.com/TheWildRosePress

And Follow us on Twitter

https://twitter.com/WildRosePress